THE ESTHER PARADIGM

SARAH MONZON

RADIQX PUBLICATIONS

Published by Radiant Publications
Moses Lake, Washington

This is a work of fiction. Characters, incidents, and dialogues are products of the author's imagination and are not to be construed as real. Any resemblance to actual events is strictly coincidental.

The Qur'an (Oxford World's Classics). Trans. M. A. S. Abdel Haleem. USA: Oxford University Press, 2008.

Scriptures used in this book, whether quoted or paraphrased, are taken from:

Holy Bible, New International Version®, NIV® Copyright ©1973, 1978, 1984, 2011 by Biblica, Inc.® Used by permission. All rights reserved worldwide.

Holy Bible, King James Version, public domain

Cover design by Sarah Monzon

Manuscript edited by Dori Harrell, Breakout Editing

PROLOGUE

Hannah Pratt stared out across the grainy hills as the wind blew a gentle kiss over the crest. The laughing desert flitted away in a game of tag like she used to play at recess. Had it only been a few weeks since the phrase "amber waves" referred to the bendy blades of grain lining the fields of her Iowa hometown? As she peered over the horizon, the dunes continuously shifting, "amber waves" took on a new meaning, even in her seven-year-old mind.

Missionaries. The name had sounded adventurous. She'd pictured herself a soldier for Jesus, clad head to toe in armor like the dress-up costume the kids in her Bible class at church played with. She'd be David, and with God's help she'd slay a Goliath. After that everyone around would believe in the God of the Bible, not...well, whatever that weird-sounding book was called that they believed in here.

"Hannah." The swish of fabric announced her mom's exit from the large tent behind her. The one that she'd thought would be fun to live in. After all, camping was a blast. But this tent was different from the one they'd used in the woods by the river back home. This tent smelled funny. Like sweaty camels. And it was dark and heavy and hot.

"Could you gather some twigs for the fire for me please, baby?"

"Yes, Mama." Their tent had been pitched along the rim of the encampment. Another reminder they were outsiders. She'd tried to make friends with the other kids, but she didn't know their games and couldn't understand anything they said. The words felt funny on her tongue when she'd try to repeat them, her only reward for the effort being the grating sound of their laughter.

She'd never felt so lonely. So out of place. When they'd moved from Martinsburg to Hallesville, she'd been scared to leave her friends, but then Jenna had spied her swinging alone and had challenged her to a race. They'd been best friends ever since. What was Jenna doing now? Mom had explained time zones on the plane ride over, but Hannah wasn't sure she really understood it all. Would Jenna be sleeping? Or maybe she was playing with the collection of Barbies Hannah had left her.

Whatever it was, Jenna sure wasn't scrounging around the hot, sandy desert looking for small twigs, hoping to find enough so she didn't have to gather any dried animal poop to fuel the fire for her mom to cook on. So gross.

A stray limb a few feet away snagged Hannah's attention. Perfect. Her feet sank into the hot sand as she walked over to the foreign wood. Bending down, she reached and curled her fingers around the bark-covered cylinder.

A sting, like the shots she'd received before they'd left Iowa, pierced the top of her hand. Tears flooded her eyes as a scream left her mouth. She pulled her hand to her chest and cradled it. Under the twig, a vile creature sped away. Looking part spider, part lobster, and part dragon, she recognized it right away. A scorpion.

She looked at her hand, angry, red, and swollen. Her heart felt funny, as if it were growing too big in her chest. Numbness spread through her fingers. She opened her mouth to yell for her mom, but invisible cotton balls filled her mouth.

Tears coursed over her cheeks as she forced her legs to move through the sand that clasped like hands around her ankles, tripping her. Knees in the hot dust, she struggled to stand. A pair of tan hands hooked under her arms and lifted. Black eyes the color of her dad's morning coffee stared down from a boy years older than her. The traditional white garment of his people hung from his shoulders to wrists and all the way to his ankles, his head covered and protected from the sun by a checked keffiyeh.

Hannah lifted her hand to show him the sting, hoping he'd understand what he saw. She hadn't learned how to say scorpion in Arabic yet.

He held her hand up, studying it a second before looking back into her eyes with a funny expression on his face. Like he'd never seen a girl before or something. He scooped her up into his arms, making a soothing noise in the back of his throat.

Her hand hurt, and she was scared she might die. She'd read that somewhere—that a scorpion sting could kill a girl. But somehow, she felt safer now that this strange boy held her.

"*Jawharat aleaynayn.*" He touched her blond hair,

rubbing it between his thumb and forefinger. "*Alshshier min aldhdhahab.*" He stepped toward her tent. "*Kanz.*"

If only she could understand what he said.

She sniffed. "Will I be okay?"

He gazed down again, the same wonderment on his face, but his lips remained closed against any more words.

She'd been found, rescued. Maybe this could be the beginning of her first friendship in her new homeland.

If she didn't die, that was.

Chapter 1

HANNAH

This was not how I'd thought I would die.

Not that I sat around imagining my death. I'm not that morbid. But never in my wildest dreams had I imagined *this*.

Along the horizon, racing toward me with frightening speed, a billowing brown wall licked the earth's surface and spit it out again—a ferocious scream that caused my heart to stutter in my chest. Six years away and this was how my beloved desert welcomed me home.

Wind whipped my long, loose dress around my legs and tugged at the few strands of hair not safely tucked in a ponytail under my hijab. I'd always been thankful the Bedouin clan my parents ministered to as missionaries didn't adhere to the more concealing Muslim headwear, such as a *niqab* or *burqa*. I had to admit, though, that having more material to cover my nose and mouth would be helpful against the dust storm about to consume me. With quick motions, I reached around my head and unwrapped the bottom of my hijab, rewrapping it around my nose and mouth. A bit of water or petroleum jelly would work even better to save my nose and lungs from the dry desert sand, but some protection was better than none.

Tiny grains of sand picked up by the wind pelted my body like fastballs pitched by major league baseball players. I hunched over, lowering my frame as close to the ground as I could. Never knew if the wind had picked up more than just the earth's surface. An abandoned tire rim or something else could decapitate a person when chucked at top speeds. It would be just like that temperamental mistress to hurl an object absently left on the wayside.

The storm was on me now.

My lungs constricted to rid themselves of the tiny particles I'd breathed in, coughing hot breath into the material around my mouth. My eyes watered with the force of the wind, and I blinked rapidly to try and rid the granules scratching my irises.

Lifting my backpack, I shielded my face and eyes, wishing I hadn't let the driver drop me off so far from where the clan currently had their tents pitched. The inside of a twenty-year-old Jeep would have served as a wonderful bunker against this onslaught. Now I had no protection.

In the thick of it, I squinted through the brown haze, looking for something to hunker under on the leeward side. The rise of a nearby dune lied of its ability to protect. Fortunately, I understood the reality of the phrase "shifting sands." Had no desire to change my death sentence from asphyxiation due to sand in my lungs to being buried alive when the wind deposited the dune right on top of my head.

A camel's bray rent through the cacophony of the storm.

My heart restarted. If ever there was an animal built to survive the temper of the desert, it was the camel. I pushed my legs forward, wishing I wore pants rather than my dress, which wrapped itself around my calves and threatened to topple me. If I could hear the camel's call, perhaps its owner could hear mine. I lifted my chin and took in a lungful of air before pulling down the covering from my lips.

"*Musaeada!*" I yelled for help in Arabic. "*Musaeada!*"

The camel answered, and I took a few more stumbling steps toward the sound. The sand made it difficult to do anything—walk, see, breathe. If I didn't find a place to wait out the storm soon, I wouldn't survive it.

A man appeared as if a mirage, the kind that might strike fear into some of the hearts of my fellow Americans after the horrifying terrorist attacks. Al-Qaeda, ISIS, Islamic Jihad, Taliban. While a few extremists built hatred throughout the world, my heart harbored no such feelings. These people were my brothers and sisters. The family among which I'd been raised.

No traditional greeting of *Assalamu alaykum* passed the man's lips, covered by the same scarf that wrapped his head in a turban. Only his dark, piercing eyes showed through the small opening of material. He studied me a moment, a question in his gaze, as if trying to place me from his memory. Or wondering about the crazy woman with impossibly light skin who'd found herself in the middle of a death storm in a barely inhabited desert.

With blue eyes, blond hair, and a fair complexion that the sun loved to torture, I'd long since become accustomed to such looks from those whose mere appearance made them better suited for this climate. I was an anomaly. But one who'd rather stay alive, so when the man pushed my head down and dragged me forward by the arm, I followed willingly.

The camel's bray sounded louder, and soon we slumped along its side, allowing its body to shield us from the spitting wind and sand.

The sheer force of the wind made it impossible to talk, so I forwent a thank you and bent over at the waist, tucking my chin to my chest and allowing my body to lean heavily against the scratchy brown hair of the big animal next to me.

The man stroked his camel's side, talking low and making reassuring noises. Growing up among the Bedouin people, I realized the importance of livestock, camels especially. They were currency, transportation, sustenance, and overall survival. I'd never truly grown fond of the stubborn beasts. Their milk too sharp and salty on my tongue, I'd missed the pasteurized cow's milk bought by the gallon at the local supermarket. Their gait too choppy, I'd missed the pony rides at the petting zoo. Their hair too coarse, I'd missed the soft cotton sundresses that twirled around me as I spun in a field of wildflowers.

But surprising enough, I'd discovered over the past six years when I'd been stateside to finish high school and then attend college, that while I'd never *liked* camels, I had come to respect them, and maybe even miss them to a degree.

Now the tally chart in the animal's favor grew, since the mammal currently shielded me from sudden death.

As quick as the storm had raced in, it vanished. Like a sprinter who collapsed after passing the finish line, the winds died, dropping the sand back to the ground.

The man patted his camel's side with two hearty

thwacks, then stood and pulled a rope connected to the animal's halter, bringing its big head around. He inspected its nose and eyes, murmuring low as he did so and pulling the scarf down from around his face.

Not as graceful as the camel, I unfolded my legs beneath me and arranged the bottom portion of my dress before awkwardly standing.

I tilted my head in his direction, lowering my gaze to his feet. It was out of respect to his culture and religion that I did so. I didn't want my actions, or lack thereof, to build a barrier between a friendship with anyone. Although I didn't have ulterior motives besides Christian love, in a country where proselytizing remained illegal, the only means of sharing Christ lay in friendship evangelism. Despite my respectful humility, I had to speak my deepest heartfelt thanks, as I knew he'd saved my life.

"*Shukraan.*"

His feet moved toward me. I held perfectly still, eyes downcast and hands clasped together in front of me. When his thumb and forefinger lightly pinched my chin, I sucked in a breath, stunned. Interaction between genders was severely limited, physical contact reserved for the privacy of the marriage tent.

Upward pressure raised my face. I found his black eyes in a fixed stare, probing, searching my own. One side of his mouth lifted, and the hardness that had creased his forehead eased away as amusement flashed across his features.

His hand dropped as the other side of his mouth lifted to join the first. His full lips, framed by a dark short-trimmed beard, formed a wide smile. He shook his head.

Based on his reaction, I should know him. But who was

he? I racked my brain but came up empty. It had been six years since I'd been around my desert family. People could change a lot in that amount of time.

My eyes narrowed as I focused on his face. His brows were thick and hung low over his eyes. Eyes that were serious and lined with the weight of heavy responsibility, even with the lightness that sparked at his discovery. The one he currently enjoyed as a secret.

I lifted my own brows in a silent request that he share his hidden knowledge, but the answer to my unspoken question was a widening of his smile. The lines his grin made on his face were not deep, and I suspected he didn't make them as often as he should. Which made me feel rewarded, even though I was still left in the dark as to his identity.

He gestured to the camel's saddle. "*Arkab.*"

I looked warily at the beautifully woven red blanket covering the wooden saddle. Remembered the way my lower back and inner thighs felt after even a short ride. I returned my gaze to the man. He knew me, and that should've put me at ease. But it wouldn't have been safe to accept a ride from a stranger into desolate lands.

"Should I know you?" Might as well ask outright, even if the directness was very American of me. But I *was* American, and even though I could assimilate, I couldn't change who I was by birth.

He continued to grin and touched the pad of his thumb to the corner of my eye. "*Jawharat aleaynayn.*"

Jewel eyes.

He ran a finger along the edge of my hijab, pulling strands of blond hair away from my face. "*Alshshier min adhdhahab.*"

10

Hair of gold.

The weight of his hand fell onto my shoulder. *"Kanz."*

Treasure.

My eyes widened. I peered at him more closely. Karim Al-Amir? Could this really be the same boy who'd rescued me after the scorpion? My first friend among his tribe?

He'd grown, both taller and fuller. But yes, now that I really looked, I could see it. This man in front of me was Karim. The same serious nature. The same shroud of responsibility and air of importance. The same need to look after his people. Of which I was yet again thankful he saw me as.

I wanted to leap forward and hug his neck. But I knew better.

It had taken two years of being back in the United States before I could comfortably look people in the eye when they spoke, and a year more to not tighten whenever I was wrapped up in someone's arms in a friendly hug. And since I'd decided to go to school in the South, the hugging thing had happened a lot.

My face broke into a huge grin, and I clasped my hands tighter so I didn't touch him in some way.

"It's good to have you back among the people." He regarded me with sincerity, but then his mouth tipped again, and he surveyed the dunes surrounding us. His eyes still sparked when he looked back down at me. "Although I see your education has not taught you to avoid trouble."

I laughed. I couldn't help it. A penchant for finding myself in predicaments? Yeah, that was pretty much my birthright. No amount of schooling could ever teach me how to steer clear of getting myself in a pickle. Although, it would've been profoundly helpful if it could have. Much more useful than my research and statistics class had been.

I let my body lean toward him a bit. Picked up the smell of burnt palm and fig. A feeling of coming home settled in the far corners of my heart. I may have been born in the heartland of the United States, but belonging washed over me amid this nomadic desert tribe. Their vibrant traditions and determination inspired me...as much as their eternal hope.

I wrapped myself around the feeling, let it clear away the loneliness of the last half dozen years, and smiled up into the face of one of my oldest friends. "If you, the sheikh's son, could not teach me such things, no hope laid within the classroom."

He laughed then, and against the laws of natural science, the sound echoed off the sloping dunes. "Come. Let's get you home to your mother and father. They have been anxious for your return."

Joy welled in my chest. The sense of urgency that had prodded me into hiring a driver to bring me this far from the city poked me again. Mom and Dad were supposed to meet me at the airport tomorrow, but I had caught an earlier flight so I could surprise them. Imagining their faces as I paraded back among the pitched community tilted my lips and urged my feet toward Karim's camel.

With a cluck, he commanded the camel to kneel. I approached with slow and steady steps from its side, wishing again for pants as I threw my leg quickly over the middle of its hump. Thankfully, my clothes were long and flowy and I could arrange the material over my legs modestly. As the camel stood with its back legs first, I leaned backward so as not to be thrown into its neck. The momentum shifted, and I moved along with it, leaning forward as Karim's camel rose from the ground. Adjusting my seat, I wrapped my legs around the saddle post to save my tailbone a sound beating.

Karim smirked up at me from the ground but didn't say anything. He knew my dislike of this particular conveyance. Once, when I was little and had still been trying to make friends and prove myself among the people, I had challenged him and a few of the other boys to a camel race. The girls had looked at me in horror, but the gleam in the boys' eyes had urged me on enough that I thought if I beat them, then maybe I would be accepted as one of them.

No and no. Not only did I suffer a lecture from the clan elders, Karim's father in particular, not to mention my own parents, but I also had to endure a sweaty, itchy cast on my left arm for seven miserable weeks.

A cluck from Karim's tongue propelled the camel forward, rocking my hips with the motion. My muscles reflexively tensed at the herky-jerky movement, but I forced them to relax and allowed my body to sway with the camel's gait.

I had so many questions I wanted to ask Karim. About my parents. The clan. I wanted to know everything that had happened since I'd left. Mom and Dad wrote letters and even a few emails when they could get to an internet café in the city. But those correspondences were a bit like a fill-in-the-blank puzzle, and I had never been really good at puzzles.

I got it though, their need not to share too much information. Even I had to be a bit secretive when my classmates and friends had asked where we were missionaries. My pat answer had always been that we served the Lord in the 10/40 window. Unfortunately, that usually reciprocated blank stares, and I would have to go on to explain that the 10/40 window referred to the regions located between ten and forty degrees north of the equator. A geographical area where the people had the least access to the Gospel message. Some of my friends would accept my response and leave it at that. Others would allow their curiosity to outweigh good manners and probe further. It was dangerous though to tell people exactly where we were and who we were sharing the Good News with. Proselytizing was illegal, and it wasn't uncommon for missionaries to be imprisoned or killed.

I looked down at Karim, the top of his head covered by his dark-blue turban. Had he taken on the full responsibility of clan leader? Married? Had children? Would his little ones be among my students?

He looked back at me. Caught me staring. I quickly averted my gaze, but I doubted he'd believe my sudden fascination with the threaded bangles edging the saddle blanket. Risking a peek out of the corner of my eye, I caught his grin.

The horizon offered little change until my attention snagged on black dots amid the endless sandy brown. Blood pulsed in my veins, and I straightened in the saddle. I wanted to leap off this lumbering creature and sprint into my parents' arms, but good sense kept me grounded. Or seated, really. Surefooted I was not. Even at this plodding pace, I'd arrive sooner on the camel's back than if I attempted to run there myself.

"If I was not afraid you'd break another bone, I'd let you experience Jamal's speed."

My fingers itched to take the reins, but Karim was probably right. I'd never been an expert at camel riding, and six years away would not have improved that fact.

He laughed and tugged Jamal to a stop, looking up at me

with amusement. "You are like a viper ready to strike at the camp with the speed of lightning but you are stuck coiled around a boulder."

Heat rose to my cheeks, though I doubted anyone could notice. My face had been flushed from the sun since stepping out of the airport. I was not chagrined, however. Even though Karim wore stoicism like a cloak, I preferred to experience the full range of emotions, ride them like a roller coaster, even. And right then I was coasting high on excitement and anticipation.

Jamal knelt, and in one fluid motion, Karim mounted behind me. The heat radiating off his chest seeped into the muscles of my back. My body swayed toward him like I had been in danger of hypothermia and he was the source to thaw me. But then Jamal started to rise, and in my unpreparedness, I was thrown into Karim's solid chest.

His chuckle was deep in my ear as he leaned forward, pressing into my back to counterbalance the camel's final movements of standing. "Ready for the ride of your life, *Kanz*?"

A double entendre? From Karim? No...surely he only meant the words for what they were—a camel ride to the clan and my parents. My years in the States had impressed upon my mind beyond what I'd thought to even consider the almost-stodgy son of a sheikh, not to mention my oldest and dearest friend, to have layered his words to mean more than he'd said.

I started to turn, to see if his expression would give me any clues, but a "hut-hut" sounded in my ear, and my body jerked. We were flying over an ocean of sand.

Chapter 2

KARIM

Hannah throwing her leg over the saddle and sliding down Jamal's side before he even came to a stop hadn't fazed me in the least. That was who she was. Exuberant. Expressive. Even after passing the age of womanhood, she still held to her childlikeness. I envied her a bit, that.

What must such carefreeness feel like? As the only child of the clan leader, my life had been planned out before I'd left the womb, the eyes of my people looking toward me, so much in their expressions. Respect. Censure. Hope. Doubt. Submission. Acceptance. Wading through the turning tides of emotion had often left me reeling, the weight of responsibility crushing my young bones until I felt like an old man in a young man's body.

A squeal rent the dry air, the joyous sound having the physical ability to tug a corner of my mouth upward. There hadn't been much to smile about lately, but Hannah bounding toward the open arms of her parents, watching her engulfed in the display of their love, eased a bit of the pressure squeezing my rib cage. Situations in life often seemed dire, but there was always hope, goodness, to be found if one but looked. And Hannah had always been goodness. And amusing. And beautiful.

Yellow strands of hair worked their way of out her hijab, teasing my gaze and causing my fingertips to tingle. I'd nicknamed her Treasure in my youth, her sapphire eyes and golden mane mesmerizing me at first glance. Never had I laid eyes on someone like her. But as the years went by, as I grew and my perspective widened, I'd realized not just Hannah but her parents as well were precious to my people. More so than any diamonds that could be mined from the earth's belly. No guile within them, they had labored tirelessly for my people, often saving clan members from the clutches of severe illness.

The cinch around my middle tightened as it often did when I dwelled upon the Pratts. They were a problem for which I'd yet to find a solution. The undercurrents of which swirled stronger with each passing day.

Tapping Jamal on the shoulder, he lowered until he lay on the ground. I dismounted and gave him a pat.

"She has returned." The voice behind me was one I'd heard and conversed with nearly every day of my life. Samlil, my best friend.

I turned toward him, a bit weary even though our hearts had bonded one to another more than brothers. "This is not unexpected."

He shook his head. "No. But is it welcome?" His steady gaze met mine for a second before moving beyond Jamal to the reunion of the Americans.

I followed where he focused. The reunited family parted

the flap to their tent and disappeared inside. We would need a feast. Though not a lot of time for preparation, my mother would be up to the task. If anything, the celebration would solidify my support of the doctors and now the new teacher.

I peered back at Samlil, trying to peel back the layers of his expression. Recently I had witnessed more to him. Hidden things that festered in his spirit. "Welcomed by whom?"

"Do not play ignorant, Karim. It is not befitting a sheikh."

"No, ignorance is not a robe I wish to don. But neither is forgetfulness." I allowed my gaze to bore into him. Let him see exactly where I stood. Although that knowledge was common, it had lately been defied. "Or has your memory so left you naked that you cannot recall when you were but thirteen years old, more in the afterlife, in Paradise, than in the present. How those doctors stayed by your side day and night, coaxing you back to the realm of the living?"

His lips pressed into a thin line. He wanted to say more. He always wanted to say more. But this time he stormed off, and I let him go, too weary to beat a dead camel.

Jamal brayed in my ear. Saliva dripped from his muzzle and sprayed my white thawb, leaving dark, wet splotches across the tailored top. I led him to water and let him drink deeply, waved over a boy to care for him, and then strode across the encampment to find my mother.

At the cooking pot behind her tent, she stirred a cauldron of aromatic lentils. Another woman crouched beside her, pounding and stretching the dough that would be cooked into flat bread.

"Our sister has returned." I bent down and kissed Mother's pleated cheek.

She looked at me, intelligence in her watery eyes. "Hannah Pratt?"

Although the Pratt family had been with us for sixteen years, their name on our tongue sounded foreign compared to when they spoke it themselves. A bit more tonal, lyrical. Like a shabbaba flute instead of a djembe drum.

"Yes, '*Ami*."

"I will prepare a *Madfoona*." She leaned against a stick to help her stand and shuffled away. Older than most mothers of men my age, my parents had conceived me late in their marriage after over a decade of trying to fill their arms with a child. My father hadn't given in to the voices that encouraged him to take another wife to produce an heir and successor. Allah had heard their cries, and I was born. If it wouldn't offend her, I'd ask one of the other women to shoulder the responsibility of the impromptu feast. As it was, .the women would rally around my mother, helping her with preparations. The banquet was in good hands. I could already taste the *maklube*, a stuffed chicken served on a bed of rice and wreathed with roasted vegetables and potato wedges. Not to mention hummus, tahini, and the small tomatoes seasoned with fresh herbs.

It was a small step. A reminder, of sorts. While not of our blood, this American family had dwelled among us for over a decade. Had respected our culture and called us their friends, never once imposing their beliefs upon us like mercenaries pouring water down the throat of a drowning man.

The disease spreading through the sheep flocks had not originated at their tent, no matter the whisperings among the most superstitious. Punishment did not come from Allah's hands for harboring unbelievers within our borders. The hand of a loving God would not fist about his followers' necks in such a manner. Instead, the sickness crippling the sheep was scientific in nature, not supernatural. They had but to find the cause and weed it out, discover a medicine and administer it.

A scapegoat would not end the shadow of darkness looming over the distant pastures, nor our clan's not-so-distant future existence.

The banquet a few hours off, I headed toward the flock and checked in with the men in charge of the sheep. Maybe things had changed, turned in their favor. Maybe the ewes were no longer aborting or giving birth to stillborn lambs. Maybe emaciation wasn't shrinking the flocks' girths and bulbous goiters weren't forming beneath fleece that fell from backs by the fistfuls.

The trek to the livestock helped center me. Reminded me who I was, my position. I could not allow my feelings and emotions to dictate my actions, not when the entire clan depended upon me. The responsibility was too heavy to allow even a fleeting moment of spontaneity. Everything needed to be thought through carefully, considered, and then the good of the many, of all my brothers and sisters, put forward. My will placed upon the altar.

Pathetic bleating cut through the arid atmosphere like a child's cry for help. My heart twisted at the sound, knowing the shepherds who had to listen to the constant pleas felt powerless and frustrated at their lack of ability to fix the problem.

I approached Mahabat as he leaned heavily on his staff, his keffiyeh billowing behind him by an unexpected yet welcomed breeze.

"*Assalaam Alaikum.*" I truly hoped peace was upon him...and the livestock.

"*Waalaikum salaam.*" He nodded at me, his mouth pinched in the corners.

I let my gaze blanket the sheep, noticing the weak and the strong had been sifted, separated. A startling contrast. While the healthy ewes and rams stood erect, their fleece full and thick, the sickly sheep hobbled, heads low, barely moving, as if putting one hoof in front of the other was a task beyond their reach.

"Any changes?" I asked Mahabat.

His gaze caught mine, the same tightness around his lips encircling his eyes. He was concerned, and rightly so. "Yes, although none good."

My throat dropped to my stomach, understanding the full range and implications. Fear had infiltrated our family. So much of our lives revolved around the animals in our care. If they began to die, we would soon follow. If not our physical bodies, then our history, our culture, our traditions...the beat of our very hearts. My dread only sank deeper, knowing who would be blamed. Knowing how malleable a mind could be and, when frightened, how a person's actions could take a turn.

He had warned the Pratts of the growing discord, the tide of hatred beginning to simmer in impure souls. They'd only smiled as if in peace, as if in possession of a hidden truth that eradicated any concern they had for themselves. Adamantly they'd refused to leave the clan, calling us brothers and sisters. Their family. While in Allah I believed this true, I had been surprised that their following of *Isa*, or Jesus, as they called him, had allowed them to recognize our ties.

A young lamb wobbled in front of me, collapsing at my feet.

"Look in its mouth," Mahabat directed.

I bent and stuck a finger between its lips, pushed down on its jaw. A swollen tongue lolled to the side, dirty blue in color.

I stood and wiped my hand against my thigh. Looking at Mahabat, I asked, "Do you know what it is?"

He peered out over the horizon. "Some symptoms are familiar. The mangy fleece I have seen before when mites take up residence among the thick wool. The boils, also not so uncommon." He shook his head. "But all of it together?"

No answer was needed. Even with our deep agricultural history, this illness had the most knowledgeable shepherds among us stymied.

Mahabat pierced me with his gaze. "Animals are dying. No lambs have been born unaffected. I do not need to tell you what this means for our people."

His tongue stopped producing words, but his eyes continued to communicate.

I needed to find a solution.

I needed to save the family.

Chapter 3

HANNAH

"It's so good to have my baby back in my arms again." Mom squeezed me to her chest, Dad right behind her, beaming down on us. Every dry and cracked place in my soul that had suffered from the drought of separation soaked in their touch, their presence. My parents and I had always been close, and just because I'd reached an age where I was an adult, didn't mean I didn't need them.

Mom loosened her hold, and I took a step back, her hand still on one of my shoulders. She squeezed and moved aside for Dad to wrap me up and squish me. He finally set me back on my feet, and we made our way to the oversized pillows lying amid the tapestry rugs covering the tent's floor.

Mom patted my knee. "Tell us all about college."

I shrugged. "What's to tell that I didn't say in my letters?"

"Oh, I don't know. A boyfriend perhaps?" Mom's eyes gleamed.

Dad's chest rumbled with a chuckle. "Leave the girl alone, Elizabeth." He looked at me with a grin. "I'm convinced women have more than one internal clock. Everyone know the first, but my theory is the second is even stronger—grandbabies."

Mom slapped Dad's shoulder. "Oh, stop it, Ethan."

"As soon as you stop trying to marry off my girl." He winked at me. "I kind of like having her around."

I loved it when they went back and forth this way. My parents, my father especially, was the most jovial person I'd ever met. Always an eternal optimist, his outlook on life, and his love for my mother especially, was unshakable.

"So, unlike the epistles that I mailed you, your letters were a bit sparse. Fill me in."

Mom and Dad shared a look that caused my belly to harden.

"Truth be told, sweetie, we've been a little worried about your timing in coming back." Dad's bushy brows narrowed into a V over his eyes.

My throat convulsed as I swallowed, intuition yelling a warning.

"The flocks have been hit with a mysterious illness. Some in the clan are stirring up trouble, trying to lay the blame for the disease at our feet."

My Americanized thought was that a few sick sheep didn't seem like much to worry about. But my Bedouin mind understood the seriousness. "How could they blame you? You didn't make the sheep sick."

Mom traced the pattern in her pillow with a finger. "They're saying Allah is punishing them for allowing us, Christians, to sojourn with them." Her eyes connected with Dad's again before resting back on me. "Which is why maybe now isn't a good time to start your school."

Breath knocked from my lungs. "You guys are leaving?"

"No. No, of course not," Dad said. "The burden for this tribe hasn't lifted from our hearts. If anything, the demonstrations have advanced the Lord's work."

"What demonstrations?" Were my parents really in that much danger? We knew the stories. Those about missionaries who'd sacrificed their lives to reach the unreached. The ones who'd yet to hear about Jesus and His loving sacrifice and redemption. Just south of us, believers smuggled Bibles among the underground churches by hiding them beneath decomposing bodies in coffins during transit across borders. Others had been shot point blank for refusing to convert to Islam or pay an exorbitant tax that no one could afford.

Those stories had never hit so close to home. For the most part, the Bedouins had accepted us, as we respected their culture and religion. We'd made friends over time, allowing them to come to us when their curiosity piqued from our peculiar differences and worship of *Isa*, Jesus.

"A few warnings," Mom hedged.

"But from them, two more men have come to me with questions about Jesus, and I've been able to share the Gospel with them," Dad said.

"Do you..." My throat worked against the dryness that had nothing to do with the sand I'd inhaled earlier. "Do you think it'll get bad enough that we'll have to leave?"

Dad's gray eyes softened. "This is our calling, your mother's and mine. Our cross that we carry to advance the kingdom. Jesus warned His followers that they'd have sufferings."

"And He promised to always be with us in them," Mom finished.

"But you..." Dad started but didn't finish.

Didn't need to. I knew where he was going.

"I'm staying."

They weren't the only ones who had a passion for the Bedouin people. The spark within me for this tribe, boys and girls I grew up among as brothers and sisters, burned hotter each day. If I left, that flame inside me would be snuffed out. My soul would be devoid of its light. No, I needed to kindle that spark until it grew into a flame and eventually, with God's help, a fire that would spread throughout the entire desert.

"Hannah." Mom's voice held a pleading tone.

I knew where they were coming from. They wanted to keep me safe, just like I wanted them to be safe. But if everyone only did what was safe, nothing would change. Eventually the rocks would cry out because the followers who were instructed to speak had shut their mouths.

"I'm staying." I looked them both in the eye, let them see my conviction and commitment. "I'm going to teach the children."

A shadow darkened the tent's opening, and my dad rose to greet the visitor. A few minutes later he reentered the large one-room dwelling, the corners of his lips pulled down in confusion.

"What is it?" Mom asked.

"The sheikh has ordered a feast prepared in honor of Hannah's return."

"Karim's father?" The old sheikh had always been kind, but not demonstrative.

Dad looked at me. "Karim has been leader these past two years. Ever since his father's death." His mustache twitched as he chewed on the inside of his cheek. A tell that something ran through his mind.

"Ethan?" Mom asked.

She saw the sign too.

Dad gave his head a little shake. "Maybe nothing."

"But?" Mom pressed.

Dad's gaze lighted on me again. "It seems, perhaps, the sheikh is making a public stand in our favor."

Did that surprise them? Karim, the most caring and generous boy I'd known, was like a mother hen but with the power of a lion. He gently gathered his chicks under his wing while snapping any intruder in half who threatened his family.

Dad's face scrunched, his mind busy. Analyzing. Organizing. Ever the scientist, categorizing the data and sifting through the evidence. Creating hypotheses.

Seemed pretty obvious to me. Karim considered us part of his people.

"Do you think it will sway social opinion?" Mom asked.

Dad's shoulders lifted. "Only time will tell."

"It's good, I think." Mom looked at me. Her eyes got a bit sad. "Although I was hoping to have you all to ourselves tonight. Especially since we have to leave tomorrow."

They were leaving? But I just got there! "Where are you going?" I left off asking why and begging them to stay, even though the little girl in me was screaming it from every corner of my heart.

Dad tapped my nose. "To pick you up from the airport."

I swatted at his hand. "In case you hadn't noticed, I'm already here."

"Right. But the plan had been to pick you up and drop off

some blood and other samples from the sheep to a local veterinarian in the city. Maybe he can help us figure out what is making the livestock sick and give us some medicine that will eradicate the problem."

"Why don't you come with us?" Mom asked.

It would be nice to spend a whole day with my parents. "I wish I could, but I need to meet with Yara. Karim mentioned she would know of a tent I could use for the school. She'd also volunteered to go with me to speak with the mothers about their children attending. Karim said he'd put a word in among the fathers."

My parents shared that look again. The one they'd developed over the years of their marriage. Communication without any words. I'd tried to figure out their secret messages, how they could know what the other was thinking just by a lift of a brow or a twitch of the lips. It had always been outside my reach, a graze of my fingertips where I thought I'd deciphered it, but then...not.

"Come on." Mom stood and held out her hand. "Let's wash off the desert and sweat from you and get you presentable for this celebration."

I let her lead me to the back of the tent, where she lit a number of lanterns. Dad left and closed the front flap, blocking out the natural light and casting the inside into flickering shadows from the lantern's small flames. Mom heated water and poured it into a large metal washbasin, which I stared at with a smirk. Far from pampered, after having to adjust to the wasteful way of life in the West, I had to admit soaking my whole body in a deep tub would be one of the things I'd miss from my time in the States.

I climbed into the water, my knees to my chest, and used

a dipper to pour the water over my hair. Even though it had been covered in the sandstorm, quite a bit of the desert still clung among the strands. The bottom of the tub turned grainy as sand slid from my body into the water. I scrubbed and rinsed and promptly got out, no desire to linger in my own filth. Accepting the towel Mom offered, I dried quickly, partly from the terry cloth and partly from the dry air that sucked all the moisture out of everything.

Mom pulled out a pale-blue *abaya* with intricately embroidered white flowers lining the hem, sleeves, neckline, and running vertically down the middle. Gorgeous. And so different from the traditional loose-fitting gowns that both the men and women wore. Although the cut was the same, the color and patterns were not. I was used to seeing bright, striking colors—red, royal blue—embellished with geometric designs and tassels. The clothes reflected the people who wore them, with their vibrancy and love of life.

"We are all the same," Mom said as she handed me the dress. "And all unique."

Mom's object lesson in the form of an outfit. It was a message she'd repeated many times in different ways. Once she'd shown me a picture of a tulip field. Row after row of beautiful red tulips, symmetrically planted, creating a stunning picture. And right in the middle, all by itself in a sea of sameness, stood one lone yellow flower.

At first I'd believed she'd wanted to reinforce in my young mind that even though I looked different from all the other children with my light skin, compared to their darker complexion, beneath the surface we were the same. We all had joys and sorrows and dreams.

But as I grew older, I learned to acknowledge that

everyone was created in God's image. Same beating heart, same lungs taking in oxygen, same blood coursing through our veins. And while we needed to embrace our sameness, there was also something completely unique and special about each person. One had to balance the similarities without losing the spark that set individuals apart.

I'd taken those little nuggets of wisdom with me wherever I went, often pulling them out. While Mom's lessons about equality had rooted in my mind—never once had I thought I was better than another because of my outward appearance— I couldn't help but think the field of red flowers looked so much more beautiful than that single yellow one. That they shone brighter and stood taller.

I took the dress in my hand, fingered the flowers stitched there. "It's beautiful. Thank you."

She helped me pull it over my head and wrapped a loose, pale-blue scarf over my hair. I rubbed my hand down the side of the smooth material. A tinkling sound clinked behind me. A bit like a wind chime made of coins. Before I could turn, something circled my head and rested like a crown. I reached my hand up and felt the head chain, the small gold circles that dripped down over my forehead. I turned to my mom, my brows raised. The women of the tribe often wore jewelry, some pieces having been inherited for several hundreds of years, but my mother and I had little adornment.

She shrugged. "It finishes the outfit." Then she turned and changed her own gown, effectively cutting off any response I might have had.

Dad reentered the tent, also changed. He escorted us to the center of the clanswomen, then left to join the men. Exotic smells already thickened the air and teased my appetite. Musicians strummed their instruments to the cadence of my heartbeat.

Mom and I greeted a group of women before finding a seat around the perimeter. In the middle of the gathering, five young ladies danced in a choreographed circle. The jeweled belts with gold tassels as well as the bangles on their wrists clicked and clanged with their movements. Hips rotated in fluid motion, arms raised as they spun. The added pieces of wispy material they'd laid over their heads flowed out in an arc as they twirled. Their ankle-length dresses in bold colors of red, blue, and purple were ornate versions of their everyday dresses. Each step they took was perfectly timed to the beat, and the women who didn't dance clapped along.

Mom looked at me and smiled as she clapped. Bedouin celebrations stirred a joy within. The music. The dancing. It was impossible not to get caught up in the atmosphere of revelry.

The dancers broke from their circle and formed two rows, one in front of the other. Their shoulders shimmied as their hips continued to sway. Down they went on their knees. Left shoulder shimmy. Right. Up again.

One line turned in a half circle until their backs faced us, while the other row marked the beat with the repeated forward then back step. They joined to form one long line now, the left half of woman with backs toward us, the right half facing us. They joined palm to palm. Two beats. Spin. Palm to palm. Two beats. All the while their hips never stopped their languid circle motion.

Six years since I'd heard this music, immersed myself in this culture. Belonging snuggled into my chest and rested there. I'd missed it. Missed the familiarity of my childhood.

Learning and experiencing new things had been exciting. The bluegrass bands with their fiddles and banjos had made my toe tap a beat. But there was nothing like coming home.

Yara dropped to the pillow at my side, leaned toward me. "You should join in on the next one."

I laughed. "I'm out of practice. They dance a little differently in the States." The Electric Slide, the only dance I'd learned one night when I'd been dragged out for karaoke, wouldn't work too well in this setting.

"Once you get moving, I'm sure it would come back to you."

Should I? I felt caught up in the moment, pulled out of myself by the rhythm and laughter around me. The music itself danced in the air, hypnotizing me to join in.

I turned toward Yara, agreement poised on my lips until my gaze snagged on two women behind her shoulder. They huddled together, their arms brushing, heads bent toward the other. Hatred shot from their eyes fixed on me. The jubilant, carefree wave that I'd been caught up in dropped me, dumping a surge like cold water on top of my head.

Yara noticed my stare behind her and twisted to follow my line of sight. She turned back around, her face sober. "Ignore them."

"Why are they looking at me like that? What have I done to them?"

Yara laid a hand on my forearm. "Nothing. They are ignorant, superstitious women."

I searched her gaze. "It's because of the sheep, isn't it? My parents said they blame us."

"Yes, but none of that is your fault or theirs. The people will come to see that soon enough."

Would they? My gaze flicked back to the women. One looked right at me and spit on the ground before she stormed away. The other held her ground, her abhorrence seething from her body. If given the choice, she'd happily rally the women here and turn this *welcome back* celebration into a mob that would drive my parents and me from the face of the earth.

All the anticipation that had driven me the last half decade withered. How was I supposed to teach and spread the Good News if the people wanted to purge themselves of my very presence?

Chapter 4

KARIM

"Are you even listening to me, Karim?" Samlil asked, disgust in his voice. He huffed his frustration, turning to the other men in the tent, his hands outstretched, palms up.

I'd tuned him and every other man surrounding me out months ago. They always said the same thing.

Karim, you need a wife.

Karim, you need sons.

Karim, you need an heir.

As if those expectations hadn't already burrowed into my mind like an adder in the loose sand, waiting to strike and sink its deadly fangs into me. I had been married before, my sense of duty propelling me to make vows to a woman arranged for me by my father before his death. Maleka had come to me a blushing virgin, the match equally beneficial to our families. Hers for the power of marrying into the sheikh's lineage, ours for the money her father had presented mine as a gift.

Duty bound us, but love had never grown. I couldn't understand why. In everything, she was the perfect wife. Obedient. Modest. Gentle. She never raised her voice in anger. She rarely used her voice at all. Meek and...boring. Our tent had become overwhelmingly silent until I thought I'd go deaf by the sheer lack of conversation. There was no zest. Like a meal that had been prepared to perfection but not a dash of salt or a hint of seasoning had been used. Completely bland.

Maybe it was selfish, but I had no wish to tie myself to such a woman again. I wanted the bright slashes against the sky when the sun edged the horizon, flinging out arms of fire in a morning welcome. I wanted a wife who could awaken the same feeling of relief and joy as when, after too long in the desert, a weary traveler stumbled upon a hidden oasis. A wife who sustained life, drank from it, and replenished, not one that merely lived, adrift in the wind.

The image of Hannah the night before danced across my memory the way the light from the camp's flames had waltzed across her fresh, pale face. A dear friend, I'd always admired her spunk, even when the clan elders had frowned and clucked their tongue at the scrapes she'd gotten into growing up. They had wanted to curb her, mold her like the women do clay at the potter's wheel. But Hannah couldn't be fashioned into the same shape as every other woman. Though she held her tongue most of the time, presented an acceptable picture, I could read her thoughts as easily as the scrolling signs in the nearby city.

"I might as well be talking to the camels," Samlil grumbled.

"Should I oblige you with a spit, my friend?" My lips

tipped in a grin, but mirth didn't reach my eyes. How could it? A smile must first originate in the heart and take root before the harvest of joy in the windows to the soul.

Light chuckles sounded from the other leaders, but Samlil's frown only deepened.

"Karim."

My mother stepped from the shadows, her presence not surprising. While others of my country might not respect the women in their lives, not so with most of the males among our tribe. My father and his father had led by example, loving their wives and daughters and not being ashamed for allowing others to see their respect and affection. Instead of making my father and grandfather smaller in the eyes of the people, their openness had increased the clans' trust in them.

"Mother." I turned to face her and opened my ears to her words. While other men, Samlil too, even though he was my friend, had the good of the clan in their minds, my mother's scope was broad enough to include me as a man and not just me the sheikh.

She placed her weathered hands on my shoulders and pivoted until my back was toward the rest gathered. She alone held my attention. "It is time, my son. For our people, yes." Her warm palm rested over my heart. "But for you as well." She leaned in and whispered into my ear. "How can you be a great leader if you do not know love?"

In this instance she missed the mark, though she looked at me knowingly.

I did know love. The love of a son. A friend. A leader.

How could knowing the love of a woman, a wife, increase my love for my people as well as better equip me to lead them?

The rumble of an engine broke into my thoughts, followed by the closing of a vehicle's door. The Pratts must be back. They had taken the only truck the clan owned into town looking for answers about the flock. Had there been information shared by the veterinarian? Medicine?

Commotion filled the air like the overcrowded streets on market day. Shrieks, shouts.

My mother's hands fell away as I turned and followed Samlil's lanky frame over the tent's threshold and out into the shadows cast by the slant of the late-evening's sun.

Bodies pressed around the rusty Toyota truck, but Ethan Pratt stood a head taller than most men. Dried blood, dark and flaky, matted his hairline at his temple and drew a line down his face like a wadi in summer. He opened the passenger door and leaned in. The layer of grime caking the windshield couldn't hide his grimace as he scooped his wife into his arms and lifted to carry her weight. He teetered, and I thought he'd crumble in a heap, Elizabeth taking the brunt of his fall.

I pushed through the people until I stood beside Ethan. Up close, his injuries looked even more awful. Swelling, discoloration. The way he swayed, I wasn't sure he didn't have a concussion.

I slid my arms beside his under his wife. "I've got her."

He blinked at me, slow and hard, before offering a slight nod and allowing me to carry Elizabeth's full weight. Her head rolled to my shoulder, and she moaned against tightly pressed lips.

"What happened?" I probed Ethan's dull, gray eyes for an answer, but he wasn't looking at me. His gaze stayed on Elizabeth.

Had it been a mugging?

"My tent," he croaked, and I followed his limp past several other pitched homes to his own.

He lit a lantern, the sun ending its shift in the sky, giving way to a gibbous moon. I laid her in the corner upon a plush pallet covered by bright blankets and stepped back, giving Ethan room to kneel beside his wife. He checked her pulse at her wrist. Kissed the spot his fingers had pressed before lying her hand on the bed. With a deft touch, he ran his hands across her middle, stopping at spots to add pressure. She groaned and thrashed when he touched the ribs on her left side. Broken.

A shadow lengthened on the floor. I turned to see my mother in the doorway, a bowl of water in her hands, bandages hanging from her arm. I took both with a thanks and a kiss to her cheek before offering them to Ethan.

Danger lurked in the shadows. Took many forms. Why, then, this unsettling feeling in the pit of my stomach? This niggle that said there was more here than a common robbery that wouldn't even hit the gossiping tongues of the hawkers?

For privacy, I left Ethan to tend to his wife. Ignored the need that pushed against my ribs to find Hannah and make sure she was all right. Repented against the relief that flooded me at knowing no harm had befallen her while her parents had suffered so severely.

"Mom! Dad!" The words were shouted in English and yet so faint that I'd hardly made them out. My gaze scanned the landscape, trying to pick out Hannah's form from among the familiar shapes of our transient town. There. Running between a cooking fire and a yapping dog, her already pale face now almost white from fright. Her blue eyes even rounder and wider in her head. She stumbled and I caught her, our hands gripping the others' forearms.

"Maybe you should wait a moment before going—"

Her arms ripped from my grip, her wide eyes narrowing a fraction in accusation before she sidestepped me altogether and entered the dwelling.

"Hannah," I called as I stepped in after her, wanting to shield her from the sight of the blood coating her parents' skin.

Already she knelt beside her father, her mother's hand wrapped in one of her own. Ethan laid a hand on Hannah's head and kissed her temple.

The bowl of water lay on the ground, its once clear contents now hued red. Ethan had had enough time to wash away some of the day's evidence.

"What happened?" Hannah turned tear-filled eyes to her father.

I should've gone. Let the family have a private moment. But need staked my feet, and I leaned in to hear Ethan's response, my breath held lest I missed any detail.

"An ambush." His voice cracked on the English words as if it hadn't been dampened in far too long.

As I unhooked the camel-hide waterskin from my belt and handed it to him, I sent up a silent thanks for the language lessons Hannah and I had taken turns teaching each other in our youth.

The liquid swished within the canteen as Ethan tilted it to his cracked lips and drank deeply. He wiped his mouth with the back of his hand before handing me back the waterskin.

"A handful of men surrounded us as we were coming from the veterinarian."

"Why?" Hannah asked, her voice raw.

It was a good question. Maybe the root to a forest of questions, even. Had the men been there by chance and seen Ethan and Elizabeth as easy targets to rob? Were they familiar or strangers? The attack premeditated or spur of the moment? Ethan's use of the word *ambush* unsettled me even more.

The large American glanced my way before focusing again on his daughter. "Another warning, is all."

My organs turned to quicksand and swallowed my heart. How could men do things such as this to each other? This was not how Allah wanted his children to act. If the men had been extremists, I could only imagine the things they'd screamed at Ethan and Elizabeth while landing blows. Their belief that such zealous acts would remove any stain of American influence by force. This was not the lifeblood of our faith. Not the pulse of the Qur'an. Did not our very name, Islam, derive from the word meaning peace?

"What did they say?"

Hannah's small voice rested in the stillness, sobriety of the atmosphere surrounding us.

Ethan kissed her again. "It doesn't matter."

In any language that translated as a father not wanting his daughter to worry. Which meant the threat had been severe indeed.

I still had questions. Had Ethan recognized any of his attackers? I didn't want to think any close brother or sister of mine from the clan would do something like this, but I also couldn't afford to be naïve. The question wasn't one I was willing to ask within Hannah's earshot, however. Nor did I believe it one Ethan would wish to answer in her presence either.

Ethan tucked his daughter's head to his chest and raised his gaze to mine behind her back. Perhaps I wouldn't have to voice the question after all. I read the suspicion in his eyes. The same that curdled in my stomach.

How far? If things continued as they were, how far would the desperate go?

I nodded my head at Ethan and turned to give them the privacy the family deserved. My feet moved in a familiar direction, my body heeding my subconscious need for peace and time to think. My limbs felt weighed down. By sadness. Grief. Responsibility. I shut the door on all the thoughts knocking. Waited to entertain them one by one. Hear their arguments and weigh their merits.

The sky was blanketed in black except for a line from apex to horizon. As if a great warrior struck a lethal slash of his dagger in the cosmos' belly, letting in a wide thread of milky light.

The cavern's mouth opened above me, and I climbed the rock's face. Hauled my body up until my feet dangled over the edge. Slowly I unlocked the entrance of my mind.

Would the Pratts heed the warnings and flee to safety?

No. They had made my people their people. Trouble had come to us all in the past, and they had never abandoned us before.

Would the threats against them continue?

I knew the answer, though I didn't want it to form on my tongue.

Was there anything I could do about the situation? Anything I could do to protect Hannah and her parents?

There lay the crux. I stared out into the rift of the night sky that allowed me to glimpse the galaxy, and willed an answer to wash over me. If it took until dawn, I was determined not to leave until I knew of a way to make things right.

Chapter 5

HANNAH

"Are all Christian missionaries so stubborn?" Yara's question held no accusation. Especially since a sweet laugh and a decided sparkle in her eye accompanied it.

I grunted as I hammered in the last tent stake. My hijab looked four shades darker around the band on my forehead, having done a good job of soaking up the sweat before it ran down into my eyes.

As of yet, I had no students enrolled in school. I swung the hammer one more time and then rose from my bent position and stepped back. The school that was now officially erected.

Were we stubborn? As a camel—which were so much more obstinate than donkeys, in my humble opinion. Although maybe driven would be a better word? What would the early disciples have called it, as time after time they were imprisoned for their faith?

If only my heart didn't quake and my tongue thicken when I thought about Mom and Dad and their beating.

Surely Stephen had not quivered in fear as he'd asked God to forgive those *while* they were stoning him. Familiar with the stories from *Fox's Book of Martyrs*, that the rivers of blood that flowed from believers willing to die for their faith watered a harvest unlike any other, I wouldn't lie and say I was ready to die. I wasn't. I wanted to live. Get married. Have babies. Grow old.

Your will. Not mine.

My Bible lay open on my pallet, Matthew 16:24–25 highlighted and underlined. I'd taken to reading the passage every day to remind myself, to comfort myself, to rally myself. I closed my eyes and whispered the words from memory, "If anyone would come after me, let him deny himself and take up his cross and follow me. For whoever would save his life will lose it, but whoever loses his life for my sake will find it."

Maybe I was being dramatic, taking the assault on my parents further than its logical conclusion. After all, we'd lived among the Bedouins for most of my life and we'd never had real reason to fear for our safety before.

"Hannah?" Yara laid a hand on my shoulder, and I jumped.

"Sorry." I forced a small smile. "Lost in thought."

Her head tilted in a way that said she understood. Though our feet traveled different paths, worry understood worry. Fear, fear. Determination, determination. Emotions were one thing that bound us all. No matter race, gender, religion, background, or worldview, not a single one of us could run from or turn off our feelings...whether they haunted us or welcomed us.

"Class begins tomorrow, yes?" Her gaze flicked to the steepled structure.

"I will be here tomorrow." With my curriculum and lesson plans if nothing else.

Her hand on my shoulder squeezed. "You will not be alone. Eamon has granted permission for our children to attend your school." Her eyes sparkled again. "More than permission. He is excited about the prospect, though don't tell him I told you that. I believe he secretly hopes all three of our little ones will grow up to be great doctors one day."

"Anything is possible." Especially if I enhanced the science curriculum and integrated it into some of the other subjects, like reading, writing, and mathematics.

The sheen in Yara's eyes changed as tears developed. "I know." Her voice cracked, and she covered her mouth with her palm. After a moment she spoke again. "I know. Eamon, he wishes to learn also. From your father." Her lips curved into a beautiful smile. "He is ready to hear more about *Isa*."

A thrill ran up and down my spine as sheer joy danced in my chest. I wanted to jump and twirl and laugh, but such a display would only draw undue attention, so I settled for a wide smile. Yara and I had been praying for years for Eamon to be open to listening to the Gospel message and the truth of Jesus's love. And now it'd happened. Prayers answered before our eyes.

Yara cleared the emotion from her throat. "Along with our children, you will have a few more students as well. At least two other families are willing to allow their children to attend, granted you keep the boys and girls separated."

Having the boys sit on one side of the tent and the girls on the other had always been my plan. From there I'd assess their levels and group them accordingly. "Of course."

"Good." Yara wrapped me in her bony arms. "It's so good to have you back, *'ukht*."

Sister. It was good to be back.

"Hannah."

My name and the familiar voice had me turning, a smile on my lips for Karim. My mouth drooped, however, as I took in his stony expression. Shoulders bunched under his white thawb. The turban wrapped around his head failed to hide the pulsing of his vein at the temple. Dark crescents rimmed the bottom of his eyes. Had he slept at all last night?

Always serious, his brooding expression shouldn't have unnerved me. Why, then, the congealing in my stomach?

"I need a word with you." His gaze darted to Yara. "In private."

My friend tilted her head toward Karim before meeting my gaze, her eyes communicating that she'd offer up a prayer for me. Which only cinched my belly tighter. Even Yara had picked up on the tension coating the air. The tension that had wound its way through Karim's sinewy muscles so tightly that it appeared any moment he might snap.

I took a step toward him, wanting to ease the frown from his forehead. "What is it?"

He shook his head. "Not here." He turned and took two steps before looking back over his shoulder. "Follow me."

I took no offense at his gruff manner. Culturally, it was acceptable. As a leader, it was expected. Those reasons weren't what made me place my sandals within the footprints he'd left in his wake. It was the guardedness of his eyes. The wariness of his tone. He wished to speak with me openly, not within hearing distance of others who might judge him for his words and actions.

I followed him to the rock face, the cave he'd shown me when I was ten. The Bedouins are a nomadic people. Transient. Always moving. But like migrating butterflies, they returned to the same destinations. Karim had a special spot in almost every place his father had stopped the clan to pitch their makeshift town. Over the years he'd shared a few of them with me.

I particularly remembered this one. It was after a big wedding feast. The first I'd ever attended in my new country. The ceremony had been so different from my aunt's wedding in Iowa. She'd gotten married in a big puffy gown, lit a unity candle, and a woman had sung "The Lord's Prayer." Afterward, at the reception, they kissed any time someone rang a bell, and we'd all eaten poached salmon and steamed broccoli. But here? I'd been fascinated by everything. That is until I had taken my first bite of the traditional wedding feast's main course...and then lost my contents in front of everyone. Their laughter rang in my ears as I stumbled away from the merriment.

Karim had followed me, a smile crinkling the corners of his dark eyes, a cloth napkin in one hand and a cup of juice in the other. I'd wiped my mouth and swished that juice over my tongue until it turned warm. Then I'd swallowed, slightly less mortified now that my taste buds had something else to cling to. Wordlessly, he'd led me up here, and we'd watched the festivities like hawks in their nest.

We sat at the mouth, our legs dangling over the edge, hands inches apart as they braced in the dirt beside our thighs. I waited. Karim would speak when he was ready.

"The elders want me to marry." His face pointed out

toward the horizon, as if he were willing the expanse to snatch his words as soon as they left his mouth.

Surprise stilled my finger, which had been drawing circles in the loose sand on the stone ground. Karim hadn't married? At thirty it was past time for him to have taken a wife and have children. At least, the way things worked here anyway.

As if reading my thoughts, he glanced at me with a smirk. "I should say, marry *again*." He looked back out at the endless desert landscape. "My wife died of a terrible fever that not even your parents could save her from."

I studied him, looking for signs of grief for his deceased wife or anger at my parents for not being able to save her. His words were spoken as if he were reciting a fact from a textbook. Something that had occurred that was far removed from him. Like it hadn't touched him personally at all. "I'm sorry."

"Every woman in the region has been presented to me." He continued as if he hadn't heard me, and I wondered if his wife's death had affected him so little or if the opposite were true. Had he been so in love with her that it was too painful to even mention the loss?

"There are many wonderful women who would make you a good wife."

The corner of his lip tilted a fraction even as his head gave an imperceptible shake. Then he turned his full gaze on me. The one that plunged deep inside my soul. "Speak to me as a friend, Hannah."

I swallowed against the dryness in my throat, the awareness that rippled from my center like a stone tossed in a still lake. I looked into Karim's face, seeing so many familiar things, memories of the boy I'd grown up with, but assaulted with the awareness of everything new. Of the *man* he'd become.

At this distance, every hair of his beard became defined. The lighter brown tones mixed with the darker ones that matched the slightly curly hair of his head. The scar that ran along his jaw from a hunting accident when he was sixteen. The faint lines that said he smiled too little. The deeper ones that said he frowned too often.

His gaze washed over me, and I was on the other side of the scrutiny. What would he discover about me? Had I changed so much in six years? Or in the seventeen since we'd first became friends?

"Why don't you want to marry any of those women, Karim?"

His gaze searched me, captured mine, and probed. "I don't want to be bound in another loveless marriage."

My lungs constricted and held. Then he looked away, and all my breath whooshed out, leaving me a little dizzy. He hadn't loved his first wife. My stomach tumbled in a funny way. I tried to make sense of everything. The things he was saying, the weird things I was feeling, the way he'd looked at me.

"It doesn't matter though. I have to marry." Steel edged his voice now as he pushed away his desires as a man and put on the responsibilities he felt as a leader.

I'd have said I was sorry if I thought that would have comforted him at all.

He turned his whole body to face me. His knee brushed mine with his movement. He caught my hand and squeezed. Looked me in the eye.

Blood fled from my cheeks as realization dawned on what he was about to say.

"I'm going to marry you, Hannah."

Karim

Often, I'd watched Hannah's cheeks turn crimson. From the heat. From embarrassment. From sheer joy. Never had I seen them drain of all color. Become as white as newly washed fleece. Mortification marked every muscle of her face, from the slackness of her jaw to the twitch around her eye.

Half of me wanted to laugh—her expression was amusing —the other half groan. Was the prospect of marriage to me that horrifying?

"Karim, I—"

"Let me explain," I interrupted. Maybe my explanation would save her from any embarrassment. And hopefully she'd see the logic in my proposal.

Her hands folded in her lap, and her spine straightened. She'd hear me but her guards were up. The wary expression in her eyes cautioned me to tread carefully but did little to hide the questions racing through her mind.

Would my honest confession do more to win her favor or set her further from me? "I said I do not wish for a loveless marriage, Hannah, and I don't."

Her brows shot to the sky.

I rushed on. "You have been a dear friend to me for many years, so of course there is love in my heart for you."

She tilted her head as she regarded me, and I met her

steady gaze with one of my own. Nothing would I keep hidden. Not from her.

"As a friend," she clarified.

I couldn't read her expression now. Couldn't tell if the way her words had come out as a whisper was disappointment or relief. "Yes."

"Then why..." She let the question hang, no doubt trying to piece together my logic.

"It is the answer that will settle many problems."

Her folded hands became folded arms across her chest. I was losing her. "The clan demands that I marry, but I don't want any of the women they've selected. You and your family have come under attack. By our marriage, two problems will be solved."

Her arms fell to her sides. "You want to marry me to protect me and my parents?"

Why did she sound so surprised? "Yes. As my wife, no one would dare hurt you or your family."

There was no missing the sadness that floated across her eyes like a cloud that dotted the blue of the sky. "No." She shook her head. "I can't."

Pride burned my esophagus, but I pushed back the pain. "Why?"

"Our protection comes from, God, Karim. Not man." The softness of her gaze cushioned her reprimand. Then she looked away, her fingers playing with the sides of her abaya. "Besides, it would not be fair to either of us to marry without love being the foundation."

She stood and walked a few steps away, pretended to be interested in the sandstone that had been washed away for so many years that it had created this cavern.

I had spent the entire night in thought and prayer. This was the only way I knew to keep her and her family safe. There had to be a way I could persuade her, have her see the logic that was as clear as the sun was hot.

Standing, I walked toward her, stopping only a foot away. I didn't say anything. Didn't move or touch her, but she stilled, aware of my presence. Silence rested in the hollowness of the cave, but my pulse beat like a drum in my ear. I waited. Listened. Not with my ears but with my soul. With the fibers of my body that made a person more than just a physical being. Deep down I felt it. Felt our hearts beat as one.

Of all that I could offer her—my protection, my name, my power, my wealth—could I give the one thing she'd protested against? My love? Was a heart even something a person could give to another, or did it have a mind of its own, falling for whomever it saw fit without giving any regard to the person for which it gave life?

Heat radiated off Hannah as I stood at her back. Her breathing had shallowed as she'd become impossibly still. Invisible, electrical currents shot through the space between us, like lightning seeking the ground. Always there had been this connection. This draw. As a boy, I'd thought it had been my fascination with her blue eyes and gold hair. My very own hidden treasure, like in the book my mother had brought home for me on market day when I was thirteen, *Treasure Island*.

The burning in my esophagus lowered until my belly ached with glowing embers.

I had to convince her. I couldn't let anything happen to my *kanz*, my treasure.

With a hand to her shoulder, I turned her to face me, saw my reflection in her eyes as if I were peering into the depths of an oasis spring. A spark of rebellion had me lifting my hand, pulling back the confining material of her hijab until a waterfall of gold tresses cascaded over my brown fingers. My gratefulness deepened that we were hidden from the censuring gazes of the clan, which would steal the wonderment from the moment. Allah forgive me for plucking the modesty from Hannah's head, the crown of her beauty reserved for her husband alone. Though I should feel shame for my actions, the delight coursing through me would not lead me to repentance.

Her gaze held confusion, and the beat of her heart that had matched mine kicked up its pace.

"Hannah," I whispered. "Please. Do you not think love can grow?"

Chapter 6

HANNAH

Seven heads bowed over makeshift desks, pencils scratching against the paper I'd stuffed into my luggage along with other supplies for the school. When I'd pushed my cart through the homeschool warehouse in Chattanooga, I'd related to how Charlie must have felt on his tour through the Chocolate Factory. Undiluted awe. But I'd bypassed the alphabet borders and brightly colored inspirational posters, zeroing in instead on essentials. Books. Paper. Pencils. Crayons. Rulers. If nothing else, I'd teach with a stick and write in the mass supply of sand, but smiles would erupt the minute a child put a crimson crayon to a fresh sheet of paper.

One of Yara's children coughed from the front, then wiped his nose with the back of his hand. He bent back over his paper and added more words.

I walked through the center aisle of the tent, boys to my left, girls to my right. Everyone worked on their assignments. The older children wrote an essay on what they'd like to be when they grew up. The younger students drew pictures of the same subject. A simple assignment, one many teachers had implemented throughout the years. But it would tell me a lot about my new charges. What were their dreams and aspirations? How well could they communicate through the written word? Their vocabulary, syntax, and overall language skills. It was an elementary introduction.

And the last assignment of the day, thank the Lord.

I had been looking forward to this, the first day of teaching these children, and yet my mind had been rebellious, never staying on task. Always straying.

I am going to marry you.

Do you not think love can grow?

When I should have been focused on helping Ahida grasp the concept of place value, Karim's words from the night before wedged their way into my head and pushed the simple math lesson out.

Even when we'd paused for the midday Dhur prayers, the children standing facing Mecca, eyes cast to the ground where their foreheads would touch, my mind wandered.

"*Allah-hoo Akbar.*" Allah is Great.

Lord... But that was it. That was as far as my prayer went before my mind seized. Like a river littered with debris rushing with its mighty current, then jamming as all the logs collided in the water's narrow ford.

The children had raised their hands level with their shoulders, then placed their left hand on their chests and their right hand over their left. "*Subhaan-Allaah wal-hamdu Lillaah wa laa Ill-Allaah wa Allaah-hoo akbar wa laa hawla wa la quwwata illa Billaah.*" Glory be to Allah, there is no god except Allah, Allah is most great and there is no power and no strength except with Allah.

Even with my log-jammed mind, the words reminded me of Psalm 48:1. *Great is the Lord, and greatly to be praised...*

That, at least, I was certain. Everything else?

The children had continued in their recitation, and I'd tried again with my own prayer.

Father God...

For a heart and mind so full, my words to the Creator were empty.

Had anyone's life changed so much in three days? Three days! That was all it had been since I'd said goodbye to my friends at the international airport in Atlanta, dreams in my head of teaching and longing in my heart to reunite with my family.

Three days. Hmm. Maybe I should be thankful I wasn't in the belly of a big stinky fish. Okay, Jonah still held the trophy for worst trifecta of all time.

"*Assalamu alaikum wa rahmatullah.*" Peace and mercy of Allah be on you.

My stomach had sunk when I'd realized I'd wasted the time of all four *rakahs*, the children's prayer time—and mine —now ended. My soul hadn't found peace, and Karim's words still swirled around my thoughts like a whirlpool.

The last child handed me her paper—a stick figure with two wooly lambs drawn in the middle—with a smile. I touched the top of her head and smiled in return. "I'm so glad to have you in class."

She waved and then turned and ran out of the tent, yelling to her siblings to wait for her.

Collecting the papers, I placed them in a woven satchel so I could take them home and read them. The sides of the tent had been rolled up hours ago for ventilation, and I was thankful for the shade the structure provided. Near the front of the tent, I'd brought in one of our large stuffed pillows, perfect for story time. Digging into my pocket, I withdrew a small travel-sized Bible, settled myself in the middle of the floor pillow, and laid the Bible on my lap. I closed my eyes, not bothering to form words I knew wouldn't come. Instead I opened my heart, thankful that the God I served knew even the secret things held there.

Not knowing exactly what I needed, I propped the Bible on its spine and let it fall open wherever it would. Looking down, I traced my finger along the book's heading. Esther. I started reading.

What girl raised in a Christian home didn't know the story of Esther? A beautiful queen, she saved her people from the evil Haman. But I read, soul open to any stirrings of the Holy Spirit. My longing for guidance drove the tracking of my eyes over the pages.

The similarities of our stories weren't lost on me, and I felt my lips curve in a wry smile. Esther had been a simple Jewish girl living among a nation that was not her own. Same, except for the Jewish part. But we worshiped the same God, so that counted in my book.

The king had the choice of every eligible maiden in the land. Yep. Karim had said the women had almost literally been paraded before him. King Ahasuerus had chosen Esther —as Karim had chosen me. But perhaps not for the same reasons. My eyes scanned the story, stumbling on words familiar: *for such a time as this.*

I tried to read on. Pushed my gaze to Esther's response to her cousin Mordecai's question, but it was like pushing against the elastic boundaries of a boxing ring. My focus kept being flung back to those words—*for such a time*.

Laughter that had been coated in a layer of sarcasm tumbled from my mouth. God had asked his followers to do a lot of crazy things in the past...even some revolving around marriage. Poor Hosea. But was He really asking me to do *this*?

I cared about Karim. How could I not? He was my good friend. And ever since I'd come back, there had been this odd awareness around him that I hadn't felt when we were children. But sisterly care and awareness did not a good marriage make. So much more was needed to form a solid foundation. Core beliefs, for one.

As if the logjam that had dammed my mind burst, arguments on both sides flooded my thoughts. I tried to still them, to listen. Discernment wasn't easy when the cacophony like that of a spring runoff whooshed in your ears.

I shut my eyes. Pictured Esther. Let her story play in my imagination as if I were watching it in a movie theater. And slowly my paradigm shifted until it lined up like the sun and moon during an eclipse. A shadow and a light.

But who was the shadow and who was the light? The sun and the moon? Was I really supposed to step into Esther's shoes and trace my life after her pattern?

I groaned and let my head fall into my hands. It would be so much easier if God would send an angel. Gideon got one. Samuel's mother. Mary.

Fear not.

The greeting of the angels. Had the two words come from my memory of their own accord, or had they been given by a supernatural prodding?

"First day went that well, did it?"

Yara's voice had me lifting my head.

"Funny. My kids look a lot happier than you at the moment."

I stood and gave her a quick hug. "I'm glad to hear it."

"Ahida is currently giving the new litter of puppies a math lesson while Ahmed is pestering his father by retelling some story he heard from you today. Something about bears."

"Goldilocks and the Three Bears."

"Right." From behind her back, she withdrew something wrapped in cloth. "I brought this for you to celebrate, but maybe it's for consolation instead?" She unwrapped the cloth to reveal a date cake and handed it to me with a raised brow.

I took the treat and bit into it, relishing the way the sweet fruit covered my taste buds. Plus the chewing gave me an excuse not to answer. Especially since I wasn't sure *what* to answer at this point.

"Maybe the groan I heard from you had more to do with Karim yesterday and less to do with the children today?"

Gracious, she. To pose it as a question instead of the simple statement we both knew was true.

I nodded and took another bite of cake, not the least ashamed to hide behind manners that dictated not talking with one's mouth full.

"And Karim said something to upset you."

My shoulders rose in a shrug—yes and no.

She eyed me with a small smile as I shoved the last of the cake into my mouth then tapped her chin in concentration. "Sort of upset you and more than overtook your thoughts." Her gaze slid my way. "And your courage."

I choked on a crumb, and she laughed. Her eyes looked

distant as she thought, then her gaze slammed into mine, her eyes wide. "He's going to marry again."

I swallowed hard before my jaw unhinged and all the food in my mouth fell to the floor. How did she—

I couldn't even finish the thought before I was wrapped up in a fierce hug. "Oh, Hannah. I am so sorry."

Umm. What? "Yara." I pulled back so I could see her face. "Why are you apologizing?"

"It's no wonder you're devastated." Her palms covered her mouth. "Karim's going to marry another woman."

Trying to follow her train of thought was harder than pushing a boulder up a mountain. "I'm not devastated, and he's not marrying someone else."

"He's not?" Her hands dropped. "So it isn't about Karim?"

"Yes, but..." I took a deep breath in and blew it out. "He wants to marry me." Although maybe *want* wasn't the right word. Compelled? Duty bound?

Modest, reserved Yara squealed. Actually squealed, then grabbed my hands. "This is so romantic. I knew. For years, I've known you two would end up together."

"What are you talking about?" I didn't even know *now* if we would end up together.

"The special bond you have. The way he's always looked at you." She gave a dreamy sigh this time, the same you'd see in a bad film right before the girl swooned.

Ridiculous. "He only looks at me differently because *I'm* different. There aren't many women with blue eyes and pasty-white skin around here."

She ignored my comment as if any sensible argument would damper this "romantic" notion she had.

"When's the ceremony going to take place? Before we move on, I hope."

Maybe I should have kept all of this to myself. "I'm not even sure there will be a ceremony, Yara."

She looked aghast now. "What are you talking about?"

"I love Karim, sure. My feelings for him are *mahabba*. A simple love of a friend. But I do not feel *sabaaba*." My cheeks flushed at the meaning of the word. The longing and ardor that resides in the heart of one madly in love with another.

"So?"

"What do you mean, *so?*"

From anyone else, her laugh would have been insulting. "Stop being so...American."

Umm...

"My father arranged my marriage to Eamon. The first time I ever laid eyes on him was on our wedding day. Now I couldn't imagine loving any other man."

My thoughts went to Samlil's wife. Theirs had also been made by their families. The result hadn't ended up as happily as Yara's. "It doesn't always happen that way, I'm afraid."

Her face fell a little. Probably thinking of some women she knew. "No, you're right." Her hand squeezed mine. "But you know Karim."

Yes, I knew him. Knew he'd never lay a violent hand to me. That he'd respect me as a woman and as a person. But what about as a Christian? He'd never said anything against my beliefs. Nor had he ever shown an interest in them.

"I'm curious," she started and then paused.

"About?"

"If you do not believe it is for love—and I have my own thoughts on that—then why did Karim offer for you?"

"He said it would benefit us both. The elders have been pressuring him to marry and the climate against my family has heated lately. He believes a union between us would solidify our place among the people and satisfy the expectations placed upon him."

Yara's eyes narrowed. Not at me, but like she was trying hard to remember something.

"I recall," she said, "a story you told me a long time ago. It was about a young woman who became a queen and ended up saving an entire nation. Doesn't that sound a little similar to your situation?"

My heart stalled...and then kicked in to high gear. I had a special phrase I called times like these. When God used someone or something to nudge me. Like a highlighter on a specific passage. Or a fluorescent light in a dark room. I called them sacred echoes. I'd read it once in a book and adapted it as my own ever since.

And the echo I heard now reverberated against every bone in my body before seeping down into the marrow.

I'm going to be a sheikh's wife.

Chapter 7

KARIM

The ewe bleated mournfully as its stomach clenched in another contraction. I ran my free hand over the bulge, feeling the lamb within while my other hand was inside the animal, waiting for the contraction to pass so I could grip the legs and help the mother with the birthing. The mother's stomach convulsed only with the constant intervals of her pains and not with any sign of life within.

If sheer will alone could make a heart pump blood and lungs fill with air, this lamb would be born alive and well. Threads of hope were all I had of that outcome. More than likely this baby would come into this world like the three others had in the last hour. Stillborn.

My grip on the lamb's legs tightened, and when the ewe bore down, I gritted my teeth and pulled. Embryonic fluid dripped from the birth canal before two tiny hooves emerged. Gentling my touch, I cooed to the mother. Her breathing had grown labored, all the energy seeping out of her. A spasm overtook her, her muscles tightening of their own will. My fingers slipped from the body fluid, but I repositioned and gave a firm but easy tug. Six pounds of livestock slipped onto the birthing bed I'd made hours earlier.

No sound. No movement.

With a cupped hand, I opened the small mouth and scooped out any fluid that blocked the air passages and repeated the process with the baby's nostrils.

Breathe. Please, breathe.

Nothing.

In an act of desperation, I bent at the waist and leaned over the too-still head, holding its lower jaw in my hand. With mouth to nose, I blew, giving the source of my life to this little body in hopes that it too might live.

I wasn't sure how long I tried to resuscitate the lamb, fighting against the denial that was losing a battle with reality. A shadow crossed overhead, and still I blew, my thoughts repeating one single word—*breathe.* Someone knelt beside me, their presence fracturing the front lines of my inner war, and still I blew.

"Karim."

My name was the white flag of surrender. Nothing I could do would save this lamb. My vision blurred, and I blinked once. Hard. Pushed back the visual signs of my emotions. I did not weep for a single lamb. I wept for the future of my people. Already we fought to keep our traditions and culture in a world that embraced convenience and technology. If we lost the nucleus of who we were, we'd fizzle out into nonexistence.

Leaning back, I let the dead animal's head go and rested my hands on my thighs. Blood streaked my forearms all the way to my elbows, and red stained the front of my tailored thawb.

"Karim."

I turned to the voice, the wall that kept all the weight of responsibility almost bursting from the compassion shining in Hannah's eyes. Her expression open, if not her arms. An expression that said she wished she could lighten my load. Share my burden.

We sat there, side by side, not saying a word. A funny thing, silence. It could stretch until you thought you'd snap, make you so uncomfortable you could barely stay still, or slowly pull from you the stress that coiled in your center like a massage that loosens the muscles.

My breathing came easier, my limbs looser. I reached for the basin of water and washed my hands and forearms, letting the grime slick away from my skin. I stood, and Hannah followed suit. When I took a step toward the other sheep in the pasture, I felt her presence just behind me. No doubt her gaze also downcast.

Why did that unquiet my soul?

When we stood amid the majority of the herd, I stopped. Following my cues, Hannah also stopped.

For the first time, I wondered why she'd sought me out. Did it have to do with our conversation the night before?

"They really are sick, aren't they?" Her soft voice held concern. I looked at her over my shoulder. Her forehead crumpled as she stared at one lamb in particular. I followed her gaze, took in the pathetic creature that had once boasted of hardy stock.

"Yes." And I had no idea how to make them well again.

"Was there something you needed, Hannah?" I turned toward her then. Waited.

"I..." Her gaze wouldn't meet mine, even though we had relative privacy. If one didn't count the sheep, that was.

"Look at me, Hannah." It was a command, but not sharp. I needed to see her eyes. Read her thoughts. I needed to feel that connection that had always grounded me in her presence.

Those sapphires turned up at me, wide and a little frightened. How inappropriate it would be for me to run my finger along the crest of her cheek. How I longed to do it. "It's just me." *No need to fear.*

Her throat worked, and then her pink lips opened. "I have decided to accept your proposal of marriage."

Relief sagged my bones while simultaneously energizing my limbs. Hannah would be safe. The embers that had glowed in the pit of my belly surged to life as desire blew a strong wind and kicked them into full flames.

She would be mine.

"But..." Unspoken words flashed across her eyes as she struggled to find just the right ones.

Other shepherds tended this herd, so I had to be careful. But I also wanted to give reassurance. I took a step closer to her, the back of my hand grazing hers. "All will be well."

"I am Christian, Karim." Her brows dipped.

Not ideal, but also not something I hadn't taken into consideration. "This I know."

"I will not convert to Islam."

So that was her worry. "I will not ask it of you. Just, as I am sure, you will not try to convert me to Christianity."

She looked away.

Oh no.

With a hook of my finger under her chin, I brought her face back to mine. Waited until her eyes raised to meet my gaze. "You will not convert me, Hannah."

Another funny thing about silence—it could speak. And hers said more than I wanted to hear. "Say it."

"I will not convert you, Karim." Her warm breathed fanned my face. The sparks grew higher.

I let my hand drop and took a half step back, filling my lungs with air not tainted by the lingering hint of her morning Arabic coffee. Looking away, I let the line of earth meeting sky ground me. When I looked back, Hannah's forehead was still furrowed.

"Something else that worries you?"

Her gaze rested on my chest, and while I was tempted to tell her to look at me again, something told me eye contact would only hinder the words emerging from her mouth.

"You've been married before." Soft words. And forced.

A loveless unity. She could not feel threatened by my memory of my first wife. Why then the concern? "Yes."

Her weight shifted as her gaze flicked up to mine but a moment before returning to my chest. "I have not."

"No." Understanding dawned and drew out the word. Heat crawled up my neck, and this time it was I who had to look away. In what manner could I reassure her that the ways between a man and wife were not something to fear? Or was it even fear? How much had her parents shared with her?

A groan lodged in my throat. I was ill prepared to have this conversation with a young woman...any woman! Perhaps my mother would be willing?

"Do you..." I cleared my throat against the thickness built

there. "Do you need to talk to another woman about..." Modesty sealed my lips from the last word. Sex.

Her blush rose all the way to her hairline. "No. I know...I mean...I'm familiar with..." Her shoulders rose weakly. "You know."

My head tilted back as I turned my face up to the sun. This was not going to work. Already there would be enough to stand between us. No matter the embarrassment, I couldn't let whatever her concern was go unanswered. But we couldn't have this conversation here.

"Come on." I marched past the far end of the pasture toward the cave. My legs ate up the distance, determination lengthening my stride. When we reached the mouth of the cavern, Hannah panted beside me, and I kicked myself for the thoughtlessness that caused her undue exertion.

In an act of apology, I slid off my outer cloak and laid it upon the ground for her to sit upon.

"Whenever we are in the area," I said as I settled beside her, "this will be our special place. Whenever we need to speak to one another without the threat of other ears hearing us, we will come here. Agreed?"

"Agreed."

I took a deep breath and pushed on. "Now, what has you concerned?"

She looked down at her folded hands in her lap. "I shouldn't have brought it up."

"Hannah, look at me."

She did, her eyes pinched at the corners.

"We have been friends for many years and have shared countless secrets. Nothing has come between our friendship, and as your soon husband, I want nothing between us now. You can trust me."

"I know. It's just...I'm a little nervous, is all."

A question pierced my mind sharper than if I'd taken the gold-edged dagger from my belt and pricked my skull. "When you were in America, were you ever with a man?"

Her eyes widened until they resembled two full moons. "Karim, no. How could you even think—"

My laughter interrupted her, for I had caught my mistake even if she had not. If anything, the tension between us over the topic had waned from my miscommunication. "I did not mean *that*. I meant, did you have a boyfriend?"

"For a short while." There she went, avoiding eye contact again.

"Did he kiss you?"

She toyed with her fingertips. "Once."

I clipped the weed of jealousy that took root. I had no right to feel such, and it would only make it that more difficult for a garden of love to grow between us.

"How did you feel when he kissed you?"

"Karim, I don't think—"

"How did it make you feel, Hannah?"

Again a shrug. "I didn't feel much of anything, I suppose."

My lips tilted in a grin. "Then he did not do it right."

She slanted a gaze at me from the corner of her eye, her mouth also bowed from my smug declaration.

I stood and offered her my hand, which she took and also rose. I led her farther into the cave's belly until the light barely illuminated the darkness.

"Where are we going?"

"To ease your fears."

At that she giggled. "From inside a cave?"

I stopped, making sure her back was to the wall. She had courage—the very fact she'd returned to teach children among a nation who did not place a high value on such, instead of staying in a life of comfort in her own country, a testament to that. But I had no idea how she'd react to my little lesson.

"I went to a concert once, about five years ago. The national orchestra played in the capitol, and I took my mother to hear it."

"She must have loved that."

"She did." I took a step toward her and placed a palm against the cool rock beside her head. "I was hypnotized, watching the conductor. Each flick of his wand produced a response in the instruments. The woodwinds soaring, the brass shouting, the percussion beating, until they all rose into a harmony that had you feeling out of this world." I let the back of my hand graze her cheek before anchoring my palm on the other side of her head. "When two become one, even in as simple an act as a kiss, it is a little like a beautifully composed piece of music. Both are the conductor. Both are the orchestra."

Slowly, I lowered my head, allowing time for her to stop the lesson if she wished. When she didn't move, didn't utter a sound, I pressed my lips against hers. A steady cadence of a drum beat from my center, determined the rhythm. I kissed her again, gently taking in her bottom lip between my own. The strings of violin and cello sang a mournful cry, and the sweetness carried me to the next bar. Hannah's hand reached up, her fingers running through the short hairs of my beard, and the music within me responded to her touch. My nails dug into the stone to anchor me, lest I lose myself in the moment. Her mouth parted, and I wanted nothing else than to continue this song we were making. I'd thought to teach her that unity could be a beautiful thing, but hadn't counted on learning in the process.

Never—I broke away, my breathing labored—never had I been stirred in such a manner.

Chapter 8

HANNAH

I wasn't one to bite my lip in worry, but this was the fourth time I'd caught myself with my bottom lip between my teeth. Cinnamon and cloves permeated the air as steam from the tea drifted upward. My parents sat on overplush pillows, waiting for me to reveal why I'd called them together for a family meeting in the first place.

I tilted the kettle, my hands shaking, and watched as the tinted hot water cascaded into the cups like a tiny waterfall. I took a fortifying breath before lifting the tray and carrying it to my parents. They each took a cup, their eyes full of questions but their lips unmoving.

Slowly I sat in front of them, smoothed out the folds of my dress. "Mom. Dad." *Prepare yourselves.*

That was the whole point of me talking to them first, after all. In respect of our cultural traditions, Karim had wanted to come to my father and ask his blessing to our union. He must have seen that in a movie once or read it in a book. I had no other idea where he'd have learned it.

That wasn't how things worked with the Bedouins. Here, the intended-groom's father or a mediator worked out the particulars, such as the dowry the groom would offer the bride's family. The reasons joining in matrimony would be beneficial to the families. No declarations of undying love fell from the groom's lips to the future father-in-law's ears, as Muslims traditionally believed love came from marriage, not the other way around.

Well. I guess we were following tradition fairly closely, after all. Except for Karim's insistence on talking to my father himself, that was.

Which was why I sat there, stalling as I brought the cup to my lips and took a drink of fragrant tea. I thought it would be better if I broke the news to my parents myself first, before Karim showed up and blindsided them. He hadn't been happy but respected my firm decision that this would be the best way to handle the situation.

I hadn't counted on how uncomfortable this would be. Especially since I knew exactly how my parents were going to respond.

"Something on your mind, Hannah?" Mom's face was still swollen and discolored. Against my father's wishes, she'd insisted on getting out of bed for a few moments. Her ribs were wrapped tightly, but I noticed the sheen of sweat along her hairline.

"Why don't you return to your pallet, Mom. You need rest to heal."

She took a sip of tea. "I think I'm okay for another few moments. Besides, you look so ominous I think I should probably stand for the news."

Actually, no. She probably should lay down. That way if she fainted, she couldn't hurt herself further.

Dad reached over and squeezed my knee. "What is it, sweetheart? You can tell us."

"Ummm...okay. I'm just going to go ahead and say it."

Except my mouth didn't want to say the words.

"Yes?" Mom put her cup down. Clasped her hands.

"Karim has asked me to marry him, and I've accepted." There. The sentence might have rushed out on a single breath, but at least it was out there.

Mom and Dad shared a look before they faced me again. Mom licked her lips, and Dad adjusted his weight on the pillow.

"I didn't know you two were in love." Mom tilted her head, puzzled. Trying to remember, no doubt, a time when Karim or I had shown anything more than friendship toward the other.

She wasn't in the cave yesterday. That thought sent a shiver down my spine. Thank goodness no one had seen us. The consequences, for me especially, would have been dire.

A Bedouin code of honor protected women. Which meant they shouldn't be touched at all by a man. Not even a graze of the fingertips. I'd shamed my family and brought dishonor to my name with that kiss.

Funny, though, that it wasn't shame that washed through my belly, but a tingling thrill and the stir of yearning. Did that equal love? No. I knew the difference between love and lust. Within the blessed union of husband and wife, lust, or passion rather, was a God-given gift. However, Karim and I were not married, so were these stirrings deep in the pit of me something I *should* be ashamed of? Maybe they were a gift as well? Like an appetizer before a main course?

Ugh. I let my head drop. I was so out of my element here.

"Hannah?"

I lifted my eyes to Mom's questioning gaze. "No, we aren't in love."

"Then why..." She let her question die.

My father stared at me, considering. His fingers drummed on his knee, his analytical mind working. I didn't need to spell it out for him. He'd figure it all out on his own.

"No matter the reasons, you know what the Bible says," he said.

This was the exact turn I knew this conversation would take.

"You can't be unequally yoked with an unbeliever."

Mom's shallow breathing became audible. "Maybe I should lay down now."

Dad helped her to the pallet and supported her weight as she eased herself into a supine position.

This conversation wasn't over, even though there wasn't anything they could say that I hadn't already said to myself. I took the pillow I'd been sitting on and moved it beside my mother's pallet, then settled on top of it.

Mom closed her eyes for a moment before opening them and staring straight into mine. "Whatever you've told yourself, Hannah, that you'll be a living witness and that will change him, convert him, may be true. But it also may not be."

Now probably wouldn't be the best time to tell them Karim had made me promise not to try to convert him. Good thing that was up to the convicting of the Holy Spirit anyway.

"There are reasons why God tells us not to marry unbelievers. Look at all the times in the Old Testament when kings married princesses from far-off lands who worshiped other gods. Nothing good ever came of it." Dad placed his large hand against the base of my head. "Marriage is hard enough without starting off not sharing the same core beliefs."

I swallowed hard, not sure I'd ever convince them with any argument or justification. I turned to look my dad in the eye. "Dad, you know why I'm doing this."

"I'm not going to sit here and allow you to make a sacrifice of yourself. You can't take this situation into your own hands." He gave me a pointed look. "You have to trust God to take care of it."

I nodded. "I am. But what if His way to take care of it is through me?"

"What do you mean?"

"Think about Esther. Hosea. Sometimes God does work in mysterious ways that don't always make sense to us at the moment."

He massaged his forehead. Shook his head. "I don't know, Hannah. I still don't like it."

Yeah. I got that. I wasn't one hundred percent convinced myself.

"Have you thought about what your life as a sheikh's wife will be like?" Mom asked. "You've never really liked being the center of attention, but if you marry Karim, everyone will be watching you, measuring you. Maybe even judging. That's a lot of pressure, honey." She took my hand. "Expectations will be placed on you. You won't be able to be as free as you have been."

All my life people had watched me because I was different. It had been hard living under that magnifying glass. Trying to be the best I could so no one would judge my parents. So no one would have any more reason to hate Americans or despise Christianity. Most of the time I felt as if I didn't measure up. Would the scrutiny increase as Karim's wife?

I swallowed hard. Would I be able to stand straight under the critical scrutiny?

"What about children?" Mom's eyes squeezed shut, and her forehead lay in folds.

I wasn't sure if my news was what had her in so much pain or if it was her body healing.

Probably wouldn't be an appropriate time to joke right then. Even if I wanted to lighten the mood with a tease about her second internal clock not needing to worry anymore. "What about them?"

"Are you planning on having any?"

I looked down at my hands. "He needs an heir, yes."

"So it is to be a real marriage?"

"Yes."

"I see."

My head jerked up to look at my mom. Her face seemed more relaxed than it had moments ago. I knew my mom wanted grandchildren, but I hadn't thought that would be what would set her mind at ease about the whole thing. If only the exact opposite weren't true for me. Even with Karim's *lesson*, I was still a jumble of nerves and insecurities.

"Hannah?"

"Yes, Mom?"

"I don't think this is a good idea, and I wish you wouldn't do it."

Okay, so she hadn't changed her mind.

"But raise your kids to know God. Though they will be the sheikh's sons and daughters, never let them forget Whose heir they really are."

Karim

Nervousness was not an emotion with which I was well acquainted. When I told people to go, they went. If I told them to stay, they stayed. It wasn't haughtiness or pride—it was my position and the respect of my clan. Not often did I have to seek permission for something, and even less often did I need to worry about the outcome.

But my mouth grew dry as I made my way to the Pratt tent, and I found myself wiping my palms on the side of my white thawb. By now Hannah would have told her parents of our plan, but I'd seen the doubt in her eyes as to whether Ethan and Elizabeth would be happy with the news. Pride pricked a bit at that. Most families would be overjoyed to have the sheikh offer to marry their daughter. Not only did I plan on protecting them, but I had a nice dowry to bestow as well. A man of morals, I would never lay a violent hand on my wife and had no desire to seek out other women.

Why should they not wish to give Hannah to me?

Those reassurances did nothing to settle the churning in my belly. I felt like a boy being sent to my father for correction after an act of disobedience. I swallowed the lump in my throat and pushed my legs forward, my gaze catching a lone man's form on the far side of the tent. I took a deep breath, thankful to have this conversation in private, as was right.

Head bare, Ethan's trimmed hair shone in the late-afternoon sun. Darker than his daughter's, it was as if the golden strands were woven through instead of coins that had been melted down and somehow transformed into cascading locks, like Hannah's.

"*Salam*, Karim."

Ethan hadn't turned, but he'd sensed my presence or heard my footsteps. Maybe a little of both. Whether he'd picked up the skills from his years dwelling among the Bedouin or it was just something innately held within him, I didn't know. Either way, I respected him, and maybe even marveled a little because of it.

I inclined my head toward him, showing my respect as his position as Hannah's father and my elder. "*Wa Alaikum Assalam wa Rahmutullah.*"

The Salam greeting was important to our religion, commanded by Allah since the time of Adam and required by the holy Qur'an. That Ethan and his family used the greeting, as well as taking upon themselves other customs such as our modesty of dress and decorum, bespoke their character. Despite our difference in religious viewpoints, we respected one another.

Hopefully, that mutual regard would be enough for Ethan to hear me out in regard to joining our families.

I took the last few steps to stand beside him, weighing my options of starting the conversation or allowing the older man to take the lead.

"You are a good man, Karim."

It was a compliment, but my shoulders tensed as I waited for the second part to land on me.

"I've watched you grow up. Seen you stretch and grow as you filled your father's shoes and took on the load that other young men would buckle under. Watched through the years your kindness and consideration toward my daughter."

I opened my mouth to respond. To assure him that kindness would not waver and that I hoped the consideration would deepen into something even more. But before my lips formed around the words, he spoke again.

"Though I've seen the intelligence of your actions in the past, this is a bad idea." He did turn to me then. Let his gaze be the punctuation to his conclusion.

"I disagree. Respectfully." I bowed slightly at the waist, showing my deference to his years of wisdom. "All things considered, this is the best course of action."

"For whom?"

Did he believe my actions selfish? I admit that I would benefit, but above all I wanted to marry Hannah for her safety. For Ethan's and his wife's. "For all of us."

"Fear is not a solid foundation for a marriage."

My brows rose, ire beginning a slow simmer within me. No man desired his courage to be questioned. To be called afraid was a dishonor. Though I respected this man a great deal, he overstepped. "I am not afraid."

"No?" He shook his head. "I am."

I gaped at that, never imagining a man would confess such a thing.

"Fear is not a weakness. I'd even go so far as to say it is healthy to feel afraid. It can alert us to danger. Keep us safe.

No, it's only when we allow fear to shackle us that it becomes the hindrance it's known to be. A wall between us and our trust in God."

Denial licked my lips.

"Whether you embrace it or not, Karim, it is fear that has moved you to offer for my daughter. Not fear for yourself but for my family." Ethan's eyes softened around the edges. "That is an honorable and noble thing."

"Then it is settled." Perhaps I was being a bit forceful, my words ringing with finality. This was the right thing, and if I had to push the man, I would.

Pain etched across his forehead, and he pressed his lips tight. His throat bobbed up and down as he swallowed emotion like a thick slice of dry bread.

"Will you..." He rubbed at the lines creasing above his eyes, then turned those pleading orbs on me. "Will you wait...until there is love between you? For a woman, the act..."

Ethan assumed I could fill in the rest of his thought on my own. Could I? My experiences with women were confined to that of my first marriage. She had been willing, dutiful. Was there more to it for the woman? I had always thought so. Was that not what my lesson in the cave with Hannah had been about?

But wait? Unnatural and not something I could conceive. Memories of our kiss fired my blood until I was sure even the thought of waiting would melt my skin. Also, too, wouldn't any distance I put between myself and my bride raise questions in her mind? There were many facets of love, and the physical unity of the body sealed and connected our souls on a level beyond our understanding.

No. I couldn't grant Ethan his request. The marriage would be consummated, as it should be. However...

I placed my hand on his shoulder. "I promise I will take care of Hannah." In all ways. Her needs would be mine to meet. Safety, provisions...love.

Chapter 9

KARIM

"You're what?" Samlil's voice thundered across the open expanse, causing Jamal's head to rise from his feed. The camel's bottom jaw moved as he chewed, the long lashes protecting his eyes lowering in a slow blink. If he could talk, I imagine he'd tell Samlil to keep it down during breakfast. I smiled at the thought and smacked Jamal on the shoulder, dust billowing from his coarse coat.

"You can't marry her, Karim." Samlil continued his tirade.

I'd put up with my friend long enough to know that his blistering came with the force of a sandstorm and lasted just as long. I only had to wait him out before I could fill his ears with reason.

"It is not done." He shook his head. "You are the sheikh. Think of how this will look to the people."

That was exactly what I'd thought about.

"You are a good and faithful Muslim. As such you cannot

bind yourself to a Christian. Do not become an infidel, Karim."

"Don't you think you're overstepping a little?"

He slammed his hand against his thigh. "No! If anything, I'm being too lenient. You know the history. The massacres during the Christian crusades. You know the threat of America. The Qur'an says we should fight, not bed their women. That we will be rewarded if—"

I slashed my hand through the air, anger wishing my grip was around the hilt of my dagger. "Enough."

Samlil's nostrils flared, and I had no doubt my expression mirrored his.

"Be careful, Samlil, or one would think you've been entertaining views not in accordance with the peaceful Allah that I serve, but that more aligned to the twisted views the terrorists have mangled to support their heinous cause."

His face reddened, and his lips pressed so thin they nearly disappeared. We faced off, each holding the challenge of the other's gaze.

The hardness seeped from his face until it transformed to a smirk. "We couldn't have that, could we?"

With another pat to Jamal's neck, I turned to the horses ground-tied yards away, willing my anger to flee my fingertips as I flicked them at my sides.

The day would be long, without peace.

I picked up the tasseled reins and stroked the stallion's dipped head. A thing of beauty, the Arabian horse. Majestic. Powerful. A stalwart heart with enough endurance and stamina to outlast the rays of the sun. A hunting expedition, we had kept the saddle and bridle serviceable. The extra frippery, the showy colors, the shine of the inlaid gold, the swish of the hundreds of woven tassels that made up the more elaborate pieces used for celebration and special occasions would only scare off the mountain ibex we hunted.

It was important to find as much game as we could and spend the next few days preserving it. Our time in this area grew short, the wells we had dug drying up. Time had come to depart and search for more water.

Hunting would not cease as we trekked the dunes. Instead, those with falcons and salukis, Bedouin hunting dogs, would shoulder more responsibility to provide the families with fresh meat from hares and other small creatures.

Checking the pouch of ammunition and securing the double-barrel rifle to my back, I mounted my horse. Samlil did the same, and with pressure from our heels, we headed toward the rocky cliffs the mountain goats liked to dwell among.

"The wedding will take place this time next year, as is our custom?" Samlil's voice held an edge, as if he already knew what my answer would be and didn't like it.

"No."

"Longer, then. To get to know her and her family better. To resolve all expectations of the union."

My spine stiffened, and in response the stallion shook his head in annoyance. Consciously I released each tight muscle until my hips once more swayed with the movement of the animal. "We all grew up together, you, Hannah, and me. You think I need a year engagement to know her better?"

"I think it wise, yes."

Betrothed to the sheikh would not offer the same level of

protection as wife of the sheikh. Not to mention, now that the idea had time to steep like a strong, flavorful coffee, I had no intentions but to take long, delightful sips from my brew. "We will be married at week's end." Barely enough time to accustom ourselves to the other in our new roles before needing to break camp and move out.

"It's not done, Karim."

"Because a thing *has* not been done does not mean it *is* not done." The trail narrowed as it began to climb into the mountain's foothills, and I took the lead. "By week's end, I will be married."

Samlil did not answer, though I imagined he continued to argue in his mind. So be it. As long as I didn't have to hear any more about it, he could stew in his displeasure until he became wrinkled by it.

A few hundred meters farther and we had to stop the horses and dismount. The craggy terrain would be easier to traverse on foot. I swung my gun around and cradled it in my hands, at the ready at the first sign of our quarry. Up we climbed, crouching behind large boulders, scouting outcropping and cliffs where the game might be hiding.

There. Past a crag cut by the flow of water from infrequent rains, a small group of ibex gnawed on a small batch of tenacious bushes. Their spindly legs supported rounded bellies, rough and knobbed horns curving from the tops of their heads.

I turned toward Samlil, got his attention, and pointed toward the herd. He nodded once before aiming and cocking his gun. I did likewise, sighting an animal that would feed a family for weeks. The shots rang out in tandem, echoing off the rocky mountain face, my shoulder taking the kickback of the firearm. Repositioning the rifle a bit to the left, I sighted and shot again. The rest of the herd scrambled away, leaving four unmoving bodies.

My grin stretched, and I whacked Samlil on the shoulder with a nod. His face transformed to the one I'd preserved in my memory. The one not hardened through the years, eyes dull and listless. This was the friend from my youth. Mischief tilting his lips and a sparkle dancing in his expression. This was the boy who'd challenged me to camel races and dared me to charm a snake.

He was not altogether lost.

"Come on." I patted his arm again. "Let's get our reward."

We hefted the carcasses to our waiting mounts and lashed the ibex to the horses' backs. Leading the stallions back down the mountain did not offer the same comfort as riding, but the cost outweighed the effort.

Hours of work lay ahead for many people. Skinning, filleting, sorting, tanning, and preserving. With no refrigeration and temperatures that hastened spoiling, copious amounts of salt would keep the meat from this hunt sustaining bellies for a number of weeks.

With everyone working together, the preservation would get done quickly. Especially since some of the more experienced men had taken over helping the women with the sheep since their sickness, leaving others to pull more weight among herding the camels.

Guilt pricked my conscious as I thought about the extra work my wedding would cause. The ceremony, the feast.

Everyone already worked so hard, their physical tiredness more felt because of the constant cloud of worry hovering over us all.

Then again, maybe something to celebrate was just the morale boost we all needed.

Chapter 10

HANNAH

It's my wedding day.

I paused after the thought, waiting for the tiny butter-flies that were supposed to be flittering around in my stomach to grab hold and lift me to soar on their magical wings. Instead, bile. That sickening feeling of churning acid that literally made it feel like my stomach was eating itself.

Cold feet, right? That was all that it was? Normal. But even if I'd pushed a polar bear to the side and hacked through feet of arctic ice and then plunged my toes into the freezing water beneath, it wouldn't come close. This was so much more than jitters.

I covered my face with my hands. How did I know I was doing the right thing? I'd justified my decision with my parents, but all those reasons seemed like drifting smoke I couldn't grasp in my hands now. Who was I to lay claim to any divine calling? To compare myself, in any small way, to Esther? She'd been considered the greatest female monarch in biblical history by many, and I was...nothing special.

Deluded arguments had made me set my feet toward a course of wispy dreams.

Dear God...

Had my motives been so self-serving? In my subconscious had I desired so much to finally come out on top when compared to another that I had misled myself into believing I was some sort of twenty-first century Esther?

But there had been the sacred echo. My reading of Esther and feeling the stirring within my soul. Then Yara coming minutes after repeating almost the same thing. That hadn't been a coincidence, had it?

My thoughts and fears echoed in my mind like the yelling deep inside a cave. Beating against the walls and tossed back at me with ricocheting speed until I thought I'd grow mad with it.

Be still.

A command I'd heard often, but this time coming at me in the voice of my friend, Rachel. She'd talked me into going spelunking with a group my sophomore year of college. I hadn't been prepared for the tight spaces we'd had to shimmy through on our bellies. Nor the large cavern hidden deep within the limestone mountain. Our group of ten had filled that space with our voices, our echoes making us sound three times our size. But then Rachel had told everyone to be still, and we'd all turned off our headlamps. The silence and peace had seeped into my pores along with the damp cave air.

I tried to clear my mind and grasp that peace now. It was there. Elusive. Just beyond the noise. If I could still myself, maybe my feet could stand firm on the foundation on which I'd made my decision, not this shifting sand that threatened to topple me.

I am called to work for God among the Bedouin.

Karim is a good man.

God won't abandon me.

I took a deep breath and let it out slowly, my spine straightening with the pressure that compressed my lungs.

It's my wedding day.

Time to get out of bed and prepare.

I swung my feet to the side of my pallet and strapped sandals on my feet. Rising, I straightened my sleeping area and peeked over at Mom's prostrate form. She smiled at me with a hint of sadness, which I answered with a forced tilt of my lips.

"Can I bring you some breakfast? A piece of fruit perhaps?"

She shook her head. "Your father already brought me something before he left this morning."

I nodded, my stomach not ready to receive anything itself. I used the cold water left in the basin to splash over my face and arms and peeked at the leather flap hanging at our tent's entrance. When would the women arrive to begin preparations?

Traditionally, Bedouin weddings lasted five days at the most, two at the least. My wedding to Karim would take place in one day. In a way, I was thankful for the lack of length. While eyebrows might rise at the unconventionality of it, I wasn't sure my nerves could handle something more drawn out. Everyone understood the urgency however, at least in that the clan had decided more than a week ago to pack up and move. The fact Karim wished to forgo a year engagement was still the topic of many conversations.

I closed my eyes, imagining the activity in the center of

our community right now. The first events of the Bedouin wedding ceremony, the *al khouta* and the *al akhd*. Karim, along with his male relatives and friends, would meet with my father for the official proposal. Being offered coffee to drink, Karim would not lift the cup to his lips until my father said yes, after which the negotiations of the marriage agreement would commence. Karim would pay my father a dowry, perhaps money, jewelry, or animals. Funny. I should have asked him what he'd planned to offer. It did kind of make a girl nauseated to think her worth boiled down to a few trinkets or livestock.

I touched the chain around my neck made of gold coins centuries old. I'd been surprised when Karim had presented it to me two days ago. My mother's ribs were still recovering, so Karim's mother, Yara, and I piled into the Toyota to head to the city, when he'd tapped on the vehicle's window. I'd clutched the wheel for leverage and pumped the handle to lower the glass. Resting his arm on the opening of the door, he'd pulled the necklace from his sleeve and handed it to me with a smile.

Gifts from the betrothed? Normal. But this? I followed the dents within the metal. This was not only a family heirloom but a piece so full of history and culture that it belonged in a museum.

I remembered looking into his eyes, trying to decipher some hidden message in the gift. Why a piece so irreplaceable instead of a simple ring? Knowing Karim, the number of layers he wrapped himself in, significance lay here. Even the approving click of his mother's tongue had confirmed it.

The leather flap opened, and morning light filtered through shadows in the tent. Yara entered first, her grin as wide as the Sahara. Other women, all friends, tailed her, with Karim's mother entering last, draped across her arms, my wedding gown.

I ached to see it. As tradition, she insisted on providing not only the cloth but sewing it herself as well. I'd tried to protest, arguing that there wasn't time to create a gown from scratch. That had been our main purpose for the trip to town —to purchase a wedding ensemble already made. But she'd dug in her heels, pushed me off in the direction of the market to collect staples such as flour and sugar. Things we'd need for our journey that the desert wouldn't provide for us.

When I'd joined her later, she had a brown paper-wrapped bundle hugged to her chest. Refused me a glimpse or to even carry the burden for her.

Now she stood before me, eyes bright though dark bags hung beneath them as testament to the hours spent on the dress which should have been spent sleeping. She stepped forward, the rest of the women making a semicircle around us. Excitement thrilled on the air as if a tangible thing, and I breathed it in, filling my lungs with the deliciousness of expectation.

Without a word, she held the package out to me with both hands. I accepted it and pulled at the tied string. Brown paper unfolded, revealing material as white and light as a cloud. Unhinged, my jaw dropped, and I looked up to find the matriarch that I'd slightly feared most my life smirking at me. Bedouin wedding dresses were usually a variety of colors, with red being a focal shade. But white...

She took another step toward me and fingered my uncov-ered hair, bringing a large chunk to drape over my shoulder. "When a Bedouin weds, they join not two people but two families." She patted my hair again, her eyes glistening in a telling way. "For you and my son, we join two worlds."

I swallowed, touched by her words and thoughtfulness. "Thank you."

She gave a small nod and took half a step back. "You and Karim, you are not two halves that make a whole. Already you are both complete." Her direct gaze pierced. "Never forget who you are."

Who I was. An American. An outsider. But how she'd said it didn't make that fact something that should be despised or shunned. While hospitable, there were still lines drawn between *us* and *them*. Lines I could never cross because of my birth, culture, and religion.

And yet I wasn't sure if I'd ever felt as accepted as I did then. My differences displayed and yet embraced. In her estimation, I'd been lined up with all the other women of her acquaintance and I hadn't been found wanting.

Looking to the cloth in my hands, I twisted my wrists and let the material flow to the ground, revealing the gown in all its glory. A simple A-line, the cut and stitching had a distinctive Western flare while still maintaining modesty. Flowing chiffon skirt tampered to a trim waist that had been embellished by a broad belt. The top and arms looked to be a little more formfitting than the everyday abaya.

Oohs and ahhs emitted from the women around us, and soon I was flocked by eager hands to help me into the gown. It fit perfectly, and I felt more like a bride than I ever dreamed I could have.

Yara removed a small wooden bowl from a bag and poured in some powder. Next she added a liquid, and from the citrus smell that hung on the air between us, I knew it to be lemon juice. She mixed the henna into a paste and filled cones with it. One woman took my hands and washed them, glancing up at me every so often with a coy smile. Soon both my hands and feet were clean. I became a canvas to these women, my hands and feet receiving the red dye in intricate designs of dots, swirls, lines, and flowers. We took breaks, drank coffee, laughed and teased. Hours passed, and then Yara looked up from her post at my right hand, sweat trailing down her temple, her smile bright.

"Beautiful."

I looked down at all their handiwork. "Yes, it is. Thank you."

She glanced down at my hands, then looked up again with a wink. "That too." With a clap of her hands, she rose. "Let's go ladies. Time to see how much the sheikh will pay us for decorating his woman."

They left the tent with giggles and twitters, women with years to their lives acting as carefree as their school-aged children. I laughed at their antics. It felt good to let the weight of the past week roll away.

I strained my ears to hear the teasing, wished I could be among the revelry, catch a glimpse of my friend-soon-to-be-husband. Was he suffering from second thoughts? At any moment would he come to his senses and call the whole thing off?

Did I want him to?

Shouts and laughter, both male and female, reached me, but I couldn't make out any of the words. The ritual of *al aadaa* was all in good fun, and I wondered if Karim would give in to the ladies' playful demands for payment or let the verbal sparring continue before making a show of relinquishing a few pieces of coin.

Yara burst through the leather flap, her cheeks glowing. Like ducklings the other women filtered in.

"You should have heard him, Hannah." Yara grinned.

"What did he say?"

"At first, he refused any payment at all," one of the other ladies chimed in. "As if all our hard work was worth nothing."

"That wasn't it at all," Yara countered.

"So did he pay, or didn't he?" I asked.

Yara's brow quirked. "At first, no. He said you were perfect and beautiful all on your own and needed no decoration to be such."

My breath hitched. He did? With my hair and eyes, I knew he thought me unique, but beautiful?

"Romantic, no?"

I nodded, still processing. "Then what?"

She tilted her hand and coins spilled out.

My eyes widened. "All that?"

"He said you were worth more than all his possessions but that we'd have to settle for the money he had in his purse."

My gaze jumped to hers. "He gave it all?"

She nodded. "All."

I looked back to the pile of money lying on the colorful floor rug. One or two in jest, yes. But what did he mean by giving it all?

Yara reached forward and squeezed my hand. "We must finish getting you ready for him."

Yara's sister knelt before me and applied thick black kohl around my eyes. She tilted my head and dusted my neck, cheeks, and ears with saffron. Gathering my hair at the back of my head, she began to fold and weave it.

"Leave it down." Karim's mother spoke for the first time since presenting me with my dress.

I could feel the sister's hands hesitate. Could almost read her thoughts. *It wasn't their way.* Then strand by strand my hair fell to my back. It seemed I wasn't the only one aware of Karim's fascination with my blond hair. His reference of it as gold before he called me a treasure would be evidence enough. His audacity to stroke it that night in the cave undeniable proof. My heart tripped a beat as my skin tingled in memory.

A light head scarf was placed over my hair, then secured with a circlet and veil made of more round gold coins. The face of a Bedouin bride must not be seen during the ceremony, and this veil of joined metal concealed my nose, mouth, and chin.

A stirring sounded behind me, and I turned toward it. Mom rose from her pallet. My heart clenched at the sight of her. For her weakness and injury, yes, but more so from guilt. She had lain silent for so long that morning that I'd nearly forgotten her presence altogether.

She limped toward me, her eyes shining. I reached out my hands toward her, and she grasped them.

"Oh, my little girl." She traced the height of my cheekbone, which jutted out from above the veil. "You are a beautiful bride."

"I'm sorry, Mama," I whispered. I wasn't sure why I felt the need to apologize, but I did. Maybe because I knew in some way I was disappointing them. That the dreams they'd held for me would now no longer be realized.

"Don't apologize. Not to me. Not on your wedding day."

She pressed on the back of my head, and I lowered it to accept her kiss on my crown, a single tear escaping and sliding down under the veil and collecting on my chin.

"Come." My soon-to-be mother-in-law stood at the entrance of our tent, holding the leather flap back, her hand extended toward us. It was time to join the rest of the ladies in the massive women's tent erected for special occasions.

I curled my arm around my mother's waist and supported her weight. For the rest of the day she would be by my side. I wasn't sure I could bolster the courage otherwise.

Chapter 11
KARIM

Darkness blanketed the night sky, the celebration in full swing. Crackling from the fires could barely be heard over the deep voices of all the men gathered in the men's tent. All day I'd cast furtive glances toward the other side of the encampment, hoping to catch even a glimpse of Hannah. Nothing. Though I knew my chances were pretty much zero to begin with. Men and women celebrated separately, and that included the bride and groom.

Samlil sat to my right, Ethan to my left. Both had been uncharacteristically quiet most the day, brooding and stewing. Or perhaps I was only projecting that? Either way, they had not been ideal, happy companions. I'd had to receive the congratulatory smiles and well wishes from those who were not as close to my heart.

The musicians started another tune on the violin-like rahaba and the dalouka drum. Men clapped and stomped in unison, their bodies moving in a centuries-old traditional dance. Along the perimeter of the tent, servers held large platters of food. Rice, lentils, meat, bread, fruits, vegetables. All the favorites were being placed on the runner on the floor. At the end, the massive main wedding dish—a whole stuffed camel. Or rather a camel stuffed with a number of lambs, stuffed with almost two dozen chickens that had been stuffed full of fish. The last twenty-four hours had been permeated with the smell of the dish roasting until the camel meat glistened brown and tender.

With a flick of my fingers, I summoned one of the men to me. He bent at the waist until his ear hovered near my lips. "I gave specific instructions to the cooks as to my bride's main course. Please see that those instructions are followed."

He inclined his head and then straightened, walking out of the airy tent without walls and toward the cooking fires.

I leaned forward and used a bit of bread to scoop up a bite of savory lentils. Ethan's hand joined me in the platter.

"What was that?" he asked.

I waved off his question. "Nothing really. Your daughter has a distinct dislike for camel meat. There should be a nice roasted chicken being delivered to her now instead."

Approval lit his eyes. "It seems you are well acquainted with my daughter's preferences."

Samlil snorted beside me, offended by the observation. As if an outsider, a missionary no less, was beneath the sheikh's time and consideration. How my friend could so easily forget the time the three of us had shared growing up, I did not know. However, Ethan's statement could cause trouble if he concluded I'd acted in any untoward manner to his kin. "A good leader notices the people under his care."

Ethan's brow rose. "So you know the favorite and least favorite dishes of everyone here?"

Pinned like a rodent under the sharp talons of a hunting falcon. I squirmed, needing to find a way to redirect the conversation without bringing to memory Hannah's embarrassment over losing her stomach the last time she'd tasted camel.

Ethan patted my knee and leaned closer. "No need to worry on my account. If anything, this eases a bit of my worries."

I didn't like that he worried about my union with Hannah at all. It called to question my character. Not a good feeling. But what could I do? Uncertainty weighed on most of the minds of the men celebrating, though their wariness lay in the choice of the bride, not the groom.

Mahabat walked from the far side of the tent. His position as head shepherd afforded him a measure of power within the clan. Since this celebration was in my honor and my duty was that of groom, I'd appointed him as overseer.

He folded himself beside Samlil and dipped a piece of bread into a platter of hummus. "It is time for the *nikah*," he said around a mouthful of seasoned garbanzo beans.

I nodded and stood, Ethan rising beside me. He would act as Hannah's representative, although I was tempted as sheikh to demand Hannah represent herself in this matter. Though everyone was having a good time, the unspoken questions and accusations hung heavy on the air. My equilibrium spun with them. If I could lay my eyes on her, perhaps all would return to focus.

A table stood in the middle of the tent, the legal contract of my marriage to Hannah on it. Mahabat walked to the table and picked up a piece of paper, reading in a loud voice the *meher*. The musicians stilled their instruments, and the scraping of hands in food dishes quieted as well.

"Karim Al-Amir, upon his marriage to Hannah Pratt, does vow his protection and honor. The symbol of which he bestows to her now."

I fished the ring I had purchased out of my belt and handed it to Ethan. The sapphire sparkled in the light of the night. Lanterns, fire, moon. Each glinted off an edge of the deep-blue gem. Diamonds were more traditional for the Western culture. Perhaps even what Hannah had expected all her life. But a piece of Hannah had always been mine, and I didn't associate her with the overrated, colorless stone. She brought life, the blue of the water my people spend their whole lives searching for. That was the treasure I'd always hold dear.

Ethan's fingers folded over his palm as he accepted the ring on Hannah's behalf. I must have had a question in my expression, my small measure of doubt that she'd appreciate my gift written on my face, because Ethan gave me a small smile and a nod.

Approving murmurs swept through the tent, and I let those affirmations reinforce my resolve as Mahabat continued to read the next section—the lifetime deferment.

"Karim Al-Amir, upon his marriage to Hannah Pratt, does offer her—" He looked up at me, eyes wide. He licked his lips.

I nodded for him to continue.

"Half of all his worldly possessions."

Tongues that had whispered approval now unfurled without restraint. A small sum, a token, was all I was supposed to give. All that was expected. In essence, in the eyes of my people, I had given my wife freedom. Which was exactly what she deserved.

If my marriage to Hannah hadn't spoken a message to my people, the gift of the *meher* did. Though by the fire sparking from some of the eyes glaring at me, that message may not have been received quite like I'd hoped.

Chapter 12

HANNAH

"It is time."

I knew it was. The growing knot in the pit of my stomach as I'd watched the moon travel the dome of the sky had wound itself tighter and tighter with each passing hour.

I nodded up at my mother, surprised she'd been the one to bring me the news.

She reached for my hand, and we walked back to our tent. My family's tent. The one that had sheltered me for years. The one that had memories and laughter woven into every fiber of goat hair. The one that would no longer be mine to call home.

I shivered, though the night air wasn't the cause. Mom squeezed my hand and opened the flap to the tent. I stepped inside, gaze darting around to all that was familiar. In the middle of the room, like a throne, lay plush pillows. The place I was to wait before being collected and escorted to another tent. To Karim.

My palms grew sweaty, and I pushed them along the rough surface of the stuffed cushions as I sat.

Karim had been married before. He had certain expectations. What if I didn't meet those? What if I was horrible at being a wife and I disappointed him?

My hands trembled, and I gripped the tassels that ran along the seam of the pillow. My parents had been open enough for me to know the coming together of two bodies wasn't something to fear. For that I was thankful. It hadn't been until I'd befriended other American Christians that I'd learned the underlying culture that produced hurdles, especially in the minds of young women, when it came to purity. The shame of feeling pleasure at a new husband's touch because of the years being told that those feelings were dirty and sinful.

It wasn't shame that washed through my core. Not even at the memory of the stirring of desire when Karim had kissed me. If anything, that lesson had taught me more than any sterile physiology class could have. That God created mankind for more than functionality, but to enjoy the life He bestows on his children. And the fact that Karim and I could possibly enjoy one another in a way that was meant for marriage was a comfort. Despite that, my body quaked. The trepidation coming from...oh dear, could I even say it?

What if I was bad at *it*? What if Karim's late wife had been exceptionally good and I ended up exceptionally...not?

Heat flushed my cheeks at my thoughts. Not so much that a good Christian girl was having them—I mean, anyone who'd read *Song of Solomon* would be familiar with the more amorous side of the Bible.

I'd tried to put the thoughts out of my mind all day and

had mostly succeeded. Whenever they'd creep in, I could shut them out again by a distraction. I swallowed hard as I stared at the dark leather flap. The one that any minute now would be raised. I couldn't ignore the inevitable that lay before me, and my thoughts battled against each other like a civil war.

Sex is a gift from God, meant to be enjoyed in the holy confines of marriage.

But it is supposed to be an outward expression, a natural culmination of love between a man and a woman. Karim has never professed to love me. Not in that way.

When you agreed to marry him, you agreed to share all of your life together. You knew what you were getting into.

But that knowledge isn't comforting me now! No knowledge is! I know about sex, but I don't know about sex. What if...how do I...what about...

All my thoughts and questions fell upon me like a pounding waterfall, made up images of the night going wrong mocking me like a tormentor until I thought I'd scream.

Mom's hand weighed on the top of my head. "Shhhh."

I hadn't made a sound, but still she shushed me. She gingerly lowered herself beside me, and I gripped on to her gaze like a lost child. "Shhh," she said again.

I sat there and waited, hungry for words of assurance. The night ahead of me was nothing to fear. Lovemaking was a beautiful act, to be anticipated. Karim was a gentle man and would not hurt me, as I'd read was sometimes the case. A few syllables of sage advice, that was all I needed.

No words spilled from my mother's lips as the flap lifted and a breeze wafted through. She kissed me on the forehead and then dabbed at her eyes, sitting back away from me.

My heart raced. I wasn't ready. I took back what I'd said earlier about being thankful the ceremony was only going to last one day. Surely there was enough water in the area to sustain us a bit longer. Tomorrow. Maybe I'd be ready tomorrow.

The bangles on Yara's wrist jingled as she motioned to me. "It's time."

On shaky legs, I stood and walked out into the night. Jamal stood before me in splendor, freshly washed and fitted with a *houdach* saddle, brightly colored tassels hanging from almost every inch of his body.

I swallowed hard as I stepped up to Karim's camel, wishing I could sneak away, wishing for a bit of privacy. The whole clan would witness the procession as I was led away from the protection of my father's tent and delivered on the other side of the encampment to Karim. Embarrassment tinged my cheeks as I mounted and swayed with Jamal's motion as he stood. My veil offered a cover to hide behind, but I still wanted to slink away. There was a difference from everyone knowing what occurred on a wedding night and having everyone's eyes on you as you made your way to it.

Already I knew the talk. Knew how hardly anyone agreed with Karim's decision to marry me. I wasn't a fitting wife for a sheikh.

For Karim, I squared my shoulders and straightened my posture. Though the people respected him, he would receive hardship on my account. I wouldn't add to it by shriveling under the accusatory stares that followed me as Jamal plodded on.

Too soon and yet not soon enough, Jamal was tugged to a stop in front of Karim's tent, his knees tapped to kneel so I could dismount. The musicians played with enthusiasm, the height of the celebration culminating in the clapping and dancing of those on the outskirts of my vision.

Karim opened the flap of his tent, his tailored white thawb reflecting the flames of the nearby fire. He stood erect, a statue of manhood, his trimmed beard not hiding the firm tilt to his jaw.

I sucked in my breath at the sight of him. With me he had always been kindness and patience. Never angered or taking offense when I did something that was culturally unaccept-able growing up. Instead he'd direct me with a gentle hand.

The man who stood in front of that tent flap resembled nothing of the compassionate boy I knew. His hard gaze slowly oscillated from face to face. As if he dared every man there to speak against him. To raise even a sound of discord within his hearing.

I waited. Waited for him to turn his gaze on me. For his face to soften to the Karim I knew. The Karim that had carried me after the scorpion sting. Had helped me back up after toppling from my first camel ride. Had kissed me in the cave.

But he didn't look at me. Not once. With his scrutiny over my shoulder, he lifted his palm skyward in my direction.

The official summons.

Head bowed, I stepped toward him, the knot in my stomach twisting tighter. My soul craved a kind word as I passed him. Something under his breath meant just for me. A small grazing of his finger on my skin that no one else would notice. But all was silent and still as I stepped past him and into the tent.

Air whooshed around me as the flap closed. I stood

without moving. Though tradition had written the procession of the day, everything was unscripted from here. Would Karim escort me directly to the sleeping pallet? Would he touch me in ways I'd never been touched? Would the orchestra play and the choir sing deep within my soul, as he'd implied in the privacy of our cave?

My muscles grew taut as I stood there. My heart raced. Like a sixth sense I could feel Karim's movements as he tied off the entrance.

Still I waited. For his touch, his direction.

He stepped past me without a word, and the displaced air from his movement took the breath from my lungs. My coiled muscles released so quickly I thought I'd drop to the floor. Instead, I took a step forward. Allowed my face to lift and take in my surroundings. I'd never been inside Karim's tent before. It was huge. My parents' tent had one large room, but Karim's was sectioned off. Which made sense. With him being the sheikh, he often had guests and visitors that he entertained in this main section.

Karim walked behind a partition, and I took another step forward, curious about my new home. The rugs along the floor were the highest quality. It must have taken the women months to dye and work such a neat and intricate weave. Large pillows bordered the center rug in an inviting manner.

Should I sit? Stay standing? Investigate wherever Karim and gone off to?

Before I had too long to decide, the partition lifted again, and Karim entered with a steaming carafe and two small cups.

"Sit, Hannah. Be comfortable."

Sit I could do. Be comfortable? I had my doubts.

I lowered onto a pillow and arranged the billowing skirt of my dress around my ankles.

Karim poured coffee into a cup and handed it to, me then poured his own and sat down. He took a drink and eyed me over the rim. The hardness had left, replaced with a hint of mischief.

There went that knot again. Tighter, tighter.

He set down his cup with a small smile and leaned toward me, his gaze never leaving my face. "May I?" His hand lifted toward my cheek.

I nodded and held still as he lifted the circlet from my forehead and the veil of gold discs no longer hid my face. He set it on the ground, then turned and removed the pins fastening the head covering. It fell to my shoulders before drifting the rest of the way to the floor.

His eyes widened, surprised my hair had been left down.

"Your mother," I said as way of explanation.

He said something, but I couldn't make it out, the music outside the tent rising in volume at the height of the song. Draining the last of his coffee, he stood and offered me his hand.

This is it.

I ignored the hammering of my heart and slipped my palm into his, his strength easily helping me rise to my feet.

Instead of leading me away, he let go of my hand and took a step back. Openly regarded me from the tip of my head to my bare toes peeking out under my hem. Admiration lit his face, and my cheeks flamed. Again.

"Your mother did a beautiful job with my dress." I looked down and folded my hands into the chiffon.

He stepped forward and kissed my cheek. Lingered. "I'll be sure to thank her later."

Later. *After*.

My vision clouded as my muscles tightened again.

He stepped back, and I hoped he hadn't sensed the quickening of my pulse. The underlying nerves that charged through my body like a lightning storm. I didn't want him to think I was having second thoughts. That in any way I would reject him.

"Would you like to see your new home?" He offered his hand again, and I took it with resolve. Now would be when he led me to the marriage bed.

We ducked under the partition he'd gone through before. The room was smaller than the one we'd left, but still comfortable. Cooking utensils were stacked in an organized manner in the corner.

"This is the women's section. My mother uses it mostly for cooking and entertaining her friends."

I nodded, not really seeing everything all the woven walls contained. Any minute now he'd lead me on. To the bedroom. Though there was a lot to take in, my mind wouldn't release its grasp of that thought alone. I was like a child afraid of the monster in her closet. I knew there was no monster, nothing to fear. And yet my hands grew clammy and my heart raced. Or maybe I was more like a world-renowned chef about to place a delicious dish in front of a critic. That critic had tasted delicious food before, maybe he'd deem mine less than desirable.

I shook my head even though I knew the movement would do nothing to dislodge my thoughts. What I needed was to be still. Get out of my head.

I scoffed, knowing my ability to stem my thoughts would be about as possible as damming the Nile river with a single chopstick.

With a hand to the small of my back, Karim led me forward and through another partition. In the middle of the room, wool quilts had been laid over henna-dyed goat-hair mats. At the head of the quilts rested two rectangular pillows. It didn't matter what country or culture a person was from—everyone would know I stood at the foot of a bed. My chin trembled, and I bit my lip, hating myself for the irrational reaction I was having to the whole thing.

"Your room," I forced myself to say past thinned lips. If I could command my tongue to work, then that was a small victory. One small victory at a time and perhaps my wooden limbs would work less like a marionette and more like a fluid human.

The heat from Karim's body radiated into my back. "Our room."

His breath on the back of my neck caused an uncontrollable shiver. Not necessarily unpleasant, but it wasn't helping me to clear my mind either.

He moved past me and sat on the bed, removed the shoes from his feet. "How was the celebration in the women's tent?"

His question caught me off guard by its normalcy. How could he ignore the suffocating presence of what was to come, as if the future were a living thing that took up space and oxygen within this very room, and ask me something so mundane? Were not his nerves pulled as tight as mine?

Of course not. Because whereas I only knew about what was to happen, he *knew*. We were on unequal ground, and I was the only one of us unbalanced because of it.

His question did remind me though. "Thank you for sending the chicken. That was very thoughtful."

He looked up at me with a grin. "Couldn't have you losing your stomach on your wedding day, now could I?"

I returned his smile and shook my head.

The tilt of his lips fell a little as he regarded me.

I tried not to squirm, not to let my gaze fall to the ground. Tried not to let the knot sink to the very bottom of my stomach. When his smile drooped, I tried not to dwell on the fact that he looked disappointed.

"Sit down, Hannah." His words were heavy, tired.

Anguish had me clenching my eyes shut before I took a step toward him. All this time I'd been dwelling on my own feelings and hadn't once cared enough to look past those to see how my friend was holding up. This day was big for both of us for different reasons. While I had been petty in allowing jealousy and doubt control my emotions, Karim had been nothing but honorable.

I sat beside him, an apology tumbling from my lips. How many brides felt the need to say they were sorry so many times on their wedding day?

He entwined our fingers and ran the pad of his thumb along the back of my hand. "You have nothing to be sorry for."

I turned to look at him. "But I do. A marriage shouldn't start as an act of sacrifice, and that's what this is. You've sacrificed marrying a woman you love so that you could protect me and my family. You deserve another chance with a woman of your choosing. Like you had with Maleka." I knew their union hadn't been a love match. Karim had told me as much before. But at least with her he hadn't been forced into the situation, the only solution to a problem he thought his responsibility.

He shook his head. "I had less of a choice with Maleka then I did with you. My father chose Maleka. I chose you."

Karim's hand came up, and he rested his wrist on the top of my shoulder, his fingers sliding over my hair. I watched his eyes track the movements of his fingers until they shifted and captured my gaze.

His eyes had always entranced me. They were as dark as midnight without the glow of a moon. So dark, in fact, that I often had difficulty discerning where his iris and pupil began and ended. Even at this close distance they melted into one another.

"Do you believe a person's soul can bond with another?" His breath fanned my face and smelled of the coffee we had drunk.

The knot in my stomach clenched in an unfamiliar way. As if it responded to Karim's question before my mind could form an answer and my voice deliver it.

Did I believe that souls bonded together?

You and Karim are not two halves that make a whole. Already you are both complete. His mother's words came back to me. I agreed with her. Plato's philosophy of love being a single soul that was divided into two bodies was a romantic idea for the movies, but not something I believed in nor thought Biblical. Helpmates, yes. Soul mates, no.

But bonding? Wasn't that God ordained? Through intimacy? *The two shall become one.*

Karim traced my bottom lip with his finger. "I have never understood it, this inexplicable drawing of my soul to yours."

I shrugged away his intensity. "I'm different." A peach in an almond grove.

"Different. Unique. Special. But those words do not define the invisible cord that connects us." He moved my hair off my shoulder and gently rubbed the lobe of my ear between his fingers. "You are sorry because you think I was forced into the decision to choose you, but, Hannah, I think my heart chose yours that day you were stung by the scorpion and I scooped you up in my arms and carried you to your parents."

My breath was coming in short bursts now. "It did?"

He moved closer, his fingers at the nape of my neck pressing me closer as well. His mouth hovered over mine. "I choose you again, today and every day," he whispered. With infinitesimal measurements he closed the gap, his warm mouth on mine.

The taut strings in my stomach began to sing like the first notes of a violin solo. Slow and aching at first as Karim kissed me. What I had been unable to do all day by sheer willpower, his simple touch succeeded—my thoughts stilled and my doubts fled. I lifted my hand and pushed the turban off his head, ran my fingers between the thick strands of his dark hair and then the coarser hairs on his cheek. Whereas his touch had stilled me, mine drove him. He deepened the kiss, the symphony within me building.

By the night's end, I had my answer.

Souls undoubtedly *did* bond with one another.

Chapter 13

KARIM

My internal clock ticked time off the predawn minutes, and I blinked the sleep from my eyes. Weight rested on my chest, the left side of my body unusually warm. Hannah stirred besides me, her golden hair fanned out over my bicep as her head nestled more snugly into the section of space below my collar bone. Desire pulled in my gut as I ran a finger along the milky white flesh of her arm.

My wife.

I'd never thought the title would belong to Hannah, but it fit. She fit. More than I ever imagined a woman could.

Protectiveness surged through my limbs, causing my muscles to ripple. Hannah stirred again, this time rolling away from me in her sleep.

I wanted nothing more than to wrap my body around hers, contour for contour. To pull her back to my chest and breathe in the scent of her. Continue to fuse the bonding of our bodies, our lives, our souls.

But intuitively I knew that in minutes the sun would

peek over the horizon, and this time of dawn was not my own but consecrated for prayer to Allah. Rising from bed, I faced the east, toward Mecca, and allowed my body to follow the rituals my muscles had conducted five times every day since childhood. Mind free, my prayer came not from rote words formed by my mouth but from deep within my heart, where worship to Allah resided.

The morning has come to me but belongs to you, Allah, Lord of the worlds. I ask of you the good of the day, its success, your aid, blessing, and guidance throughout.

Rustling from the bed drew my attention, and though I knew I shouldn't, I peeked from under heavy lids. Hannah's arm rose from under the blankets, her hands rubbing at her eyes. My heart clenched at the sight of her, and I repeated my plea for guidance. She sat up and caught my gaze with a smile. With no thought, my lips hitched upward. It took concerted effort to close my eyes and mind once again to outward distractions.

Allah deserved my undivided attention.

The next words of the Fajr prayer seemed especially important at this time. I bowed my head even further in reverence.

Shelter me from the evil of this day and the evil to come.

Though I'd argued the disease wasting away the livestock was of a natural cause, the air bred a taste of something sinister. I could not concede to a supernatural cause. Did not think the illness and devastation a curse from Allah. But something more than environment was at play. And the thing with evil intent, it did not content itself with benign infliction. Instead it ate and drank and grew and bred until its black fingers had spread to touch any life near.

The air beside me stirred, and though I kept my eyes closed, I was aware of Hannah's presence. Was she, a Christian, also taking part in sunrise prayers?

Closing the door yet again to outward wanderings, I shepherded my mind to thoughts of worship.

All praise to you who has forgiven me today and not destroyed me due to my wickedness.

My body rocked forward so my forehead touched the ground. With reverence, I ended the prayer and stood.

Hannah knelt by our bed, her hands folded, head bowed, eyes closed, and lips moving. All the years I'd known the Pratts, I'd never heard a Christian prayer. The way she knelt spoke of humility, a posture familiar to me and one I respected. Were the words she spoke simple recitation, the going through of motions?

As quickly as the question entered my mind I dismissed it. No one could commit to their God in the way this family had by a nominal faith. Although they rejected the great prophet Muhammad and his teachings—the ways to practice religion that were familiar to me—their hearts were still open, their worship still pure. Did we not, after all, serve the same God, though I called him Allah and they referred to him as Father? The God of Abraham our father, the father of Ishmael, was who I served. The God of Abraham, the father of Isaac, who my wife and her family served.

"Amen," Hannah said under her breath, then raised her face to me.

I sat on the edge of our bed and faced her. Her cheek was wrinkled where it had pressed against the pillow. My hand itched to smooth it out. One touch to an ember, however, could produce a flame, and now that the sun had risen, duties beckoned me outside this chamber.

Still, I lingered. "Good morning, wife."

Her cheeks produced a rosy hue. "Good morning, husband."

Husband.

As much as I hadn't predicted ever calling Hannah *wife*, the punch of hearing her call me *husband* from her soft voice nearly knocked me over. Hunger for her rolled in my belly and produced a groan that nearly escaped into her hearing. Our friendship had been the seed of our love, our marriage its planting. Time and attention would be the sun and water. With both, germination would occur, roots would form, and the product would be something both delicate and strong, sweet and savory. But restraint was needed as well. If I doused the seed with too much water, it would drown before it ever had a chance to live. Too much sun and it would wither away.

Uncertainty crawled into her expression, and I realized I had let too much silence span. I opened my mouth to speak, reassure her in some way, but the bleating of ewes and the shuffling of feet reached our ears. Beams creaked as the skeleton of tents were disassembled, the skins falling to the ground below.

I leaned forward and kissed Hannah on the forehead. "I have to go," I said as I stood. There was much to do, and as leader I had to oversee it all. Hannah had been a part of many such preparations. She understood.

Hannah

I watched Karim's back as he exited the partition and then the tent itself. Wrapping my arms around my middle, I scolded myself at the emptiness and insecurity his departure caused. Was I a small girl who needed pats on the head and assurances that all was well when there was no evidence to the contrary?

As much as logic told me he was needed elsewhere and that responsibility was what had pulled him from my side, a chasm cracked in my chest. Even with the time we'd spent together the night before, I needed a few more moments. Some time to bolster my confidence in our new relationship. Convince myself the lasting impression of his lips on mine, his touch on my skin, held more meaning for him than the desires of the flesh and the pressing demands to produce an heir.

In the deepest recesses of my heart, I knew Karim cared for me. Loved me, even. As a friend. But it was like wading in a river. I'd only stood in the shallows before. Yesterday I'd plunged all the way in. And right now, the current was so strong, it attempted to drag me under instead of offering me its cool freshness.

I bowed my head again, in need of strength in my unknown from an all-knowing God. When I'd finished pouring my heart out, I rose and dressed for the day. There was much to do, and none of it would get done if I spent all my time closed within this tent or within the confines of my own head. Neither would produce many results.

I packed up the quilt, rugs, and pillows and stored them in a corner of the tent. Only a day had passed since the wedding, but at this point, I was ready to throw time out the window. In a week it would be tradition to return to my parents' tent with various foods to show I was well taken care of and happy. But where would we be in a week? I knew we were leaving, but so much was happening, Karim hadn't informed me of our destination.

Ducking under the partition of the women's section of the tent, I gathered a few of the richer foods and fresh fruits left over from the wedding feast and bundled them together in a thick cloth. At this point, I wasn't sure where my parents would be, but with Mother's injuries, she wouldn't have been able to go far. More than likely my parents' tent would be one of the last to be taken down.

I kept my gaze to the ground, in adherence to the culture, yes, but also to avoid any knowing looks that might be cast my way. Already I had felt on display, but now, whether true or imagined, the scrutiny of my brothers and sisters dug deeper.

The sides of my parents' tent had been rolled up to allow a breeze to drift through, the roof still providing much-needed shade. I expected Mom to be sitting or reclining, but she stood off to the side, arranging their belongings to travel.

She noticed me and smiled, moving aside what she was working on to shuffle toward me. I met her in the middle with an open arm.

When we separated, I handed her my offering.

"What is this?" she asked as she uncovered the food I'd gathered.

"I'm a few days early." She'd lived here as long as I had. Knew the culture and customs.

Tears glazed her eyes, but she blinked them back. "Thank you for this." She set the bundle down, then busied her hands with packing. "Shouldn't you be busy packing your own household now?"

"I am sure my husband would be pleased that I took a small measure of time to assure my family of his good care of me." Why did I sound so formal?

"I'm sure your husband would."

I turned toward the tenor voice I knew so well. "Karim."

"Wife." His gaze bore into mine, but his face remained cool. No crinkles around his eyes. No smile upon his lips. Not even a softening. It was the face I'd encountered in the sandstorm. The same one I'd witnessed many times as he strode through the encampment.

Serious.

Withdrawn.

I wanted to do something to crack his veneer. Touch him. Crack a joke. Hip-check him. Something that would shock or shake the shroud he cloaked himself in. Transform him into the man I saw when we were alone.

Mom moved around me with small steps. "Ethan is not here at the moment."

Of course Mom would think Karim was here for Dad. As much as possible, genders stayed separate.

Karim held himself straight. "No matter. I have already spoken to him. Both of you will travel with Mahabat in the Toyota. With your injuries, it will be the easiest way, although I fear the jostling will still cause you great discomfort. The sickest of the livestock will go with you, and I pray between Allah's mercy, Mahabat's experience, and your husband's medical knowledge, no more sheep will be lost along the way."

Mom bowed her head. "I thank you for your kind consideration."

"Yes, thank you, Karim." I wanted to walk to him, give him a hug of thanks (I guess those years in the South rubbed off on me more than I thought), but his body language said *do not approach.*

"I wonder"—Mom's head remained bowed—"will Hannah be traveling with her parents, in relative comfort and safety?"

My lungs froze. I had never heard my mother be so bold with anyone but Dad before. She'd phrased her question so that if Karim answered in the negative, he'd be admitting to not putting my safety first.

I looked at him. Watched his mouth pinch and his eyes narrow. He, however, did not look at me. Not even a glance. Nothing to gauge my response.

In a tight voice he replied, "Hannah stays with me." Without another word, he turned and stalked away.

"Mother." The second syllable fell long on my tongue, drawing out the reprimand I felt.

She looked up, no apology in her expression. "It is not wrong to want to keep you safe."

"Karim will keep me safe. As a friend, he always has. Now that I am his wife, don't you think he'll be even more on guard?"

"From scorpions, and sandstorms, and scrapes of your own making, yes, Karim has protected you."

The silence that followed spoke what she hadn't. Things had changed. The social climate had shifted. There was no telling where the danger originated.

Which was the whole point of Karim marrying me in the first place. For protection, safety.

"Besides," Mom said with a smile, "I thought you'd relish the chance at traveling by vehicle instead of trekking the distance by camel."

My legs, back, and bottom protested the suggestion of camel riding. The long days, endless motion, unbearable heat. Maybe I should try to convince Karim to let me ride with my folks.

But that would mean who knew how long away from him. No matter how strong the current, I wasn't going to let it sweep me away without a fight. And in this battle, my only weapons were the biblical decree.

Leave and cleave.

Chapter 14

HANNAH

In an unprecedented decision, Karim divided us into three separate caravans. My parents and Mahabat traveled in the truck with the animals too sick to journey under their own steam. The majority of the women and a few of their husbands shepherded the remaining flock and prized Arabian horses. Both their routes included cities, known public wells, and ways to receive help along the way should they need it.

The final caravan, the one made up of the clan's camels, a majority of the men to tend to them, and a handful of women, was headed into the heart of the region with its harsh climate and desolate wildness. Not many creatures were equipped to handle the conditions, but the Bedouins had learned from the survivors, the thrivers, and had spent centuries making a way where no man had succeeded before. We'd all meet up again in a few weeks' time.

Ewes and rams bleated as they started off toward the east. I shielded my eyes from the morning sun and watched as the herd moved, the shepherdesses hedging the perimeter. Off in the distance, two men stood with their heads bent toward each other. Their keffiyehs hid their profiles, and I couldn't make out who they were. One man pulled a vial from his sleeve and handed it to the other man.

What were they doing? What was in the vial?

I squinted but couldn't make out any other details.

They separated, the man now in possession of the vial moving toward the retreating sheep, the other making his way to the front of the camel lineup.

My palms grew sweaty as I adjusted my grip on my camel's lead rope. Natural curiosity and my heightened sense of carefulness had me making hypotheses. Was there some sort of medication in the vial? But that wouldn't make sense. Medication would come from my father, not another man. Maybe something for the sheep? A salve of some sort in case one of the animals caught itself on a thorny briar?

There was no way to know, and dwelling on it would drive me crazy.

I waited while last-minute checks were being made, then we'd be off. A few were already mounted upon their camels' backs, but I preferred to walk as much as I could. There would be a time, I knew, when the sand would become so soft and deep that I'd have no choice but to endure the jostling of my camel's gait and rely on the surefootedness of her wide cloven hoof.

That day wouldn't be today, however.

I leaned to the side from my position in the middle of the pack with the rest of the women to get a clearer view of the front. Karim held his back straight and head erect. He turned and surveyed the group of us, jaw firm. Then with a loud "hut, hut," he twisted his wrist and swatted Jamal on his rump with a switch. The animal plodded forward, and those of us in line followed.

Plodded. A good word, and appropriate as hour after endless hour I put one foot in front of the other, the sun beating down on my head and shoulders. I was thankful for the shield of fabric that protected me from sunburn, but it did nothing to ward off the oppressive heat. Dry beyond warm, it felt like I was being baked in a global oven.

By midday my legs felt both leaden and like Jell-O. Ironically opposites. The earth crunched under my foot with each step, the sand shifting under my weight. My throat was dry, and the only thing I could think about was water. And this was only the first day. The first half of a day, even. How was I going to survive the many weeks it would take before we reached our destination? How had I survived it before? Food and water were rationed for good reason, but already I wanted to drain my canteen, then fill it again and pour it over my head.

And I hated it. Hated the weakness. Not in all my years of desert dwelling had I grown accustomed to the oppressive heat. The time spent in the States only making me that much more ill prepared. The South was hot, for sure, but nothing like this.

I looked back over my shoulder to the travelers behind me. Surely no one else in the caravan was suffering from a thickened tongue that felt like cotton balls had absorbed all the moisture from their mouth. Surely they did not suffer from a one-track mind that was already driving them to the edge of delirium.

Why couldn't I be stronger?

I readjusted my grip on the rope and straightened my shoulders.

I would be stronger.

Swallowing, I ignored the sweat that dripped down the center of my spine. Ignored the glare of the sun that cast waves of heat to dance in the air. Ignored the way my thighs quivered as I took another step.

If I couldn't do this, then the people wouldn't respect me. If they didn't respect me, they wouldn't allow me to teach their children. They wouldn't listen to me when an opportunity arose to share about the love of Jesus. They'd scorn Karim for his choice of wife.

Five hours into our trek. Hundreds of miles to go. The distance, the journey through it, weighed upon my shoulders. It was more than physical. More than forcing my feet one in front of the other until we reached the oasis and date grove Karim's friend managed. It was also spiritual, emotional.

My future hinged on this expedition.

Karim broke from the lead and signaled with his hand. We led our camels into a tight circle and gave the command for them to lay down. We formed a circle within their circle, using their bodies as backrests as we sat. Dried fruit and meat were passed around along with a skin of water. When they reached me, I carefully took only my share of both.

The water, warm and stale, tasted like only water from an animal skin could. And it was the best thing I'd ever held in my mouth. I followed it with the jerky, my teeth slowly grinding the chewy meat. Dried dates ended our quick lunch with quiet satisfaction. The natural sugars gave me much-needed energy.

Karim had made the rounds, checking on the people and

animals. He approached me and held out the waterskin again.

I shook my head. "I already had my share, thank you."

"Your cheeks are as pink as a desert rose. Another drink would do you good."

My eyes slid closed as I tipped the mouth of the skin to my lips. It wasn't weakness, was it, to accept the kindness of help when needed?

I handed the skin back to Karim.

"You should ride." He continued to regard me in that piercing manner of his.

My gaze shifted to the lounging animals around us. "I'd rather walk."

His lips thinned, but he said nothing more. Another moment of scrutiny, then he turned back to Jamal. One swift motion and he was on the camel's back, the animal on its feet.

We hadn't fed or watered the camels. There was no need, and we hadn't packed any provisions for them anyway. All they carried upon their backs was for our survival. The fact they could last up to six months without water and we could only survive five days at the most, spoke to how much better prepared they were for the even harsher climate we were about to enter.

Those who'd ridden earlier now took a turn walking and vice versa. To my observation, I was the only one who did not yet take advantage of the transportation afforded me.

The rest of the day followed like the first half had.

Plodding.

My view consisted of tan sand, tawny camel hair, and the azure sky. Conversation was minimal, and I found myself making up stories to occupy my mind. I couldn't have it go back to the broken record of *water, water, water*.

My imagination and shallow knowledge of history painted another caravan cresting a ridge to my right. The leader, Caucasian like me. European clad in the uniform of a WW I officer. He held himself erect, his bearing proud and commanding. Behind him, a train of two dozen camels. The wind nipped at his blond hair and whipped at the British flag soaring in defiance against the Turks. Had he come from destroying the ongoing construction of the rail line, or was he on his way there?

The image disintegrated like the figment it was, but I smiled anyway. I might not have known all the history of the famed Lawrence of Arabia, and I wasn't even sure if he'd made any appearance in this particular area, but he'd serve well as a distraction. I could fill in the blanks of my knowledge with whatever fancied me at the time. Perhaps he too felt most at home among the native people who befriended and followed him. Perhaps he even fell in love with one of their sisters or daughters.

It didn't really matter. In my imagination, I could make him do whatever I wished, and I had more than ample time on my hands to create a myriad of adventures for him as we crossed the desert in time to help in the date harvest.

When the sun neared the horizon, Karim lifted his hand again in signal.

We'd camp here for the night.

My body wilted in gratitude at the thought of rest. If allowed, I could lay down right then without a pallet or anything and easily sleep the night away. My damp skin would crack when the sweat dried, and I was sure I would awaken with sand in all sorts of interesting places, but I didn't care. To not move and simply be, let the exhaustion that had chased me the last hour finally catch up and overcome—it sounded like bliss.

Karim approached leading Jamal, and held out his hand. "I will take care of your camel for you. Rest."

He didn't have to convince me. Without any decorum, I plunked my behind down on the ground right there. The less-than-ladylike act did nothing to earn the respect I sought in the eyes of my brothers and sisters. Instead of sitting, I should be making myself useful. While in America, I'd silently smiled at my friends' lack of endurance when it came to the physical. Now I was on the other side of the coin.

Suppressing a groan, I hefted my body up and pushed past the wobbliness of my legs, moving at a snail's pace to the small group of women who were preparing the beginnings of an evening meal. A small fire had already been built, although I had no idea how they'd managed it in such a short time. Had I sat in a daze longer than I'd thought?

The fire had been banked, hot coals pushed to a flat surface. In a bowl, the ingredients for flat bread were being mixed.

"Here, let me help." I reached into the bowl and pinched off a good portion of the dough, forming it into a round cake between my palms. Back and forth I tossed it, stretching it rounder and rounder. When it was the right shape and thickness, I gently laid it on top of the heated coals and ash. A long, thin stick lay to the side of the cooking area, and I used it to sweep more coals and ash on top of the flat bread.

The women chatted around me as they worked, but my tongue was as heavy as my eyelids. I had no energy to force words. Sharing in their meal preparation was as much as my body would allow me to participate. When I knew the bread would be done, I used the stick to push away the coals and ash on top and retrieve the flat loaf. Gray and dirty, I took it to a nearby rock and threw it down on top of the stone. Ash billowed away from the bread, and I repeated the process until it was as clean as food could be when cooked in such a manner.

A stack of loaves lay under a cloth, and I added mine to the others. The smell of steeped coffee hung bitter in the air, still hot but dropping by degrees as the sun slunk lower in the sky.

Cooking complete, the fire stoked to leaping flames, we arranged ourselves around its light and ate.

There was something universal about a campfire, I'd found. Whether huddled around the crackling warmth in a crowded campsite in the Smokey Mountains on Memorial Day or eating bread produced from its heat in the desolate desert of a far-off land, the dancing flames held a mesmerizing, hypnotic quality that loosened muscles and tongues alike.

Never had a better story been heard or told than around a campfire.

I smiled and listened as Samlil regaled us about his legendary hunting trip. How he'd tracked a herd of majestic white oryx, the only animal more suited for desert living than the camel. So majestic, in fact, that the legend of the unicorn originated from its horse-like body and long, regal horns. He'd been so overcome upon seeing them that he'd forgotten to raise his rifle and shoot.

Karim sat directly across from me and caught my attention. He winked. Neither of us quite believed Samlil's tale, but we'd never say so.

Stories flowed around the circle, and I hid a yawn behind my hand. Karim stood and walked a crescent shape around the fire until he reached my side. He sat to my right, and I was more than tempted to lean my head on his shoulder and close my eyes.

"Tell me about your country." He spoke low, asking for a story that would be more for the two of us than for the whole gathered group.

"What do you want to know?"

His gaze held mine. "Everything."

At that, I laughed. "Everything is a lot."

He smiled in a way that said he knew and he'd asked anyway. "Tell me something I have not learned by watching movies from Hollywood. Describe to me something you have seen with your own eyes, experienced by your own hands."

Karim's understanding of the West consisted of the memories I'd shared growing up—but those had been painted by the perspective of a child—the rare movie he might see in town, and whatever news he heard or read about in a newspaper slanted by political agendas. Deciding what to share was like choosing a single water particle from an entire ocean.

I stared into the flames, sifting through experiences I'd had the last six years. "Before Samlil started in on his oryx story," I said quietly, "I was remembering the last time I'd sat around a campfire."

He continued to watch me, his silence an invitation to continue. "In America, when you go camping and have a fire, there is a rule about what food you must eat."

"You must eat a certain food?"

"Oh yes. It's called s'mores."

"What is this s'more? Are they delicious?"

I licked my lips at the memory of them. On that trip, I'd eaten six without any shame. "Very. You take a marshmallow—"

His eyebrows dipped. I'd lost him already. "A marshmallow is a soft, white, sweet, fluffy type of dessert. You spear it on a stick and roast it until it has an outer shell but a gooey inside. Then you place it on a cracker made of ginger and sugar, a square of chocolate on that, and finally another ginger sugar cracker." I closed my eyes. "When you bite into a s'more, it is warm and sweet and gooey and crunchy all at the same time."

I opened my lids to Karim's fixed stare. Not on my eyes, but a few inches south to my lips. My stomach flipped. I was no longer remembering a late-spring evening in the Smokey Mountains a few years ago when I enjoyed a dessert sandwich, but a night not so distant, last night even, when I enjoyed...my husband.

In a graceful move he stood, bringing me along with him. Turning to our group, he said, *"Tusbah al khair."* *May you have a good morning.*

He didn't wait for a response. The wishing of our morning to be full of light. Instead he placed a hand to the small of my back and led me away from the crowd, away from the fire and the light, and into the darkness, where our warmth would only be found in each other.

Chapter 15

KARIM

Regret curdled my stomach like milk gone bad. I deserved the discomfort. Deserved so much more. Hannah's face as it blanched, her eyes rounding with hurt, whipped against my heart like a lashing.

I'd take it back, if I could. Reach out and grip my words before they reached her ears and swallow them down. But words couldn't be unheard, and they couldn't be unspoken, even if the syllables never should have been formed in the first place.

The frustration I'd let overtake me in the moment had cooled faster than a fire being doused with water. Nothing justified what I'd said. Our tiny sapling of growing love, trampled under my careless foot.

My intentions had been good. I'd been watching her, although I doubt she'd noticed. Her face was burned, her lips chapped. Stubbornly she'd led her camel day after day, as of yet not once taking a break and letting the animal carry her upon its back.

It stung a bit, her refusal to ride. I knew her hesitation, her dislike, even her underlying fear. But didn't she know *me*? Didn't she know that I would have chosen for her the safest, most docile and dependable creature among the herd?

It wasn't the lack of trust she showed in my ability to care for her that had caused me to speak this morning, however. No. Her utter exhaustion forced me to my declaration. She'd barely been able to pull herself to her feet, though she'd thought to hide how her muscles quivered, how her limbs seemed to have gained double the weight, how they were so difficult for her to move. I couldn't let her keep doing this to herself. If she didn't ride, she'd push herself over the edge, where I'd never be able to bring her back.

My words had been gentle, I'd thought, as I sat across from her and watched her loop her hijab over her head. "Hannah."

She'd looked up at me, and I'd taken a moment to frame my words. Too easy it would be to command her to ride. I was used to instructing others, and even in my previous marriage, it was what I'd have done. Maleka had been meek and obedient, more like a child. Hannah wasn't like that. She would take offense to my tone, the American independence bred within her rising to the challenge of being told what to do.

"I think it best if today you ride." There. Not a command, but she now held awareness of my wishes.

"I'd rather walk." She'd stood and turned, shooing me and my concern away like a pesky bug.

I tempered the quick flash of pride that bolted through me, annoyance following like thunder. On the one hand, I was glad she still felt comfortable being herself around me, that the events of the last weeks and the change in our relationship hadn't caused her to behave in a way different than before. She still felt comfortable to speak her mind when we were alone. But on the other hand, things *had* changed. We had both been thrust into new roles—that of husband and wife. And as husband, the responsibility fell to me to take care of her, to make sure she was safe. Even safe from herself if her stubbornness put her in danger and caused her harm.

And perhaps, as I thought back on it, I didn't quite enjoy my word being challenged. Not that I had never been challenged before. As a young sheikh, the elders often questioned my decisions, but ultimately, they would see the wisdom of what I spoke and heed my counsel and leadership.

If Hannah had only submitted to me...

But she wouldn't be Hannah then, would she? She wouldn't be the headstrong girl who'd grown into the beautiful woman I'd married.

As long as I was listing the "if onlys," I had quite a number to apply to myself.

If only I hadn't been so arrogant.

If only I had exhibited more patience.

If only I hadn't spoken out of frustration.

But I'd marched around to face her and had lightly pinched her chin to raise her face to mine. "And I'd rather you ride."

She'd jerked her chin out of my grasp. It had felt like a slap. "You don't understand."

How could I not? Wasn't it I who had been by her side when she'd tumbled from the camel the time she'd thought to race with the other children? I the one who'd tended her wound the time a young camel had spooked and bitten her? I the one to soothe her anger when her new clothing had been soiled by the green saliva an ornery camel had spit along her front? And yet she said I did not understand.

"It is you who do not understand." My nostrils had flared. "Do not understand the body's limitations. The way the sun will suck out all the moisture from your bones. The way your heart will race, muscles cramp, and weakness will weigh you down as if you were dragging around another body on top of your own. How your stomach will rebel first, followed by your entire body until you lay unconscious in a heap on the desert floor."

Her gaze had hardened. "I'm fine."

She may have attempted to convince herself, but I would not be so deceived. The evidence stood in front of me. Already she swayed unsteadily on her feet. "You are not fine." If she wouldn't heed my advice, she would obey my command. I stared into her eyes, communicating my unbending decision. I wouldn't be argued with any longer. "You *will* ride today, Hannah."

Her spine straightened despite the fact she'd already been holding herself erect. "I will not."

My frustration had quickly transformed to anger. I beat a fist against my thigh. "Maleka would have listened—"

That was when I'd stopped the flow of words, but they'd already hit their mark. I'm sure if I'd unsheathed the dagger from my belt and pierced her skin with it, I wouldn't have caused her as much pain.

Eyes wide with a telling sheen backdropped by a face pale despite long days in the sun gaped at me. I'd taken a step toward her, hand outstretched, apology on my lips. But she'd turned, literally ran away from me. I had followed at a slower pace, and when I'd come upon the rest of the caravan, had found her upon the cursed camel's back.

I'd won, but in the winning had lost so much more.

Hannah

If the desert decided right then to kick up a storm, I wouldn't run. Wouldn't seek shelter. I'd thank it, grateful to be swallowed whole. But the stagnant air around me didn't so much as stir. The sun continued to beat upon my skin like a branding iron, and the swaying of the camel beneath me poked like a stick at an open wound.

I tried to block out the pain, ignore the way my heart bled as if a serrated knife had been taken to it.

I was overreacting. Karim hadn't done anything truly awful. His words were even true. If Maleka had been here, she wouldn't have argued with her husband. No doubt she'd have heeded his words and obeyed like a good little wife should.

Tears pricked my eyes, and I blinked rapidly to keep them at bay. Crying would only speed up the process of dehydration, doing more harm than good. As if crying really ever did much good.

I stared off to my right. The landscape was beginning to change from hard rock cliffs to soft sand dunes. I tried to conjure up Lawrence and his entourage again, something to occupy my mind and take it away from reliving the moment this morning.

How was it whenever I was compared to another person,

I never come out on top? Always found wanting. Never quite good enough.

My parents, bless their hearts, hadn't meant to compare me, I don't think. As an only child, I'd never been pitted against a sibling. But we'd been thrust into a culture that wasn't our own, and we'd wanted to assimilate, to be accepted. So often I'd hear, "Hannah, you must be like the other kids. You can't lift up your skirts and show your legs when you run." "Hannah, watch how Anya interacts with her peers. You are older now—you cannot be looking the men in the eye. Show humility and respect." "Hannah, we have to be like Jesus, to be a living example to these people who do not know Him. You can't be acting like that. It's not what Jesus would do."

And if not my parents, then the other clanswomen. Compared to their children, compared to all infidel Western-ers. Compared and always found lacking.

It hadn't stopped when I'd been in America either. Some were less vocal, but still I saw it in their eyes. Their wish that I'd be "normal." More like them, less like I had been raised in the middle of nowhere among a tribe of nomads.

My eyes slid shut slowly against the pain I'd tried to mask with a willing spirit and a ready smile. It hurt though, this feeling of never being good enough. Of people wishing I were someone else, someone other than me.

Karim had never made me feel like that. Until today. And knowing that even he wished I were someone else...

It cut deep.

Had he been harboring those thoughts for long? When he'd married me, had he wished I were Maleka? Or at least more like her? Did he long for me to be more compliant and less independent? More meek and less vivacious?

When he held me at night, when we made love, was it Maleka who filled his thoughts, haunted his memories? Had she pleased him more than I did? Did he yearn for her while holding me?

In how many ways was I a disappointment to him?

I opened my eyes and sniffed. Lawrence refused to appear and distract me with his escapades of wartime bravery.

Would Esther be as stubborn, or would she be accommodating? Maybe she would even understand.

Though our stories were separated by centuries, we had a lot in common. She was also a foreigner in a foreign land. Her husband had also been married before. Although, in one point I conceded to an advantage. Esther shared her husband, King Ahasuerus, with not only his previous wife's memory but also a number of concubines.

I shuddered at the thought of sharing my husband with other women in that way.

I could see her in my mind though, in the palace, in her room, handmaidens around her, fanning her with palm branches. Gold bracelets encircled her wrists, an intricate crown upon her head. Turning my thoughts from reality, from the pressure in my chest and my view of the backside of the camel in front of me in the caravan, I journeyed into my imagination. My escape.

Esther's delicate face scrunched slightly, worry lining her brow. I was a spectator to this drama, notwithstanding it was one of my own making. But I could not converse with her, could not ask her all the questions I'd gathered every time I'd heard her story.

Did the king love her, or was it merely her beauty that had caused him to name her queen? Had she loved him in return?

The crease in her brow deepened, and my questions turned more to the moment. Or rather, which moment. Had she just found out about Haman's nefarious plans? Something that would destroy all of her people. Or was her distress even more personal? Was her husband now visiting one of his concubines? Something that would without a doubt destroy her heart.

The pressure in my chest increased, twisted, like a rag between two hands that sought to wring out every drop of water from it. As if I were feeling the betrayal Esther must have felt.

And wasn't I? Karim didn't want me. He wanted Maleka.

I fisted my hand and pressed it against my mouth to keep in the sob. I didn't want my pain to become public knowledge. The teary-eyed American who couldn't pull it together, who couldn't make the journey like a real Bedouin—the men in the caravan would compare me to the handful of other women journeying among them. The ones who worked just as hard for everyone's survival and did it with dignity and perseverance. It would just be another instance in which I'd fall short.

The only way to move forward was to learn from the past. No one wanted me to be me. Instead they wanted me to be more submissive, less headstrong, quieter, gentler, meeker. My parents had called it a mirror, a reflection of Christ. But no matter how much I tried, I'd always fall short of being like

Jesus. Even when I emptied myself and filled myself again with the Holy Spirit, the vessel was still a broken, sinful human.

So I'd stitch closed the rip in my heart Karim's words had opened. I'd don the robes of humility, meekness, submission. Hide myself under the covering of these cloths.

I'd be all things to all people and nothing to myself.

Underneath my breath I whispered goodbye to the Hannah nobody wanted.

Chapter 16
KARIM

Tension crackled on the air more than the fire in front of us. Samlil regaled the group with another tale, this time a folklore passed down from generation to generation. The others sat in rapt attention as he wound the story through its intricate details. My ears were closed to the telling, tuned only to Hannah beside me. I'd asked again for a story from her about America, her time there, if she wished, or the land of her birth in general. It had become a special time between us these last evenings. Though I knew her well, a lot could happen to change a person in six years. Through her stories, I felt she was opening up those missing pages of her life where I'd been missing.

But that book was shut to me now. She hadn't denied my request for a story, but what she'd shared, the simple descriptions of the rolling hills of Tennessee, were impersonal and lacked the depth and openness of our previous times around the fire.

I'd apologized earlier for my thoughtless words, and I'd do

it a thousand times more if it would build a bridge across this rift I'd created between us.

I picked up her hand and studied her unresponsive fingers. She didn't flinch at my touch, of which I should be grateful, yet neither did she lean into it as she'd begun to do. My heart squeezed at the loss. My loss, yes, but more so hers.

I had shattered her trust. Broken her in some way that all that remained in my hand was an empty shell.

My Hannah had a voice that spoke against injustice. And surely I had not been just with my words. She should be yelling at me, putting me in my place.

I gazed around the group gathered. Perhaps in private she would feel secure enough to speak from her heart, and we could find a way together to make this right.

As I'd done every night, I stood and offered my hand to her, wishing those around the fire a good night. She slipped her palm against mine, her gaze cast to the ground as I led her away from listening ears and prying eyes.

Earlier I'd arranged our bedding close enough to the others for protection, far enough away for privacy. I led her to the pallet and pulled her down beside me.

Without a word, she unwound the hijab from her head and finger-combed her long, silky tresses. Taking up a brush, I scooted on my knees behind her and gathered her mane in one hand, running the teeth of the brush from the crown of her head to the tips of her hair that rested near her waist.

"I'm sorry again for what I said. I take my words back."

She didn't move to look at me, but her shoulders slumped a little. I didn't want them to slump. I wanted them to snap like a whip ready for a fight.

"Words of truth should never be unspoken."

"And words of anger should never be spoken at all."

Her body shifted. Even in the dim light of a waning moon on a cloudless night, the pain in her eyes shone. "Sometimes anger is what is needed to show the reality of one's heart."

She started to turn away, but I caught her hand. Pressed it to my chest. I could feel my pulse through her fingers. "That is not the reality of my heart. It has never and will never beat for Maleka."

Her chin dropped to her chest, the hair I'd been brushing a veil over her face. I lifted the hand covering hers to tuck the strands behind her ear. The moment my grip no longer anchored her palm, it fell from my chest to her lap.

I stared at her profile, willed her to turn her face toward me.

"I don't want to fight, Karim. Besides, if I'd listened to you in the first place, none of this would've happened."

"You are not to blame. I lost control, and that is unacceptable."

"We should just forget it ever happened." She removed her shoes and tucked her feet under her legs.

"Pain is not easily forgotten by the one who feels it or the one who unintentionally inflicts it. We cannot simply choose a memory or feeling away."

She lay down on her side, her back to me, and curled her legs up to her stomach. "I'm tired."

Should I continue to press or let it go? Perhaps this was her way to cope. Though I wished to talk about the matter, perhaps she needed time and space to deal with it on her own.

I bent down and kissed her forehead. "Sleep well, wife." Turning, I laid on my back and stared up into the starry sky.

Tension radiated like heat off Hannah's back, and the bond of our souls seemed stitched with discord.

I didn't like it. Not one bit. But what could I do, if anything?

As the night deepened, life in the desert awoke. Hiding under the sand from the death rays of the burning sun, wildlife found safety at night. Relative safety, for both prey and predator alike emerged at this time. When the first glow of morning crested the horizon, the ocean of sand would bear the mark of the tiny footprints of the scarab beetle. Perhaps even the sideways serpentine pattern of a horned viper in search of a small rodent like a jerboa to feast on.

My thoughts were as active as the desert nightlife around me. When the sun arose, they'd return to their hiding places and shelters of safety. I, on the other hand, could not bury my head in the sand. My problems would not go away at morning light. Still there would be threats looming against the Pratt family. Still our flocks would be suffering from an unknown disease.

I glanced at Hannah's sleeping form beside me.

Still my wife's heart would be broken by my own hand.

When we were children, what had returned a smile to her lips after a trying time? I racked my brain to remember. There had to be something. A lot had been asked of her when she and her parents had received permission to live among us as one of our own. Hospitality is a way of life for our people, but the Pratts hadn't sought lodging for a time or season, but for good. Hannah and her parents had been willing and the clan patient, but there had been times, for Ethan and Elizabeth as well as Hannah, when the expectations had been a little too high and the allowances a little too low.

What was something that had eased Hannah's hurt in such cases? Something that brought the joy and vibrancy back into her life?

Singing.

Like a melody on the wind, I remembered her girlish, high-pitched voice raised in song followed quickly by fits of laughter. Sometimes Elizabeth would start the song and coax the lyrics out of Hannah. But once she got going, the silliness of her songs never failed to wrap around her and fling away the melancholy.

One particular time I'd found her down in a wadi, her arms hugging her bent knees pressed tightly against her chest. As I'd descended toward her, I'd heard the telltale sniffs. Then she lifted her head and seemed to stare off into the distance for a few moments before she started to sing. The song was in English, and while I could catch a word here or there, ultimately I hadn't a clue about what she'd sung. The ending of the verses seemed to conclude with similar sounds, and after three or four verses, she burst into laughter.

I sat beside her and asked what she'd been singing, but she only tilted her head and looked at me funny. No surprise. Her family had been with us a few short months by then, and Hannah's Arabic had been about as good as my English.

I sang a few generic notes and shrugged my shoulders, then pointed at her, hoping my rudimentary sign language would cross our communication barriers. Light dawned behind her eyes in understanding, and she sang another verse.

I shrugged my shoulders again, at which she pursed her lips to the side in response. She concentrated for a moment, and then her whole face brightened. She sprinted to a nearby bush and found a small stick in the underbrush. After she returned to my side, she pushed the point of the stick to the ground and began to draw pictures.

The first was an oval with stripes. Which didn't make a whole lot of sense to me. Next, she drew the tail of a whale. I knew because my father had once taken me to the coast and we'd seen the native group of humpbacks. On the tail, she drew lots of small circles.

I looked at her, brows low over my eyes. Either there was something I wasn't getting, or American songs were seriously crazy.

The third picture was of a flying bug of some sort with something hanging down from around its neck.

Hannah had dropped her stick and covered her giggles with her hand, and I'd left as puzzled as before.

Later, when we both were more familiar with the other's native languages, I'd asked her about the song. Apparently the striped oval was a watermelon that grew by a bay where there was a horde of silly animals that wore silly clothes and did silly things.

Even after I understood her words, I didn't understand the song. I never understood any of the songs. A particular favorite of hers being a ballad a cucumber sang about his undying love for his lips.

Americans were weird.

The chirp of a locust rubbing its legs together filled the night's silence.

Maybe if I caught him he could accompany Hannah

tomorrow when I asked her to share another of her nonsensical songs with me.

Chapter 17

HANNAH

I awoke with my eyes gritty. As if sand had made its way behind my lids in the middle of the night and danced along my irises. I sat up and rubbed the heel of my palms against my closed eyes, hoping my tear ducts would do their job and wash away the discomfort. Water was scarce, and I didn't want to have to ask for some merely so I could rinse out my eyes.

I lowered my hands and blinked rapidly. There, that was better.

Or maybe not. Without the physical discomfort, I was no longer distracted and was keenly aware of a deeper pain. Or lack thereof. A void really. Emptiness. Hollow. As if I had gotten up and walked out on myself, and yet here I still was.

I shook my head, knowing my thoughts sounded crazy. How could I be both gone and here? Body and spirit could not be separated. Yet, that was what it felt like.

I shook my head again, harder this time. Feeling sorry for myself would get me nowhere. It wasn't going to come up with lesson plans, something I probably should have been doing on these countless miles rather than conjuring up images of Lawrence of Arabia. No one looked favorably upon wallowing. The next time I was pitted against another in a brutal game of comparison, it would only tether about my legs like an anchor and sink me.

Karim crested the nearby knoll, two small steaming mugs in his hands.

Didn't matter the rations, there was always coffee. I grinned as I accepted the cup and forced out a cheerful "Good morning!"

Karim didn't think I could bury the memory of him comparing me to Maleka. I'd prove him wrong. I'd tuck that little gem along with all the others into the deep, dark recesses. A locked door I never opened.

"I was thinking," Karim said as he drained his coffee in one shot. "I haven't heard you sing since you came back."

My heart froze in my chest.

I'm sorry, Hannah. We've chosen April to fill the soprano spot. Maybe you can try again next year. The memory leaked under that closed door like smoke from a burning building. I hadn't tried out the next year, or any year. I hadn't sung at all after that. I wasn't any good, and no one wanted to hear me. To be fair, I hadn't given up after one setback. That had just been the last rejection I could take.

I glanced at Karim. He stared at me in that searching, serious way of his.

"I've, uh, been busy, is all." I deflected. "With the attack on my parents and the wedding. You understand."

"Of course."

I exhaled, relived I'd darted around that mine.

"We have a few moments now, before we need to pack up and head out."

My pulse thundered louder than the annual Bedouin camel races.

"Teach me another one of your ridiculous songs that I can never understand."

I laughed, but it sounded high and squeaky to my ears. "If you won't understand it anyway, then what's the point?"

I turned and began to pack up our belongings. The faster we were ready to go, the faster we could get going. I'd gladly mount that camel's back if it meant Karim would drop this topic.

Already he knew enough of my shortcomings. I didn't need to add to the list. For all I knew, Maleka had the voice of an angel and he'd often sat and listened to her serenade him at night in the privacy of their shared bedroom. If I sang something even as nonconsequential as "Down by the Bay," my go-to silly song of choice when I was little, I'd be mortified if his lips turned down in disappointment.

I couldn't fail his expectations another time. Not so quickly after the camel-riding fiasco.

"The point is they make you laugh." He didn't turn away when a flash of vulnerability entered his eyes. "I miss hearing that sound."

There hadn't been much to laugh about lately. What was it I'd thought to myself after I'd realized it was Karim who stood before me after the sandstorm? After I'd registered the lines creasing his face had been there not from laughter but from hardship?

A sigh escaped my lungs. I'd said, if anything, I'd wanted

to see him smile more. Laughter was contagious. If he missed hearing it from me, then maybe he'd join in.

I looked at him out of the corner of my eye, a sly grin spreading on my lips. Only one song would do. Win or lose, there would be a reaction.

With an air of innocence, I opened my mouth and sang the song dreaded among all parents far and wide. The song that circled and circled but never ended. By the fourth go around, Karim's brow quirked and the lyrics were leaving my mouth on bursts of giggles. But I didn't give up. I kept singing. And singing. And singing. Until Karim doubled over in a fit of laughter, his hand held up in surrender.

"Stop! I give up." He wheezed. He planted his hands on his knees and looked up at me from his hunched position with a grin. "That one is worst of all."

I lifted my lips in a cheeky smirk. "I know."

He shook his head with another chuckle, then walked up to me and planted a firm kiss to my lips. When he raised his head, all mirth was gone. "Thank you. That was the best thing I've heard in a while."

Things shifted between us. Maybe not quite to the way they were, but the deep ache in my chest that had pulsed since Karim's rejection lost a bit of its sting. I couldn't hold on to it. Had already consciously decided not to. But this was more than just forgetting a hurt against me. Whereas I'd thought I'd need to say goodbye to who I was in order to make things work, Karim had remembered something about me that was all...me.

Even if I didn't have the voice of a songbird, he'd still wanted to hear me sing silly songs that made no sense to him, all because he knew they made me giggle. Like when his mother handed me my Western-styled wedding gown, I felt accepted for who I was. It went against his words that he'd wished I was more like Maleka and less like myself.

Which left me a little confused and unstable. Like a baby learning to take her first steps and falling on her face, I had to decide if I would be content to remain immobile or if I was willing to endure a few tumbles in order to experience the jubilation of a full-out run.

Karim gathered our belongings, and I walked beside him to the rest of the group who were tying their possessions on their pack camels. I stroked my camel's long neck before climbing onto her back. Never one of grace, it took me longer than the others to mount and get in position, so I figured it would be a good idea to get a head start.

My camel did not agree with me. As soon as my weight set upon her hump, she turned into a wild thing and flew through the air, twisting and turning her body in a way that would make a rodeo bull stand up and take notice. My thighs gripped the saddle on instinct, my hands threading through my camel's coarse hair. Out of my peripheral vision, I thought I saw a man approach with his hands out. Thought I heard the shouts of others over the beating of my heart in my ears.

Then in a dash, my camel sprinted at full speed, and I was thrown forward, my arms hugging the base of her neck. Her shoulder bones collided with my jaw, and my teeth rattled in my head. With my face down, I took in the ground that sped by at an alarming rate, causing my muscles to tighten even more. As if bred for the million-dollar camel races in Dubai, she ran at full throttle.

Should I loosen my grip and slide to the ground, or would I get trampled over by her wide hoof?

Shouts reached past my panic this time, and I glanced quickly over my shoulder. Keffiyeh flying, Karim bent low over Jamal the way I'd only seen jockeys do. It felt like forever before he was by my side. Our knees almost touched with how close he'd managed to direct Jamal. His arm reached out and hooked about my waist, and he hauled me off my runaway camel and pulled me to his side.

Jamal slowed, then stopped. When Karim's muscles eased, I slid down Jamal's sweaty side, my feet unsteady beneath me. Karim leaped from the saddle, his feet planting firm in the sand. I looked up at him the same moment his gentle hands cradled the sides of my head. His brows pulled low over his dark eyes as they scrutinized the planes of my face.

I gripped his wrists. "I'm okay."

"Are you sure?" His voice quaked.

As soon as my head dipped in a nod, I was pulled against his chest, strong arms crushing me.

We stood like that a moment, each needing the physical assurance that all was well. He stepped back and looked at me again. "What happened?"

"I don't know. As soon as I mounted, it was like she become possessed. Is there such a thing as a camel curse?" My laugh came out forced and fell flat.

He tucked my head back to his shoulder without a word, his chin grazing the top as he looked past me. I followed his line of site to the wretched beast I'd never ride again. She stood a distance away, belly heaving.

With hands to my shoulders, Karim put me aside, gaze focused on my rebellious camel. "Stay with Jamal."

Slowly he moved toward the lone animal. In a low, soft tone, he sang a song—a lullaby to soothe. She didn't shy, didn't bare her teethe, didn't charge. She didn't do anything that would contradict the docile temperament she'd previously shown on the journey. The one before she'd decided it would be a good idea to try and kill me.

He ran a hand along her neck, and with quick movements, removed her saddle.

What were those dark, thin lines that ran down her middle? Sweat? I squinted, trying to see better. My eyes popped open. Blood.

Dread filled my gut. No curse, real or imagined, would be able to draw blood. Someone had purposefully tried to sabotage my camel. The only conclusion—they'd wanted to scare me, injure me, or kill me. If the first, they'd succeeded. My pulse still hadn't slowed to its normal rhythm.

Karim inspected the camel's side, then stooped and prodded the saddle and blankets that were strewn on the ground. Sunlight glinted off metal that he jammed into his belt. He gathered the reins and slowly led the camel back toward me and the rest of the group. Fire flew like daggers from his eyes. His jaw hardened. Even so, the sounds coming from his lips were nothing but soothing.

I felt like that camel. Jittery and out of sorts. One quick movement or loud pop of noise would have me bolting.

I swallowed hard before I spoke, wanting my voice to sound strong despite how my body quaked. "What is it?"

He gathered Jamal's reins and placed them in the same hand as the others. The two animals stood side by side as

Karim placed his arm around my shoulders and squeezed, his lips pressing to my temple.

"Someone placed a blade beneath the saddle. Naturally she sought to get far from the pain, but her thrashing and running only plunged the weapon deeper."

I looked behind me, saw the dried blood on her tawny side, the open wound near the base of her hump along the ridge of her back. "Will she be okay?"

"Yes." His expression tightened. "But whoever did this won't be."

Chapter 18

KARIM

There was a murderer in our midst.

The fact they hadn't succeeded wasn't the point. Their objective had been to harm my wife. To kill her. Their heart was against her, and so mine was against them.

I scanned the faces of the men and women that stood as statues as they watched Hannah as I walked up with our camel's following behind. Shock registered on some, relief on others.

Samlil stepped forward, hand outstretched to accept an animal's lead. "Praise Allah, you both are all right."

I handed off a tasseled rope. "Indeed."

His gaze roamed us both, then turned toward the camels. His eyes widened—forced or sincere?—at the sight of blood.

I hated the suspicion that twisted my thoughts. That I could even entertain the idea that one of my closest friends could sabotage my wife.

Could he?

He'd made his displeasure at my choice known, but so had the majority of the clan.

I rubbed at my forehead, wishing for insight, wisdom, and discernment that was beyond me.

Hannah sagged at my side, and I placed a hand under her elbow to sustain her.

This wasn't how things were supposed to play out. Instead of protecting her through our union, had I put her in even more jeopardy? Elizabeth's question the day we broke camp—the one about in which caravan Hannah would travel —mocked me. Had my selfishness in not wanting to be separated from my wife caused her harm? If the saboteur was one of our number, then surely it had. With her parents, Mahabat, and the ill sheep, Hannah would've been safe and relatively comfortable. But I'd dragged her through the innards of the desert, convinced I was strong enough and capable to protect her from harm.

How foolish my pride.

The back of my fingers grazed Hannah's arm as they slid downward and then threaded through her own. If the clan wanted to look sideways at my public display, so be it. She needed to feel safe, and I needed to know that she was.

One of the men had gone and retrieved the discarded saddle and blanket and now set the items down a few feet away. Hannah's camel shied away from them as if a hyena were concealed beneath, ready to laugh at her before sinking its teeth into her neck.

Hannah shivered beside me. "If it's all right with you, I'll walk."

I shook my head. "It's not all right with me."

Her hand loosened from my grip. "But, Karim—"

I kept ahold of her fingers. "You won't ride her." I jutted my chin to the skittish camel. "Though she is sweet natured, I won't risk that she has associated you with her pain and therefor holds a grudge against you."

She shivered again.

"You'll ride with me on Jamal."

Her teeth captured her bottom lip, but she didn't say anything. I could imagine her thoughts. That more than one person riding a camel was fine for the tourists who wanted to experience a quick ride, or even children at play. But two adults on a long journey through treacherous territory?

Two more days and we'd be at the date grove. Jamal was strong and could bear our weight. When he grew tired, I'd walk. But not now. Now I needed to hold my wife. If it be weak of me, then call me weak. I wouldn't be strong again until I was sure of her safety.

The caravan assembled, and I took my place at the lead. With Hannah in front of me, Jamal rose to his feet and journeyed on.

My palm rested on the flat of Hannah's stomach, my hips swaying in unison with Jamal's gate, hers jarring with each step. Even after a kilometer, her spine still held erect, a good distance spanning from her back to my chest.

With this posture, she'd wear herself out in hours. With a hand to her shoulder, I gently pressed her back to me, but she wouldn't budge. "You need to relax."

"I'm trying. This is the best I can do."

A deep sigh expelled my lungs, but I didn't push. Instead I settled more fully into the saddle, the gap between our bodies widening. As much as I knew Hannah, there was still more to learn. Like what would help ease the tension from her coiled muscles. I had an idea, but would she would agree?

"On long journeys," I said, "a caravan leader often sings to the camels. It helps soothe them and keeps up their spirits during the vast distances."

Her head turned slightly so she could look at me out of the corner of her eye. "I'm not singing 'This is the Song that Never Ends' to the camels."

I let my lips tilt up. "Good. No one wants to hear that again."

"I'm not doing a marching cadence for them either."

"I don't even know what that is."

"Hmm..."

Maybe it would be easier to show her what I meant. Taking a deep breath, I filled my lungs, then opened my mouth to the long, low tones of a song my people had sung for many years. I kept my voice quiet, but even so, my words filled the void of the open space around us. Soon others joined my song. Men's voices that ranged in volume and pitch. We sang of the earth, the sky, the stars. Of life and the God who gives it, beautiful and flowing like a rare river from a deep spring. Of the majestic hawk that soars against a crystal sky and the cunning snake that slithers across the ground.

Jamal's rhythm matched the timing of our lyrics like a harmony, and inch by inch I watched Hannah's rigid spine release until, by the end of the song, her back had nestled a spot against my chest, her head on my shoulder.

Our song neared the end, but I hated to see her tense up again, so without missing a beat I transitioned into a melody. Like a choir, the voices behind me followed. After three songs, however, my mouth grew dry. We needed to progress without the accompaniment. Hopefully, Hannah had relaxed enough that the lack of singing wouldn't trigger her back to such a severe posture.

To my shock, when our song concluded, she started one of her own. Quiet, yet clear.

"Bless the Lord, O my soul; And all that is within me, bless His holy name." Her voice echoed, though there was nothing except the crevice that protected my heart to bounce the sound back from. She paused to take another breath. "Bless the Lord, O my soul, And forget not all His benefits: who forgives all your iniquities, who heals all your diseases, who redeems your life from destruction, who crowns you with loving kindness and tender mercies, who satisfies your mouth with good things, so that your youth is renewed like the eagle's."

She held the last note, and the beauty of the lyrics falling from her lips captured me.

"Sing another one," I urged.

She nestled deeper into my chest, and my belly tightened, fueled by the simple act that demonstrated her trust in me.

"I will extol you, my God, O king: And I will bless your name forever and ever. Every day I will bless you. And I will praise your name forever and ever. Great is the Lord, and greatly to be praised; And his greatness is unsearchable."

Reverence coated her sweet voice, and I realized the song she sang was praise to her God. My heart clenched, both with an ounce of fear and a measure of admiration. Quickly I glanced over my shoulder and searched the faces among the caravan. Could they hear her words? Did they understand her language enough to know the things she was saying?

"I will meditate on the glorious splendor of Your majesty, And on your wondrous works. Men shall speak of the might of Your awesome acts, And I will declare Your greatness."

My brothers' and sisters' faces wore passive expressions, and I sighed with some relief. None showed the strained markings of one heated due to hearing heresy. Though nothing Hannah had said was heresy. God was great and greatly to be praised.

I wished to hear her keep singing, to hear the rest of the song and the place of worship in her heart from whence it came. But prudence urged me to stop the flow of her lips. Though the area was deserted save our company, any religion practiced and expressed beyond the teaching of our great Muhammad was illegal. On my vow to protect my wife, I had to be faithful in this as well.

In private she could be free to express these beliefs, but it was not safe to sing thus in public. No matter how beautiful.

"Hannah." I cringed at the forcefulness of my voice and the way she stiffened at it, then drew away from me.

Her eyes blinked then widened with a look of horror.

Hannah

How could I have been so stupid? Or maybe not stupid, but definitely careless. After all these years one would think I knew better. I *did* know better. And yet without conscious thought, in a moment of rare serenity and deep security, I had forgotten caution and let the worship well up and bubble over.

I couldn't apologize though. No one should ever apologize for praise and worship. No matter the danger and no matter how much it angered those around. Daniel didn't hide his prayer thrice daily, and Paul and Silas sang from prison. If anything, my actions had run from the same source as theirs. There was a time to be silent and a time to speak. I often couldn't tell the difference of when I should do the one and not the other but had trusted the Holy Spirit to lead me.

With caution, I turned to look at Karim. To gauge his reaction to what he might consider blatant rebellion. Against his desire for me not to outright proselytize as well as the illegality of it.

Though it had been just songs, they originated from the Scriptures. It was something my parents and I had done as far back as I could remember. A way to buoy us up when things got heavy and weighed us down. We couldn't quote scriptural promises to each other. Not in the hearing of others. So we'd set them to tune and made them songs. When we saw one of our family burdened, we'd hum the tune knowing the other person could supply the lyrics—the Bible passage filled with truth to sustain us.

What had I expected to find on my husband's countenance? A face of stone etched in displeasure? Deep lines that furrowed his brow in anger? Exasperation? Intolerance?

He looked weary. And weren't we all? Long days of walking or riding perched on a hump could tire a body down to the bones. Yet his wide shoulders still held straight with an almost regal quality. No, his tiredness didn't hinge on the physical. He was soul weary, his eyes themselves weighed down with heavy burdens.

Take My yoke upon you...and you will find rest for your souls.

I longed to share with my husband the promise Jesus gave in Matthew for His people, but I swallowed the sacred words and felt the burn of them in my throat. Desire rested like a gnawing ache in the pit of my stomach. One only known to those who experienced the unceasing throbbing of loving someone who had not accepted Jesus as their personal Savior. Helpless, but not hopeless.

Open his eyes, Lord.

Maybe then Karim could see and experience the peace that came by surrendering one's burdens into the hands of a Creator God.

"It was beautiful, my treasure." His lips grazed my temple. "But maybe you can sing your songs in private next time."

I nodded, knowing that for now, he was right. There would be a time, however, when God would require me to speak. Whether to one receptive person or a crowd. God's love could never be silenced and was not meant to stay hidden in a shroud of privacy.

Chapter 19

HANNAH

As much as I'd tried to keep the mantra of *water, water, water* out of my head, that was all I could think about. I dreamed of mountainous waterfalls in the Blue Ridge Mountains. Of rock jumping into cool, clear depths. Of summer rain showers and crystal-clear springs. I even dreamed of tiny droplets of dew glistening on broad leaves.

Instead all that surrounded me was dry and brown. No sign of life or relief.

My tongue worked against the roof of my mouth in an attempt to produce saliva. Something to alleviate the parchedness.

The air shimmied on heat waves, and exhaustion pulled my body down and against Karim behind me.

"We're almost there."

I wasn't sure if I believed him. It felt like the trip would never end. That he was only placating me like a parent would a child. But then, like a cartoonish mirage, trees jutted out of the tan landscape. Where there were trees, there was water. Life-giving, refreshing, glorious water.

Wide fronds fanned out from the tops of the trees. Date palms.

We'd arrived. Finally.

With a surge of energy, I sat up straighter and strained to make out any shape that wasn't an evergreen. My parents and the other caravan had to have arrived already. My heart raced, and I hadn't realized until then quite how much I'd worried about them. No one had tried any more *demonstrations* while we were apart, had they?

Jamal let out a long bray that shook his body. Instinctively, my thighs tightened.

Karim's hand splayed across my stomach as he pulled me closer to his back. "You're making him nervous. We'll be there soon. Just relax."

Relax. While my broken record had been *water, water, water*, his had been *relax, relax, relax*. How could one relax on a beast that had nearly killed you more than once? Even so, I'd tried. And not letting my pride get in the way, had succeeded a time or two. Although I had to give Karim the credit there. Without him I'd have internally combusted from nervousness. But whenever I got wound up, he'd start a slow, almost mournful song that calmed me, and I'd melt into him, the beat of his heart continuing to soothe when the song ended.

He gave me strength when I felt weak, grounded me when I felt awash with fear. A small part of me almost wished our trek wasn't about to end, because riding with him had given us time together.

Like separate strands of yarn in a weaver's loom, our lives

were entwining fiber by fiber. Was the tapestry of our marriage strong enough to withstand the difficulties and strains of life? We'd no longer have hours on end to spend in each other's company. His responsibilities would pull him one way—the tug of clan leadership strong—while mine would pull me another—teaching the children and gentle witnessing. I feared without the third strand in our braid—a central relationship with a mutual Savior—our cord would be easily broken.

A man of middling years wearing a spotless robe and a full beard separated from the onlookers and approached our caravan. He smiled wide in welcome. "*As-salamu 'alaykum.*"

Karim pulled Jamal to a stop and had the camel kneel. He dismounted, then turned and helped me to the ground. I stood there, eyes downcast, as he stepped forward. "*Wa 'alaykumu as-salam.*"

"It is good to see you, old friend."

"And you."

The man, who was undoubtedly this clan's sheikh, tickled my memory. Karim had reminded me of his name—Daher Samaha—but at the time the name did nothing to conjure up a face. I'd been among these people before, but it had been over a decade. Before returning to the States, I'd missed the last trek to the date harvest, having spent a week in the hospital due to MERS, a viral respiratory virus.

Daher slapped Karim on the shoulder. "Come. Water your camels. Refreshments have been prepared in your honor."

The men walked on toward the small village while others stepped forward to help with our camels. I was all too happy to release the animals to someone else's care and added a soft *"Shukraan"* to the teenager who led Jamal away.

With hands behind my back, I followed my husband's footsteps.

Though Bedouin, no tents of camel and goat hair were pitched. Instead, permanent homes of stone had been erected. It didn't come as a surprise. Few clans still adhered to the traditional and ancestral transient lifestyle. Many made their dwellings outside of cities where food, water, and employment were more easily accessible.

Daher Samaha held a unique position that had been passed down to him for generations. One of power that had been challenged by war more than once. He controlled the water for the region. Nestled in the foothills of a jutting, craggy mountain, the early monsoon dumped life-giving precipitation and then cradled the liquid more precious than gold in deep caves. For centuries, this water had been dammed and then farmed. Daher's responsibilities lay in protecting the water supply as well as issuing its rations among the neighboring clans for farming.

Karim had told me the man had steel in his veins. He had to in order to retain control over something men were willing to die for. Lack of water was a reality every citizen of the region faced, not just the Bedouins. Even scientists in the forward-thinking cities wrestled with answering the need. I'd laughed when Karim had told me one city's plan to create rain. I thought he'd been teasing me. Turned out he was serious. The plan was to create a man-made mountain to push air up into the atmosphere to create rain clouds.

Tinkling metal like the sound of soft laughter met my ears, and I raised my head. A petite woman approached, the bangles around her wrists and the veil covering the bottom half of her face announcing her approach. Though I couldn't see her lips, the skin around her eyes crinkled as she smiled at me.

"I am Radina, wife of Daher. Welcome to our village." She lifted her hand to me. "Come. Your mother has been quite anxious for your arrival."

"Thank you." I bowed slightly to her. "I am Hannah."

"I know." Her eyes, heavily lined with black makeup, sparked. "We have heard many things about you around the nightly fire."

My feet stumbled, and Radina laughed. "Did you not think speculation would circle when word reached us that Karim had finally taken a bride? Some of our own women had hoped to claim that title." She looked at me again, and even veiled, kindness shown in her face. "I see the rumor that your beauty had hypnotized him was correct."

How to respond? I dared not argue the point or explain the underlying necessity of our marriage. Without another option, I merely smiled in reply.

A group of four children ran in front of us, their laughter dancing in their wake.

"We have also heard that you are a teacher?"

Though she knew it to be true, she posed it as a question rather than a statement. So that I could refute the claim? I had no wish to.

"Yes. Although my lessons were cut terribly short by the journey."

She pointed to the children's retreating backs. "As you can see, we have a number of Allah's blessings running around here as well. Daher thinks it would be wise to embrace your time among us as another blessing and have our children learn from a real teacher."

The way she emphasized her husband's name made me think the idea had been more her own than his. I grinned. "I would love nothing more."

Her hands clapped and the bangles jangled. "Perfect. I have already arranged a tent set up between our village and yours." Her feet slowed until she stopped and turned toward me. The confidence of moments before fled, replaced with uncertainty. "I..."

"Yes?"

Her chest rose and fell as she took a deep breath. "I would like to learn as well."

Wanting to set her at ease, I gently squeezed her forearm. "I would be honored."

She smiled, her confidence returning. "Come, now. Before your mother takes it upon herself to search you out."

I followed Radina through the alleys between the monotone buildings, my heart a little lighter.

Chapter 20

KARIM

"It is good to see you again, old friend." Daher sat on a chair in the main room of his more-than-modest home, one ankle resting on the opposite knee. He leaned back as if he hadn't a care in the world, though the twelve-inch dagger he wore on his belt contradicted his posture.

"And I, you." Though our paths crossed but once a year, Daher had been a good friend for many years. We both understood the challenges of leading and the responsibility of holding the lives of others in our hands. Often I'd sought his advice on a matter, the nearly ten years he had on me adding experiences to his life that weighed in wisdom. Once I'd fought alongside him when another clan sought to overthrow his position and take all the water for themselves.

"How was your journey?"

"The desert was gracious to let us pass."

"Indeed. And your new wife?" Not so much as a brow rose on his face as he popped a fig into his mouth. "She did not wilt under the scorching sun?"

I studied his face. Unreadable, impassive. Curious to the story there, but would not outright ask. Had he already come to his own conclusions? Had those of my people who'd arrived ahead of us filled his ears with lies and prejudices against Hannah and her family?

"Though my wife is as beautiful and delicate looking as a rose, her roots run deep, which give her a strength not visible to every eye."

Daher's mouth relaxed, yet I'd never call the action a smile.

"I know a thing or two about strong women." His propped foot fell to the floor as he leaned forward and winked. "They are the most beautiful of all." Reaching forward, he grabbed another fig from the wooden bowl. "Now, tell me about this problem you've been having with your sheep."

I opened my mouth to explain our dire yet befuddling situation, when the front door swung open and slammed against the wall. A small boy of about eight stepped in, his eyes wide and his chest heaving as if he'd run as fast as his spindly legs could carry him.

Daher stood as a soldier at the ready. "Asoud, what is it?"

Instead of addressing his leader, the boy turned to me, his mouth gaping like a fish that had been taken from the water. "Your"—deep, gasping breath in—"mother." Two more deep breaths.

I was on my feet, my hands clasping the boy's bony shoulders, my pulse thundering like the hooves of my prized Arabian stallion. "What about my mother?"

He flinched away from my grip, and I realized I had

squeezed too hard. I let my hands fall but pinned him to the spot with a hard stare.

It was taking too long. For him to get his breath and form his words. For me to get answers about my mother. Impatient, I spun him around and pushed on his shoulder. "Take me to her."

But he doubled over, his hands on his knees.

"Where is she, Asoud?" The calm in Daher's voice grated on my frantic nerves.

The boy pointed out the door. "Grove."

Lifting my thawb from around my ankles, I sprinted in the direction of the date grove. While there were many trees, the sound of frantic voices and the clump of bodies huddled in one spot directed my path. Without a word, people shifted and let me through. My heart stopped before my feet did. Pale faced, my mother lay on the ground, her eyes closed and head supported in Ethan's lap.

I felt Daher's presence come up beside me but didn't have the time nor inclination to acknowledge him. All my focus zeroed in on the prostrate form that had given me life. Like water in a wadi during the first days of summer, the color seeped from her skin. Her lips parted, and a high-pitched whistling sound emitted with her exhaled breath.

My eyes shot to Ethan, who had already focused on me.

"Listen to me, Karim. I need you to fetch my medical bag. It's sitting near the entrance of my tent."

I swung around in search of a runner. No way would I leave my mother's side.

"Karim, it must be you."

Ethan's strident words sunk into my brain and ceased my searching, as if he'd hooked my neck with the loop of a shepherd's rod. "You know exactly where my tent will be pitched. You have seen my bag hundreds of times before and will know what to look for."

My body swayed over my feet. Ethan needed his doctor tools, but my mother needed me.

"Go! Now!" With the authority of a general, he barked his orders.

I let my eyes fall to my mother once more before sprinting with all my strength. With every step, the distance seemed to grow instead of shorten. A never-ending, ever-widening expanse. One that would open up and swallow me, keeping me from bringing the help my mother needed.

We'd camped a kilometer away. The distance necessary to keep relations between the clans amicable and privacy intact. No one wanted to infringe and overstep the hospitality of a hosting clan, and the space afforded each party to remain gracious.

Blood pumped through my veins in a pounding rhythm as an invisible band tightened around my chest. I tunneled my focus, ignoring the pain of each breath and the stabbing in my side.

Graciousness be hanged. My mother's life weighed in the balance, and I wasted time beating my feet against the sand as I dashed too far away all for propriety.

Blessedly, the Pratts' tent was pitched along the perime-ter, and I barreled through the heavy leather flap. Immedi-ately turning, I nearly tripped over the black bag that I'd seen Ethan carry around for over a decade. Its weight felt good in my hands. Tangible. I gripped it like I had the ability to wrap my fingers around hope and then exited with as much force as I'd entered.

My shoes slapped against the earth, the hot sand pouring in and then out of the holes on the sides with each step I took. Digging deeper, I pushed my body to pick up even more speed. Every minute counted the way my mother counted on me.

Daher gripped my elbow as I stormed into the throng, propelling me the last few feet while also slowing my approach. Ethan's bag fell from my hand and landed at his side. With deft movements, he unclasped the top and rummaged around, withdrawing a stethoscope. He placed the tubes at one end into his ears and laid the circle piece of the other end on my mother's chest. He moved it around, listening. It seemed like ages before he removed the earpieces from his ears.

"What is it? What's wrong with her?" My muscles coiled like a leopard ready to pounce.

Ethan's blue eyes raised to meet my gaze. "Your mother is having difficulty breathing. She passed out—"

A moan interrupted, followed by soft stirring. My knees hit the sand, and I scooped up my mother's hand and pressed it to my cheek. "'*Ami*. You're going to be okay."

Her eyes blinked, and her hand lay limp and clammy in my own. Up and down her throat bobbed as she worked to speak. Fear pooled in her eyes as she looked at me and then Ethan, who still supported her head.

I followed her gaze. "She's going to be all right, isn't she, Doctor?"

Ethan looked down and ran a thumb across my mother's forehead. "Of course." He raised his face to me. "But she's very sick and needs to go to the hospital right away."

"The closest hospital is nearly a hundred kilometers

away." Daher spoke from just behind my shoulder.

Ethan shifted his gaze to the man at my back. "Then we've no time to lose."

My fingers twitched to fold into themselves, but I still held my mother's palm in my hand and didn't want to cause her further pain by my thoughtlessness. Her eyes had drifted shut again, and though my heart squeezed for her, I was relieved she rested in consciousness instead of unconsciousness. I leaned forward and lowered my voice, not wanting to alarm her further. "Is it so serious?"

"There's fluid in her lungs, which is indicative of pneumonia, an infection in her lung sacs. The hospital will need to do chest x-rays and put her on intravenous antibiotics."

I could feel tension building between my eyes, drawing my brows together. Fluid in the lungs sounded a lot like drowning to me.

Mother's wheezing grew louder, a testament of the difficulty she was having drawing in enough oxygen. I ran my thumb in small circles across the back of her hand like she used to do for me when I was sick as a small child.

Drowning in a desert. I shook my head.

"Because of your mother's age, she is at a higher risk for complications and needs to be in a facility that can combat anything else that may arise."

"Such as?"

"A number of things, really. Blood poisoning being one of them."

Sounded as bad as drowning. I looked down at the sweet woman, not liking how the corners of her eyes scrunched as if in pain. Gently I scooped my arms under her body and cradled her as if a babe.

Not long ago I'd had to carry Ethan's wife in such a way. And now my mother. The sheep...the sabotage against Hannah's camel... Would trouble never cease to compound at my door?

Ethan jogged ahead of me and retrieved the keys to the truck. By the time I made it to the rusty old vehicle, he'd opened the passenger-side door. With as much tenderness as I could, I settled her in the middle, draping my arm around her shoulder and tucking her body close to mine. Her chin tucked into her chest, she rested against me. With my free hand, I cranked the handle to roll down the window as Daher stepped closer.

I had to go with my mother to the hospital. She needed me. But Hannah needed me too. I had failed her once in keeping her safe. If I left, she'd be like a sheep without a shepherd and the wolves could devour her. My promise to protect her would crumble like old mortar overbaked by the hot sun.

I looked to my friend, his shoulders wide with years of labor, stance firm. My family was not his responsibility, but my choices were limited.

Ethan turned the key in the ignition, and the engine rumbled to life.

I'd run out of time.

My eyes locked with Daher's. "My wife."

Not much of an explanation, but he understood and gave a small nod as he stepped away from the vehicle. He knew what I'd asked and had accepted Hannah temporarily as part of his family, and therefor under his protection.

Staring at the side mirror, I rolled up the window and wished I'd been able to kiss my bride goodbye.

Chapter 21

HANNAH

Counting time. It had become my reality. The only constant in my ever-changing life. When had it started, this habit of measuring days? Not long ago I'd looked forward to graduation, a classroom of my own, the opportunity to return to the land of my childhood, sharing Jesus's love with the people of my heart. Had the whirlwind started then? Somehow getting sucked into a tornado that was both of my making and not? From happily single to married to my oldest friend in a matter of days. Now, less than a month later and displaced, I found myself once again alone. No matter how much I wished it, I couldn't slow time down or speed it up. All I could do was mark it.

It had been two days since Karim had left without a word. Daher had found his wife, and Radina had told me the news. I'd run as soon as the sheikh's wife had said Karim's mother had fallen ill. Ran all the way to first her tent and then my father's. Both empty. Steps had echoed behind me, and that was when I'd slowed enough to hear the rest. The three had left immediately for the hospital—my father, my husband, and his mother.

Two days I'd wrestled. I should be there. My place was by my husband's side. Especially now as he waded through a difficult time. I should be there to give him strength. To comfort him.

But he'd left me behind.

I hated the insecurities and their ugly voices that shredded my confidence. In no way should I take it personally. His mother had been ill, and they'd needed to leave immediately for the hospital to get her the care she needed. With the three of them on the single bench seat, there would've been no room in the cab for me.

Except, how long, really, would it have taken to fetch me? I would've run with all my strength to get there as fast as possible. Minutes, surely. That was all sending word would've delayed them. And I'd have gladly hopped into the bed of the truck. Would've been happy to breathe in the dust kicked up by the tires if it meant I could help Karim during this difficult time.

But I'd been left behind. Without a word. Without a care?

The insecurity again. Because if Karim hadn't cared, he wouldn't have appointed Daher over my safety.

But had it been duty or something more that had caused him to momentarily think of me before he'd left?

Fingertips touched my arm, and I looked to my right.

Radina cocked her head as if wondering at my thoughts, but only asked, "Are you ready?"

Life had surprised me too often lately to say I'd ever be ready again. But I couldn't voice that, so I smiled and nodded.

Date harvest started today. A day that spelled hard work but was accompanied by joviality and family. Besides my mother, whose ribs still hadn't healed enough for her to offer much help, I was without any family and felt no reason to laugh.

I almost felt robbed. This was to be the first memories made with my mother-in-law. She would teach me things as a woman among the tribe that I hadn't learned as a child. We'd share stories of Karim and bond under the shade of the wide palm canopy.

Would we ever have such an opportunity now?

Jesus, You are the Great Physician. Please heal her. Give her more time to know You...give me more time to know her.

We made our way to the grove, both clans already present at the trunks of the towering trees. Yara looked up from her work and smiled.

I tried to switch my thinking, focus on the task directly before me instead of what was taking place in a hospital a hundred kilometers away. While I'd helped with the harvest in my youth, it'd been some years since I'd had anything to do with the fruit besides eat it.

Radina led me to a row and stared up at the wide fronds. "These trees belong to your husband and your tribe."

My eyes widened. I'd thought all of the trees in the grove were owned by Daher and his people.

"I'm not sure how long the trees have been in his family's procession. Perhaps they were the ones who'd originally planted them." She pointed to the next row over. "Those are the trees belonging to the poor."

"The poor?" How could the poor afford date palm trees?

"Yes. We have around one hundred trees in this grove. Ten are dedicated to those who work within the grove year round, and ten are dedicated to the poor. It is what Allah would have us do."

Sounded like tithe and the biblical decrees to help those in times of need.

Radina turned to me. "How many years has it been since you've helped with the palms?"

My forehead scrunched as I tried to think back.

"That long?" Radina chuckled. She looked back at the row of trees and reached out to touch one of the thick, scratchy brown pieces that made up the trunk. "Did you know these palms do more than just provide food for our tables and shade for our heads? On the coast, they use the trunks to create boats for fishing. The women use the branches as brooms for their homes. The leaves can be woven into rope and bags, and the trunks themselves make excellent seating." She looked back at me. "They take care of us, and in return, we take care of them."

I shielded my eyes against the sun as I craned my neck and peered up into the fronds, trying to look at the tree and see all that Radina did. Large clusters of purple fruit hung low, heavy like a pregnant woman ready to deliver. My mouth watered to sink my teeth into the fresh flesh. Bedouins ate dates in many ways. *Shegig*—dried without the stone but the skin still on. *Aguwa*—skins removed, the naked, soft fruit mashed with sesame seeds. My favorite, though, was a fresh fruit fallen to the ground accompanied by a strong Arabic coffee.

"They are just like us, those trees."

I swallowed a laugh, not seeing the similarities. Unless she meant we both had prickly edges. Or that we required great care to grow.

"Palm trees are dioecious. They are either male or female."

My brows rose. One didn't think of gender when it came to plant life. "Really?"

"They need each other for survival, for their seeds to scatter and germinate. If it wasn't for the workers who remove the pollen from the male trees at the exact time and then hand pollinate the flowers of the female tree at least three times, there would be no harvest. No ripe fruit ready for the picking."

A slight breeze picked up and blew through the fingerlike branches, causing them to rub together and make a shushing sound, drawing my attention back to them. My mind worked to wrap itself around Radina's words and the deeper meaning within them. The fact she used her beloved palms as an example of an object lesson was clear. The meaning, however...I still struggled to unravel.

She wasn't the first to use a tree as a lesson, and that was the direction my thoughts took. To the two parables Jesus told of fig trees. One budding and one barren. The buds of the tree were a sign of readiness. The barren tree, however, had had three years in which to bear fruit and still produced nothing. Frustrated, the owner commanded the vinedresser to cut the worthless tree down. To which the vinedresser pleaded to give the tree one more year to bear fruit.

The three lessons didn't have anything to do with one another. Did they?

I studied Radina, surprised to find she returned the scrutiny with equal intensity, as if measuring me by some invisible scale. With a softening around her shoulders, she reached into a woven bag slung across her chest and removed a small leather-bound book.

My breath caught. It couldn't be. Frantically, I looked to the left and right. No one paid us any attention.

"You are not the first Christian that has come and tended to my tree." With reverence, she caressed the top cover of the Bible. A book illegal to possess, the consequences of ownership severe. She raised her face to me, her dark eyes clear. "Three times these palms need pollination to bear fruit." She took a step toward me and pressed the book into my hand, keeping hers on top so that the Bible was sandwiched between our palms. "Help me to bear fruit, Hannah."

With clarity, like a curtain dropping to reveal the masterpiece it'd covered, I realized Radina was the budding fig and I the barren. The revelation reverberated inside me like the deep resonation of a bass drum. Almost an entire life living among the tribe, and I couldn't conjure up one time in which I'd shared my faith. Not verbally. Not like this. Not even with Yara. Her conversion had been a result of my mother's loving administrations, not mine.

I'd taken care to live my faith, evangelize through friendship, but now I saw, like the changing images of a PowerPoint presentation, the moments of opportunity I'd let slip by without a word about a loving Savior who had died for all our sins. And their need of Him.

With humility, I laid my hand on top of hers. "It would be my honor."

She smiled with a radiant glow that almost had me believing I could hear the angels rejoicing in heaven. "Date harvest in the morning, school lessons in the afternoon, and"—she wiggled her brows—"should we say harvest lessons in the evenings?"

Laughter—something I'd been sure only minutes before wouldn't be a part of my day—tumbled from my lips. "I can't think of anything better."

Is this the reason I was left behind, Lord? Was it Your doing all along?

"Good." She slipped her Bible back into her bag and then reached out and grabbed my wrist, pulling me to a group of women sitting in a circle. A large mound of dates still connected to the bunch residing in the middle of them all. "Now, let's see how many of these bags you can fill." She handed me a large yellow plastic bag and took a seat on the ground.

I shook the bag out to fill it with air and opened it at the mouth before sitting. Reaching forward, I grabbed a cluster of dates and then began pulling the individual fruits from the strands.

Ahead of me, a man stood at the base of a tree, a long piece of rope in his hands. He wound the rope around itself to create a type of harness, which he placed at his lower back and the back of his thighs before reaching the rope around the base of the tree. Secured, he flicked the rope up, then placed his bare feet on the trunk. With agility and speed that surprised me, he climbed the tree that reached straight into the air, yet another rope dangling from his hand. He looped the loose rope around a thick branch, then hand over hand pulled the rope, a wide basket attached to the other end. A long knife with a hooked end that I hadn't noticed before appeared, and he sawed at the stalks bowed under the weight of the ripe purple fruits. The date bunch dangled in his hand as he lowered his arm, releasing the fruit into the basket. Down the basket scaled into the arms of another man, who emptied its contents, the basket rising again for another load.

"Not those." Radina's words drew back my attention.

She nodded her head at the dates in my grip, and I looked down.

"Separate the yellow ones from the rest that go into the sack. They've not fully ripened yet and will need to be left out in the heat to do so."

I placed the two unripe dates to the side and slid another three into my bag, feeling the stares of the other women. Their bangles tinkled against each other as their hands moved to separate the fruits from the strands.

I'd become the center of the gossip mill in Radina's clan the same as I'd become in my own. That familiar feeling of self-doubt stole over me. Were they only curious, or did they see me as unworthy? My lips wobbled as I attempted to smile at two of the women across from me who openly stared. They quickly dropped their gazes back to their work.

I scanned the circle. Still forced my smile. Resemblances could be seen anywhere if a person had their eyes open wide enough to see them. Women, all working together, their hands making deft movements in a pattern they'd perfected over years of practice. Though the setting was different, the clothing, the language, the food, I couldn't help but notice the resemblance to a southern front porch, rocking chairs, and women shucking peas out of their shells.

We were all more alike than some liked to acknowledge. Did these women see that?

Radina's gaze met mine, her smile warm before returning to her work. Were more of these women like Radina? Ready to hear of Jesus and His love?

Dear Lord, give me the words.

Chapter 22

KARIM

"How is she today, Doctor?" My question preceded me as I followed the doctor from my mother's curtained-off hospital room. She could still hear our conversation past the fabric partition, but perhaps separating the physician from her keen, laser-like gaze would allow him to shake off whatever power she held over him.

In any other situation, watching this knowledgeable, grown man shrink a little under my mother's glare would be humorous. The men of my tribe had become used to her ways and accepted them because of the power she held in our family unit. This man, however... It was as if it were his own mother in the cot, ready to swat his backside if he spoke something against her wishes. Like the fact that she was ill and needed to stay at the hospital to regain her strength and fight the infection. So he'd acted like a teenager about to get disciplined whenever he was in her presence and been tight lipped around her, causing Ethan and I to stalk him in the halls just to get straight information out of him about her condition and progress.

He turned and tapped a pen to the clipboard in his hands. "Her oxygen saturation levels are rising, which means we should be able to take her off the ventilator later today, if things continue to progress the way they have. Her body is responding well to the antibiotics, and she hasn't had a return of fever for the last twenty-four hours."

"Does that mean we'll be able to take her home today?"

The doctor's gaze moved to the partition, his weight shifting from one foot to the other. "Even though she's demanded that very thing, I'm afraid she must remain here at least one more day, perhaps two." He looked back at me. "I'm sorry."

I scrubbed a hand across my cheek, my beard scratching my palm. "Thank you for taking care of her."

He nodded, then turned and strode down the hall to another patient.

I let my head fall, my chin against my chest. The muscles in the back of my neck stretched, and I took a deep breath, hoping some of the stress built there would leave on an exhale.

Unfortunately, when I raised my head, I still felt wound tight.

Ethan approached, two steaming Styrofoam cups in his hands. He held one out to me.

Warmth seeped into my fingers as I held the cup to my lips and took a long drink. "Thank you."

He stared at me over the rim of his cup as he sipped at his coffee. Licked his lips as he lowered his hand. Silence enveloped us. He assessed me as if trying to uncover a diagnosis from my expression.

"Worry never solved anything, you know." A small smile tipped his lips. "My grandmother used to say, 'Why worry if you pray, and why pray if you worry?'"

Catchy, but his grandmother wasn't responsible for the survival of an entire clan of people, a dying culture we fought to keep alive, a herd of livestock with a mysteries disease, a wife and in-laws who were being persecuted for their beliefs, and a mother who lay helpless on a hospital cot.

My thoughts and responsibilities were weights I carried with chains around my neck, slumping my shoulders with each tick of my mental list. They all pressed in my mind, garnering for my attention, and here I was, helpless to address any of them.

Ethan's strong hand clasped my shoulder. "Everything will work out, son."

He couldn't know that.

As if reading my thoughts, he said, "I know, because I pray. I've given it all to God, and He's big enough to take care of it."

"He's shown you the future then?" I didn't mean to be disrespectful in my sarcasm, but I'd prayed too. Five times a day, in fact. And yet I'd received no revelation from Allah. The sheep were still sick. Hannah and her parents were still in danger. And now my mother was in the hospital. Even so, I knew Allah blessed me. I continued to have faith in his word.

But the truth hadn't altered. Prayer hadn't changed my circumstances.

Ethan tilted his head and regarded me with a secret

smile. "The big-picture future, yes. How all of this will turn out, no. Still, I know, in the end, everything will work out. Even if it isn't the way we think or hope."

I had no wish to enter into a religious debate with the man. Especially not here in public where anyone could hear us. Ethan took too many risks. If he wished to believe in Jesus as the son of God, that was his religious right. But in a country where such talk could get you in severe trouble, he should keep his personal beliefs to himself.

Thankfully, Hannah had already learned that lesson. She lived a faithful life, but I'd never heard her trying to convince another that her religion was the only right one.

What was she doing right then? Did she miss me like I did her? I'd never thought it possible, this feeling of restlessness I had simply because I was away from my wife. I found myself reaching for her in the night, only to have my fingertips graze the cool sheet beside me. With equal parts cruelty and kindness, my memory reminded me of the feel of her skin, the smell of her hair, the sound of her laughter. The last few days I'd walked around as if part of me was missing, and my soul ached to be reunited with hers.

The tense muscles in my neck loosened as I thought of Hannah. Imagined her among the women harvesting dates waiting for my arrival so she could return to her place in my arms.

Ethan chuckled besides me, and my face heated under his knowing look. "Missing my daughter?"

I cleared my throat, embarrassed and ready to deny the claim, but he held up a hand.

"It's good. That you miss her, I mean. Makes me feel a little better, actually." He leaned back and hooked a finger over his chin, his eyes narrowing as his gaze probed my face. Then he laughed. Not a light snicker but a deep roar that shook his belly. When he'd regained his composure he said, "I can't believe I never saw it before. I must have been blind!"

What was he talking about? "Saw what?"

He shook his head like he hadn't heard me. "All these years and I never saw it."

At the risk of sounding like a toddler asking a parent the same question over and over, I repeated myself. "Saw *what*?"

His head turned right to left again before resting in the center, his face bemused with a smirk.

My chin dropped and brows rose, silently demanding an explanation.

"That you love her. Have loved her since you were children."

I brushed off his assessment. "Of course I have always loved her. We grew up together as the best of friends."

His eyes softened. "No, Karim. You *love* her. She is, and has always been, your treasure, has she not?"

His gaze held mine captive. Wouldn't let go. Hadn't I said the same things to Hannah on our wedding night? I'd meant them, but as I let Ethan's words soak into my conscious, they grabbed hold of my center.

And then it all came to me. Like a blast of cold air on a hot summer day. The rightness that had settled into my bones that first time I'd swept her up into my arms and carried her to her parents after the scorpion sting. The way I'd always sought her out because simply being with her made me feel better than how I felt without her. The way her pain had been my pain. Her joy my joy.

The way I'd been listless and incomplete when she'd been away.

The way I'd finally felt whole when she returned.

The way I knew I could never live without her.

Ethan was right. My heart was filled with love for Hannah.

Chapter 23

HANNAH

"Is this right?" Questioning eyes stared up at me as one of my students held out her paper.

We'd been going over the alphabet, and I'd had the students practice making their letters. Something I'd stayed up the night before reviewing. Just in case. The Arabic alphabet comprised of twenty-eight letters and was written in cursive, each letter flowing into the next. I'd learned to read and write in the language the same time I'd learn to speak it, but there hadn't been much opportunity to practice in the States, so even though I was pretty confident in my abilities, nervousness had me hitting the books for a refresher.

I scanned the neat handwriting of letters in *abjadi* order and then pointed to a letter three quarters of the way down the line. Bending at the waist, I held the paper so my student could see where I pointed. "See here? This should be the letter *t* and have two dots above, but you have added one dot below, which now makes it the letter *b*."

Her mouth formed an O, and she took the paper and

returned to her seat, eraser end of her pencil to the paper fixing her mistake.

I straightened and rubbed at my lower back. Bending over the date strands that morning had pulled at my muscles, which still protested the bumpy ride on a camel's back. It'd been worth it though, that long, arduous journey. Worth it to see so many students working diligently to learn.

Pencils scratching against paper brought a smile to my lips. No more beautiful sound than that.

I'd been shocked when Radina and I had reached the tent after noon prayers. I'd expected to see maybe a handful of students, but bodies, young and old alike, crammed under the shade of the pitched canopy. Daher's approval of learning had encouraged any who had time to spare to increase their knowledge. The parents who'd accompanied their children had already learned to read, so I'd given them books on subjects that interested them to occupy their time while I worked with the younger students on more rudimentary lessons.

Movement at the corner of my eye brought my attention around. My heart slid to a stop at the sudden approach of a man whose face bore the thunderous look of an oncoming storm. Like a raging bull charging a matador, he barreled into the tent, his nostrils flaring with his every breath. His gaze shot around the open-aired room like daggers, and he snapped his fingers. Three children of various ages popped up like daisies, although I feared the delicate flowers were about to be trampled.

I took a step forward, head down enough to show respect but still high enough to keep him in my vision. *"As-salamu alaykum."*

Spittle landed at my feet. "Peace is surely upon me, but not you." His gaze traveled over the students gathered, and his lips curled. "Nor any of you who turn your back on Islam to embrace this—"

"Watch yourself, Farid." Radina's voice held warning.

"No. You watch yourself. Though you be Daher's wife, you forget yourself." His arm swept the group. "As you all have forgotten."

So far, it seemed he was alone, but that didn't settle my pulse. Schools had become targets to extremists, and it wasn't a stretch to consider that any minute we could be surrounded by men with guns. Had I not read accounts in the news of such things? Hundreds dying because they simply wished to receive an education.

Keep us safe.

I kept my head down, hoping that my show of humility and nonengagement would send him on his way. Anything to get him to turn around and leave as quickly as he'd arrived. Maybe then my lungs could expand to their full capacity and I could take a much-needed breath.

But the silence that hung only seemed to invite the man Radina had called Farid to continue his raging.

He thrust an accusing finger at my chest. "And you. Sheltered princess that you are, you probably don't even realize why we all hate you, do you? Why we despise America and all that wicked country stands for."

I held my tongue, not believing he actually wished an answer.

But he stepped forward and barked, "Do you?"

My head shook along with my hands, and I whispered, "No." Shame filled me at my answer. I'd often wondered why the animosity bred so deep among these people, but, as Farid had accused, my parents had sought to shelter me from the glaring hatred, often leaving me with the clan when they needed to make a trip to the city for medical supplies.

"Well, let me educate you, teacher." His scowl deepened. "Your ignorance is why we hate you. The fact that you don't even know. None of you do."

You. The separation of *us* and *them.* He'd drawn the line, and I'd been placed on the side of the enemy.

"You teach but know nothing." Farid spit again, this time his warm saliva landing on the hem of my *abiya.* "What of Sabra and Chatila?"

Did he wish an answer? Fear clawed along my spine as those names offered no recognition. Would his verbal tirade soon turn physical?

Not the children, Lord.

I looked sideways and locked eyes with Radina. With a flick of my chin, I mouthed, *Children. Go.* And then held on to hope that she'd understand my meaning and get the innocents out of danger. Farid was a ticking time bomb ready to explode.

He stalked even closer toward me, his children huddled behind him. "Ignorance!" The beams holding the tent erect shook at his volume. "The blood from Sabra and Chatila still cry out, in need of vindication. Though you Christians profess a loving God, it was Christian militiamen who slaughtered over eight hundred people, not sparing even the women or children."

But that was not us, I wanted to scream. Not true Christ followers and not Americans.

My thoughts must have reflected in my expression,

because he folded his arms over his thick chest. "Though your hands were not stained red, your *benevolent*"—he spat the word—"country is not innocent. Do they not shower money upon the murderers? Feed the lion that devours our people?"

Radina slunk around the perimeter of people, whispering words into ears and then pushing them down on their hands and knees so they could crawl away unnoticed.

"Stop!" Farid bellowed.

Everyone froze, no one daring to twitch a muscle or even blink.

"I am not the threat here, my brothers and sisters." His voice softened until he seemed to be almost pleading with them. "If you do not see that, then you are blinder than I had suspected. It is not education I am against, and will continue to teach my children at home in the ways of Islam, as is right." His back turned toward me so he could face those he'd named his family. He held their gazes as he entreated, "If you allow the Western lies to infiltrate your thinking, you will be lost for all eternity." With that he strode forward, snapping his fingers again.

Only one child glanced back at me before falling into line behind his brothers and following his father out of view.

As if someone had pushed the Play button after pausing a show, the stillness erupted with movement and talking. As for myself, however, I felt like I was set on slow motion. My legs quivered beneath me, and I reached out to grab a pole for support.

We were safe. There had been no guns that had opened fire on us. No one had lost their lives for a simple lesson on the alphabet. The outcome could've been so much worse. We could've been added to the statistics, a headline on national news.

Thank you, Jesus.

Voices rose. The fog that had been hovering over my head ascended with the noise. Lines were being drawn again, some agreeing with all Farid had said, while others defended the new school and the education I offered.

I should say something, but weariness dragged my bones. All I wanted to do was slump toward the ground. Confusion and not a small amount of fear twisted my gut.

A hand tapped my arm, and I let my weight pull me down to one knee. A boy with soulful eyes offered a wobbly smile, his two front teeth missing. He lifted his hand, a paper pinched between his fingers, and I took it. Like nothing had happened at all to concern himself with, he turned and skipped around those loitering about who argued among themselves. At the edge of the tent he turned and waved. Though my limbs felt heavy, I returned the gesture with a forced smile. I looked down at the paper in my hand, my heart melting at the picture he'd drawn of me teaching in the tent, at the bottom of his alphabet-filled paper.

Determination hardened behind my breastbone. I wouldn't be scared off. Not by Farid, not by anybody. If God was for me, no one could stand against me. Not when I'd been called to do this very thing.

It didn't take much convincing to dismiss the rest of the class, although I wondered how many of them I'd see return the next day. If the situation were reversed, would I dare to attend?

"You are a gifted teacher. And brave." Radina approached with a small smile. One I identified with. Relief made our lips bow, but the seriousness and aftereffects of our fear held our mood in a subdued grip.

"I'm not brave." A brave person wouldn't still be trembling all over. "As far as teaching..." I shrugged, brushing off her intended compliment. "I've always loved learning, so it's natural to want to share that with others."

"You're being too modest. On both accounts." She waved her hand as if she could disturb the memories of our recent ordeal as easily as smoke from a fire. "One, we had another teacher here so our children could learn without having to move to the cities. Farid approved of him since he came from a good Muslim family." Her face clouded. "But he had no patience for the children's mistakes and often took to beating them to keep them in line."

"How awful!"

"Indeed. Needless to say, Daher did not suffer his actions, and the man learned a hard lesson he will not soon forget." Her eyes brightened a fraction, almost to their regular brilliance. "He will be happy to hear my report on you, though maybe not so much of Farid's actions."

I swallowed hard. "Your report?"

"Of course. Nothing happens within a twenty-kilometer radius that my husband does not know about."

What would Daher do to Farid when he learned about the man's outburst? Though the experience had frightened me to no end, Farid hadn't threatened me or anyone else. Not really. Maybe the best course of action was to just let the incident go. That was what I needed to do. I couldn't dwell on it, or I'd be too paralyzed by my fear to do what I needed to. Teach. Share Jesus's love.

Wait. Daher knew *everything* that happened? Even...

"Even—" My throat thickened around the thought. I tried again and took a step forward, lowering my voice to a whisper. "Even your harvest lessons?"

"Especially those."

My heart seized in my chest, and my gaze darted beyond her shoulder, expecting officers this time to approach and arrest me on the spot.

"He has been having dreams, my husband. Of *Isa*. He wished to speak with your father of his dreams, but perhaps I may learn from you, then return home and share with my husband all you have said."

Dreams. Like Daniel? John? Had an angel visited Daher like Gabriel had Mary?

Direct my words, Lord.

Never had I felt so unprepared. So unworthy. But I wouldn't be a barren fig tree any longer. I'd be the branches and remain in the Vine. With Him I could do anything and bear the fruit He'd planted.

Chapter 24

HANNAH

"A re you sure you don't want to lead tonight?" My words came out in a rush and slightly high pitched, a testament to the nerves that raced around in circles in my stomach.

Mom smiled, all softness and confidence, though not in herself. She directed that attribute to me. Though her ribs still pained her, the eye that had nearly swollen shut had reduced in size, the bruise almost completely gone now, so I knew she could see clearly. Must be she chose to see what she wanted even if it wasn't there. Confidence was the last thing about me.

"You're going to do great."

I'd settle for coherent. What if Radina left more confused than when she'd arrived? What if I didn't have the answers to all her questions? I had to trust that the Holy Spirit would bring them to my memory. That alone was the only thought that kept my hands from shaking.

Although not from sweating. I ran my damp palms down the skirt of my fitted abaya and took a deep breath.

"I'll pray without ceasing, Hannah. God will be with you."

I nodded at the same time as a greeting shouted from the other side of the tent walls. Shoulders back, I strode forward and welcomed Radina with a smile. My lips wobbled, however, when two more women followed the sheikh's wife into my parents' tent.

Radina and the women greeted my mother with the traditional greeting, and she responded in kind.

"Hannah"—Radina turned to me—"may I present Qitarah and Bahira?"

I smiled warmly and invited them to sit upon the low couches. Searching out Radina's gaze, I raised a brow.

"Qitarah and Bahira also have questions and seek to learn more of *Isa*. I didn't think you'd mind two more students." Her look held a note of challenge and strength, as if conveying they all knew the costs these harvest lessons could exact. They were willing to pay the price. Was I?

In Jesus's name, I was. "I'm so happy you were able to join us."

Radina nodded in approval and pulled out her pocket Bible, handing it to me.

Instead of accepting, I turned and reached behind me to my mother, who placed a stack of six books in my hand. She'd worked quickly to uncover the hidden Scriptures so each woman could hold one for themselves.

I passed the books out, two to each woman.

"A Qur'an!" Bahia exclaimed, her face scrunched in

confusion. "But I thought we were to learn of your Messiah from your Bible."

One could not jump a hurdle when one had not even taken a step. "Tell me—do you believe the Bible to hold truths given by Allah?"

Uncertainty came in the loss of eye contact and the thinning of lips. Around the circle, the women avoided my gaze. "Then we begin in the Honored Qur'an, a book you *do* believe holds truth from Allah." I opened the book they'd been taught from all their lives. "All-E-Imran reads, 'It is He Who sent down to thee, step by step, in truth, the Book, confirming what went before it; and He sent down the Law.'" I looked up from the page. "The Law here is of Moses, the Taurat."

"Yes," Qitarah whispered.

I continued reading. "'And the Gospel before this, as a guide to mankind.'" Placing my finger where I'd left off, I looked up again. "The Gospel is of Isa, which is the Injeel. The Holy Scriptures we call the Bible. As the Qur'an says, they were given to all mankind." I read a few more passages that showed that through Isa al-Masih, Jesus the Messiah, the son of Mary, the Gospel was sent to guide and enlighten all who followed Allah.

Radina leaned forward. "But what is Isa's purpose? Is he another prophet or something more? Why do you Christians worship him?"

Like forks in the road, my brain stalled on which path to take. I could show them Jesus in the Qur'an, the passages calling Him the Holy Son of God, who they called Allah, and how He was conceived supernaturally. How we all have sinned and are in need of a Savior sent by the mercy of God.

Passage after passage we could turn, first through the Qur'an and then the Bible. Would it be too much too soon? I could further press on them the trueness of the Scriptures through their own honored book and then send them home to discover at their own speed Jesus' goodness. Or...

"Let me tell you a story, one you are familiar with but with meanings deeper than your current understanding."

"What story?" Radina's mouth turned down. She thought I'd skirted her direct question.

I held her gaze, asking for patience without words. "Of Father Ibrahim."

"The father of our father Ishmael." Qitarah spoke in her quiet way.

"That's right." My smile held encouragement. "Allah called Ibrahim away from all he knew—his family, his country, his home. Ibrahim obeyed without question even though Allah had not disclosed the destination to Ibrahim or whether or not he'd ever return to his homeland again. Ibrahim set aside his own comfort and preferences because of the confident relationship he'd developed with Allah. He understood that Allah's ways were always best, even if he didn't understand them at the time."

"It is a lesson of submission we'd all do well to learn," my mother added, and we all nodded in agreement.

I picked up the story. "Many years later, Allah directed Ibrahim again. This time obedience cost a much higher price. That of his own son."

Bahia's brow furrowed. "We understand the importance of this story. It is written in Sura 26.69 to rehearse the story of Ibrahim. But what significance does it have to Isa?"

Their curiosity sent a thrill through my center. "I'm

getting to that. But isn't it interesting the Qur'an emphasizes the rehearsal of the story." My brows lifted high on my forehead. "Must mean there is much significance and equal things to learn from the telling, no?"

Radina waved her hand. "Continue so we may understand."

"It is important to note that Ibrahim communicated so much with Allah that he recognized the voice of God when he heard it. And the love in Ibrahim's heart for Allah outweighed that of even his own son so that he moved to obey the voice he trusted."

"I cannot imagine sacrificing my own son," Qitarah said.

Bahia agreed. "Nor I."

Unbidden, I pressed a palm to my flat stomach. Would it round soon with Karim's heir? A baby made of our union but not a profession of our love? Pain seized me, but now was not a time to succumb to its hold. It was not a time to dissect the swirl of feeling that threatened to pull me under, their range from despair to exhilaration.

"I think the three-day journey to Mount Moriah were ones of misery." Mom picked up when my silence stretched too long. "How he must have pleaded in prayer for Allah to make another way."

I smiled my thanks to Mom for saving me and refocused my thoughts. "Alone, Ibrahim took his son away from the others in order to sacrifice him. But the son was observant and questioned his father about the lack of a lamb for slaughter."

"God will provide himself a lamb for the burnt offering," Radina said slowly.

I could see her mind working to sift out the meaning there.

"The Qur'an says Ibrahim's son was ransomed with a momentous sacrifice."

My heart lifted in gratitude, as it always did upon reflection of the greatest sacrifice of all. "Momentous indeed. The ram caught in the thicket that saved Ibrahim's son pointed forward to the greatest sacrifice. The one whom Allah would send to be a sin offering for us all." I leaned forward and rested my elbows on my knees. "You see, Ibrahim's son represented all of humanity. We all deserve to die for our sins. But like Ibrahim's son, we were spared the sacrifice of another in our stead. Allah's own son, Isa al-Masih, died so that we might live eternally."

A twig snapped outside the tent, causing the blood in my veins to freeze. By the wide, doe-like eyes of the other women, the sound hadn't come from my imagination. My heart pounded in my ears. I strained to hear past it, to discern any other noise beyond our tight circle.

A horse whinnied from the pasture, and another answered. Karim's prized Arabian equines holding a conversation in the interim of ours. But nothing else. No footsteps. No voices. Nothing that signaled we'd been overheard.

Yet twigs did not snap on their own.

Radina rose, her gaze pointed. "I think this year's date harvest will rival even that of last year's."

Qitarah looked at the sheikh's wife with a question in her eyes, but Bahia understood.

"Allah is abundant with his blessings." Radina nodded and stepped lightly to the door flap, Bahia continuing on the conversation as if all that went on within the moveable walls was a gathering of women on a social visit. "There may even be enough surplus to sell in the markets."

Slowly Radina lifted the flap and stared out into the night. I prayed for the fullness of the moon to shine brighter. If we'd been overheard, our fates were nearly sealed.

The flap settled back into place. Radina turned, relief evident in the slackness of her jaw.

"Nothing?" I asked.

She shook her head. "None that I saw. Perhaps it was but a mouse on the run from a hunting predator."

Better a mouse be prey than us.

Chapter 25

KARIM

It felt good to stretch my legs, even if the guilt of doing so chewed on my insides like a dog with a bone. Only two places I should be—at the hospital with my mother, and if not there, then at camp with Hannah, overseeing my family's contribution to the date harvest and managing the tribe. Not to mention keeping an eye on my wife so she didn't fall into danger. And yet here I was, on a stroll through the city streets as if a tourist without care.

A man and woman smiled brightly as I passed them, staring into the phone the man held out at arm's length.

I rolled my eyes and glanced up at the sky. The sun had barely moved on its course.

I would not be welcomed back at the hospital. Neither by Mother or Ethan. Both had insisted I get out for fresh air for my benefit. More so for them to get a break from my hovering and foul mood.

But the cloudless blue sky nor the gentle breeze had

managed to lift my sour disposition. I stomped down the dusty street, the muscles tight in my face. Not even the men who passed met my gaze. The scowl drawing my brows down enough of a deterrent for even a polite greeting.

A domed roof topped with a crescent, four spires jutting to the sky in a square around the central arch, drew my attention. Prayers in a mosque. I should be elated to worship Allah with others faithful to him, but my spirit protested. I was not in the right frame of mind. Distracted and foul, I would not come before the great creator with so unworthy a heart.

I turned aside and strode down a narrow alley that emptied into a large court. More people littered the outer meeting area lined with brightly colored urns filled with tall potted plants. From the garments alone I deduced I'd stumbled onto a main tourist attraction. Fellow countrymen, their pristine white thawbs testifying the wealth and power within their possession stood beside men clad in business suits as well as those so immodest as to wear clothing that showed hairy calves and scrawny arms. My lips curled at the women who disrespected our culture and went with head bare and too much skin showing.

My mood darkened even further, the blackness of which sought to steal completely the light.

Light of the world...follow Him and never walk in darkness. Like a whisper in my ear, the strains of one of Hannah's songs she'd sung while I'd held her in my arms on Jamal through the heart of the desert came to me in her sweet voice. The lyrics washed away before I could catch them in my grasp, but the memory lingered, turning the black to gray. Even just a shadow of her brightened my life, but how I ached for her nearness like I never thought possible. For the feel of her to again rest against my chest. To cover her body with my own. For our souls to unite in beautiful harmony. To hear her voice and see her smile.

In comparison, my life had again become the dull and colorless existence it had been before her. I needed her beside me to blow away the thick layer of drudgery and reveal the vibrant colors life could be.

I let my head fall to my chest. Lifted a hand up beneath my keffiyeh and pulled against the tightness in the back of my neck. Self-pity tasted bitter in my mouth and rotted my thoughts like a too-ripe piece of fruit.

If I dug deep enough, the roots that tenaciously held and sprouted my temper had little to do with the circumstances and trials that surrounded me like bandits and more to do with the lack of control I had over them. No matter what I did, the Pratts continued to be threatened, the sheep refused to get well, my mother continued to age and weaken.

The warrior and leader in me demanded action. To protect, to guide, to strengthen. And yet all my fighting was as good as chaff in the wind.

It couldn't last much longer, though, could it? Because the truth was we, as a people, would not last much longer. Soon we'd succumb to the change of time, and the history and culture we'd preserved through generations would also blow away until not a trace of it could be found anywhere.

My fist slammed against my thigh as anger rose. I refused. Refused to give up and surrender like a coward. With every breath in my lungs and every ounce of blood in my veins, I would defend all I held dear.

Who is the stronghold of defense in your absence? My thoughts provoked. Fight drained from me, but not all. Daher was worthy to the task, though I should have set a man from my own tribe in charge of things until I returned. Samlil. It should have been my friend who was more like a brother to me. Though too sympathetic to extremists, he would stand against any threat to our people and way of life and had a commanding presence that the men respected and would follow.

But for now, despite the fact I longed to be in another place, felt the urgency of responsibility upon me, I stood where I needed to stand—supporting my mother who had long supported me. Which meant I needed to shed every vestige of the darkness and be the light she needed in order to heal.

Raising my head, my gaze collided with the building on the opposite side of the courtyard, the same that had drawn the crowds milling around me. Against a backdrop of a city carved out of sandstone, here stood a masterpiece of color and architecture. It drew me to it, that darkness that had more than hovered around me since entering the city, now retreating in the brilliance of the light bouncing off the glass mosaic tiles.

A wall of arches invited all within her shelter. I accepted the invitation of sanctuary and stepped through, my gaze traveling up the length of the hall and down the layers of symmetric curves that reached points all along the ceiling. Pieces of tile of varying shape, size, and color adorned the walls and ceiling in a beautiful pattern that reflected the artistic eye of the architect who had erected such a masterpiece. Hues of blue that captured the palette of the sky set the backdrop with thin veins of brilliant yellow and small clusters of white. The pattern repeated, beckoning the eye to follow its movement.

"Beautiful, isn't it?"

I turned to the voice at my side. A businessman in a suit, his arms loosely folded across his chest, regarded the ceiling of undulating arches.

"Hard to believe that millions of tiny, inconsequential pieces, when put together to form something bigger than themselves, could result in something so magnificent."

I looked again at the walls, zeroed in on a specific section, and scanned piece by piece. Individually, the tiles were not remarkable. Some simple squares still intact, others broken with jagged, raw edges. Only by widening my range of focus could I see the pieces and how they worked together.

"It's all about perspective, isn't it?" The stranger smiled and let his arms drop, his lips puckered to form the whistle that accompanied him as he strode away.

Was my perspective askew? I looked again, tried to fit the metaphorical pieces to those of reality. My gaze traveled from the base of an arch line and followed it to the top of its apex. And held.

The keystone. The piece that held it all together. Without it, all would crumble and fall.

For my people, I was the keystone. I led. I counseled. I provided. I protected. Which meant I alone bore the weight of all upon my shoulders so their load could be less troublesome.

My inspection continued past the ceilings until it stalled on the far wall. Another arch, but this one different. Instead of a wedged keystone at its apex, it led the eye up to the very top, where it ended in a high point, directing its viewer to continue his inspection all the way up to the heavens. This keystone did not look down upon itself and its own strength. It pointed up to the Strongest of All.

Without shame, I fell to my knees and pressed my forehead down to the cool ground. *Forgive my presumption. Fill me with wisdom.*

Rising to my feet, I felt lighter. Though Allah had set me in a position of leadership, all did not rise and fall with me. A firmer foundation held us together.

Hawkers from the street over shouted above the din of the tourists in the courtyard. My stomach rumbled, reminding me breakfast had been many hours ago. Ethan would enjoy the succulent street fare over what he'd lately consumed. Mother as well, if the doctor could be persuaded.

Makeshift booths had been erected along the narrow roads, wares ranging from dried goods and fresh foods to household items and souvenirs. A small cart with steam rising from the side stood ahead of me. I picked my way through the crowd toward it. Unlike other sellers who specialized in one or two preparations, the closer I came the more my mouth watered at the smorgasbord of offerings.

Manakeesh, a round bread and my mother's favorite when prepared with cheese and herbs. Tabbouleh packed with parsley, mint, tomatoes, and onions. I'd often seen Ethan partake of the bulgur wheat salad at mealtimes. Ah, and my favorite. Kofta. Succulent balls of minced lamb dripping in a spicy sauce and easily eaten off the skewer while on the go.

I placed my order and waited as the man filled containers with each and set them in again for me to carry. After paying the man, I browsed the booths on my way back to the main thoroughfare to return to the hospital.

A booth of flowers caught my attention, and I stopped for a bunch of jasmine. If the manakeesh did not soften my mother up to forgive me for my mood, these delicate white flowers, her favorite, would aid me in my quest for pardon.

Chapter 26

HANNAH

How had I missed it all yesterday? I could only blame it on the wonder, on the stage lights igniting my memories and bringing them into focus. My childlike delight coming back to me at watching a barefoot man scale to the top of a tree more than a dozen feet into the air in a matter of seconds. But now the edges of my focus faded, and I could take in what I'd not observed yesterday—the life in the midst of the lifeless.

Beyond the people, life thrived here.

Wading in the cool pool of water up to its knobby knees, his head cocked back causing his neck to form a Z shape, stood a heron, lazy after catching his breakfast—a nice-sized fish he'd gulped down. Around him flew small birds, their green feathers reflecting the rays of the morning sun as they twisted and turned in an aerial game of chase. Their song filled the air, and I imagined them taunting each other that they couldn't be caught, then protesting when their playmate did just that.

A green-backed, round, fat toad, mostly submerged under the water, let out a loud croak.

And if I looked harder, I'd see more. An entire food chain nourished themselves at these waters, from the tiniest insect to the most cunning mammal.

The rushes along the edge of the water brushed against each other with a gust of breeze, the sound happy, as if they took delight in the little songbird's game. I smiled and watched as I bent down and let my fingers graze the surface in lazy strokes.

"'God, you are my God. I thirst for you, my whole being longs for you, in a dry and parched land where there is no water.'

"Psalm 63:1," I whispered to myself.

Could anyone ever understand a parched land with no water better than I? Had not my mantra a few days ago been *water, water, water?* And yet David declared he thirsted for God in such a way.

Change my mantra to "my God, my God, my God."

Maybe if I thirsted only for Him, my mind wouldn't stray to self. I wouldn't loathe my thoughts that hovered around self-pity, doubt, and insecurities.

Because I wouldn't have them, so filled I would be of Him.

Even though I drank from His Word, my human vessel bore a crack, and I leaked out the worth He poured in.

Like a dog that returns to its vomit, I couldn't stop thinking about Maleka. How she might have looked—beautiful, no doubt. How she must have acted—with proper decorum that no one could find fault with. But the train-wrecked thoughts revolved around Karim *with* her.

"I thought I might find you here."

I turned and smiled at Radina. "Just taking a moment to soak in the beauty before heading to the school to prepare for today's lessons."

She waved a hand. "No need to explain. I often find myself by the shore in reflection."

She knelt beside me, content to watch the resting heron and the playful songbirds. After a few moments, she turned to me. "What troubles you? Please, if I can help, I would like to."

Dare I share? She'd only think less of me for my weakness. And yet I longed to know more about my husband's previous wife. "Did you know, Maleka? Karim's first wife."

She studied me for a moment before nodding slowly. "Maleka came from our tribe. I knew her well."

I swallowed down my misgivings and gathered my courage about me. "What...what was she like?"

Radina settled into the short grass and leaned back, her elbow resting on the ground. "You and Maleka are night and day."

A comparison of differences as drastic as the other.

"Maleka was like the moon, obedient and submissive to first her father and then her husband, like the moon is obedient in its orbit around the earth. She shone, though not with brilliance, and her moods waned and waxed."

Without a beat, she continued. "You, Hannah, are the sun. You shine your light upon all you see, igniting their lives with rays of color. And unlike the moon who orbits the earth, the earth orbits the sun, ever turning his face toward it."

She sat up and rested a hand on my arm. "I have never seen Karim look at another woman the way he gazes at you.

Love shines in his eyes for you." She stood up and brushed off her backside, then looked at me pointedly. "The sun should never wish to be the moon, nor be jealous of it. Now"—she clapped her hands—"do you know where our water comes from?"

I was taken aback by the quick turn in conversation, still trying to process all she'd revealed. Gathering my thoughts and her words, I tucked them aside for later inspection, and then caught up to the new topic she presented.

"About eight kilometers from here, deep within the mountain, resides a dam hundreds of years old. A heart of water. Our ancestors carved a canal through the rock and the land, veins in which the heart pumps its life-giving liquid." She pointed over her shoulder. "Do you see my husband there?"

I looked and nodded. Daher stood beside a tall pole, a trio of men rounding him. Their faces turned to the sky, then around in a circle.

"Daher is the keeper of the water. Rocks cemented into the ground surround that pole, telling Daher the times in which to share. When the shadow passes a rock, he releases the stopper to a canal that leads to one of those men's farms. When the shadow reaches the next rock, his time for water is up. Fifteen minutes afforded to each farm a day. Fifteen minutes of water that has been held in the mountain's belly for centuries."

"That's incredible."

"It is. To think of rain that fell in the days of my great-grandparents is the water that sustains us now is a wonderful thought indeed." She turned back to me with a smile. "Now, can I escort our esteemed teacher back to the school?"

Friendship and love for this woman filled my heart. I hooked my arm through hers. "I'd like nothing better."

As we left those still working to cut down the dates from the trees, worry began to gnaw at me. Farid's children would not return for more lessons, but would the man be content with that, or would he return to cause more disruption?

"If you're afraid of Farid, then settle your mind," Radina said. "My husband spoke with that man after I reported all he'd done. You have no cause to fear him."

Maybe not him, but who was to say another wouldn't take his place? Maybe one more violent? And hand in hand with that thought, I hadn't forgotten the noises outside the tent the night before. Someone or something had eavesdropped on our Bible study. If a some*one*... My heart stalled.

And then started again.

God was in control of all. I had but to be faithful to what He put before me.

Children's voices skipped along the arid air, and I was surprised again at how full the school tent was. With the side walls rolled up, students spilled even beyond the shadow of the canopy.

I greeted them all with a smile, crouched down to meet the smallest face to face. Some brave with curiosity reached out dirty fingers and stroked my cheek and eyebrows. They had probably never seen a white woman with pale skin and blond hair before. I stifled a giggle as I imagined their reaction if I unwound my hijab and let my hair fall down my back. Already their eyes rounded as they stared into mine, mesmerized by the strange blueness of my irises.

In a way, they reminded me of Karim and his instant fascination upon laying eyes on me. My cheeks warmed at

SARAH MONZON

the remembrance of his gaze on our wedding night. Heated with desire yet tender with amazement. I'd felt like the treasure he'd always called me.

Lest caught in a daydream that could lead to nowhere, I directed the children to sit and stepped to the front of the class to begin teaching.

Two hours later with equal parts exhaustion and invigoration, I waved goodbye to the last student who ran down the dusty trail back to the village. I smiled and shook my head, amazed that the heat couldn't sap the energy out of the little ones like it did me. I turned back around to clean up the supplies from the day, when my eyes snagged on a bright piece of red material lying on the ground off to the side. Had someone ripped their clothing?

Not a dress in need of mending. I bent and picked up the object, fingered the dark yarn twisted into a braid that ran down the back. A beloved doll. One I'd seen before in a precious little girl's arms.

I held up the doll to Radina, who'd stayed to help me clean up before meeting at my parents' tent for another Bible study. "My friend Yara's daughter left her doll here. If I hurry, I can return it to her mother before the meeting."

"Of course. I'll see you at your mother's tent shortly."

I watched Radina go, then lowered the sides along the perimeter of the tent to secure it for the night. Ensured that all would be safe until the next day, I lengthened my stride toward the pastures Karim had rented from Daher during our stay on his lands. Yara should be among the sheep at this time.

A small knoll separated from where they'd pitched the schoolroom to where the animals grazed. Standing on the top,

I rested with my hands on my hips and surveyed the land. White sheep dotted a lush green field, one Daher must irrigate with the water dammed deep under the adjacent mountain. Surely with all this fresh vegetation, the livestock must be getting better.

I let gravity pull me down the hill while scanning the fields for Yara's signature purple headdress. Her favorite color, she wore it daily.

No fence enclosed the animals, and as I walked among them, they made their way to my side. My spirits sank. Still, their skin clung to their bones in an unnatural way, their eyes droopy and leaking. Instead of them kicking up their heels and prancing around, they either stood in a trancelike stillness or lumbered and stumbled to reach me.

Overcome, I fell to my knees and hugged the closest ewe around her neck, tears in my eyes. They didn't deserve this, innocent animals as they were. Whatever *this* was. It baffled me how no one understood this illness. People who had spent their entire lives around sheep, learned about them and their care from their parents and grandparents, didn't have a clue as to cause or cure.

Mischievous lips brushed against my shoulder, followed by the graze of teeth as the ewe sought to take a bite out of my clothing. With a laugh, I pushed her aside and then swiped at my eyes.

My laughter died, replaced by hopelessness. How long had the sheep been like this? No wonder Karim found little reason to smile, that the lines in his face had nothing to do with humor. I wanted to help, but how? Maybe one of my classmates who had majored in veterinary science would like to have an adventure and see this as an opportunity for a short-term mission trip. Surely someone familiar with modern science would know how to heal our herd. I'd have to talk to Karim about it when he returned.

I patted the ewe's head, then stepped around her. If I didn't hurry, the ladies would be waiting for me. Thankfully, I spotted her bright head cover a minute later and waved. She smiled and waved in return, then met me halfway.

I held out the doll. "I thought someone might miss this if not returned promptly."

"Ack! Thank you." She held the doll to her chest. "I hate to think what bedtime would be like without the doll. My daughter can't sleep without it. Thank you for returning her."

"No problem. I'd love to stay and chat, but I need to be heading back." I reached to give her a hug. "Soon, though, we need to sit and catch up. I feel like we haven't talked at all since..." My cheeks heated. "Well, since the wedding."

Yara smiled with glee. "And I've been dying to hear how married life is for you."

Laughing, the heat in my face reached volcanic proportions. "Soon." I turned and walked away to the sound of her giggles.

My mind wandered as I trekked across the field, not really paying attention to much except my feet in front of me so I didn't stumble over a loose rock.

"And I'm telling you, they can't handle any more. If you continue with this, they will all die and we along with them!"

Angry voices brought my head up. Two men gestured wildly a dozen and a half paces to my right. Ahead, a small, squat tree beckoned. I nearly dove behind its protection. With tempers as high as they were, little doubt remained that whatever the men discussed, they did not wish for it to be overheard.

The other man spat. "Then so be it. You focus too much on the small picture, which is of no consequence. You must broaden your scope. We fight a great war for Allah, and in battles there are casualties. Karim has brought this upon himself for first allowing the infidels to live among us, polluting us with their heresy, and then adding insult by marrying one of them."

My stomach bucked and rose to my throat, but I held my breath. Though I wanted to dash away, I dared not even stir lest the slight movement attract their attention. I'd be no better than an antelope in the scope of a rifle.

Bang! Hannah's dead.

But if I could remain undetected, maybe I could learn what the two had schemed and report back to Daher and Karim. Maybe the threat to my family would finally end and the sheep that we all depended on would begin to be restored to health.

"What of our families? If you continue to poison the sheep, Samlil, our way of life will be over. We'll be forced into the confines of the city, and the voices of our ancestors will cry out in our souls. We'll rot for need of space and freedom."

It couldn't be. Samlil? The same boy who once taught me how to play mancala and who had mesmerized me with his retelling of Aladdin time and time again? Karim's best friend?

But...why?

I asked the question, but I also knew the answer. Just as he'd poisoned the sheep, he too had been poisoned by the propaganda of the extremist groups. Those who claimed to be *hanif*, a true and pure believer who rejected idolatry and upheld and protected true Islam. His vision of a loving Allah had been clouded with hatred and intolerance. The same pit any could fall in, no matter what religion they professed to believe.

Tiny feet scuttled across my sandal, increasing my heartbeat as I glanced down and swallowed a scream. Large pinchers and a bent tail that ended in a sharp point that I remembered with clarity stood in the small space between my feet. My lungs constricted as I stumbled backward without thinking. Then froze. Samlil and his crony presented more of a threat than the scorpion.

But it was too late. Already their conversation ceased.

I held my breath, hoping they'd attribute whatever noise I'd made to an animal.

Which was exactly what the other man did.

I squeezed my eyes, relief wedging between the invisible band around my chest so I could breathe easier.

"I'm going to make sure," Samlil said before the sound of his sandals digging into the sand as he walked filled the wake of his plotting.

Go! Run! I had no other choice. If I stayed, I'd be no better than a sitting duck. If I ran, I'd at least have a slim chance of escaping.

My feet betrayed me and slipped as I stumbled forward. *Go!* My brain screamed at me.

Too long before the balls of my feet found passage on the shifting ground and dug in, flipping the grains behind me as I ran with all my worth.

Samlil cursed behind me.

Too close behind me.

"Hannah! Stop!"

Did he think I was crazy? I'd overheard his entire scheme and he thought I'd just stop so we could have a friendly chat? My parents' beating, the knife under my camel's saddle... Samlil had been behind it all.

"Stop!"

My lungs and thighs begged the same, but I couldn't. Not when the man who wanted me and my parents dead was right on my heels.

Chapter 27

KARIM

I was surprised to see Ethan standing outside the hospital entrance and smiled in greeting. But when his gaze collided with mine, my smile fell. Worry etched deep into his features, making him seem years older.

Mother.

The bags in my hand dropped to the ground, and I ran the remaining distance. My legs felt wobbly beneath me, so I gripped Ethan's shoulder all the while cursing myself at the weakness.

"What happened?" If she'd taken a turn for the worse while I was gone, I'd never forgive myself.

"Calm down. Your mother's health is stable."

"Then..." Why did anxiety cling to him like fleas to an animal?

Ethan shook his head. "Go see her." He patted my back as he stepped beyond me. "I'll gather the bags you dropped."

I didn't need a second invitation. Whatever Mother had to say must be serious if she'd sent Ethan as a lookout. My nerves stood like little soldiers at attention awaiting a command. I took a deep breath before pulling back the curtain partition to her space. If she was agitated for some reason, I needed to stay calm and not let her get too worked up.

She bolted up in her bed the minute the metal hooks holding up the curtain slid across the metal rod.

"My son..." She reached her hands to me. Her damp cheeks bore witness of the tears she'd shed, the reddening of her nose saying those tears might not be over.

I took her hands in mine and knelt beside her bed. "What is it, Mother?"

"I have had a terrible dream. You must go back. Now. You've not a second to lose."

I stroked the back of her hand and looked at the machine she'd been hooked up to. The numbers seemed higher than I'd noticed before. Couldn't be a good thing. "Shh. Calm down, Mother. Tell me your dream."

She squeezed her eyes shut. Tears leaked out of the corners. "It was awful. Simply awful." Her eyes flashed open. "You have to save her, Karim. Quickly. Before it's too late."

"Save who, *'Ami?*"

"Hannah." Her grip tightened on my hand. "Save Hannah."

I jumped to my feet. My mother's hand still in mine jerked with the sudden movement. I gentled my clasp and laid her hand back on the bed. Gave it a pat.

My muscles coiled until I thought I'd snap if I didn't move. Three steps brought me to the end of the room, and I turned and paced three more steps. Back and forth. I looked to my mother. "It was just a dream, right?"

"It was a warning, my son. She is in grave danger. You must go to her."

My heart ripped in two. Love for my mother and her need of me tugged with my love for Hannah.

"I will be fine. Ethan will stay with me and we will hire a driver when they let me out of the hospital. Do not delay a second longer." She made a shooing motion with her hand. "Go!"

I kissed her on the crown of her head and whispered an "I love you" and then raced out of the room.

Hannah

A hand grabbed a fistful of my clothing and yanked me backward until I fell hard to the ground. Samlil blocked the sun as he towered over me, the sneer to his lips complementing the victory in his eyes.

"Allah has looked favorably upon me this day."

I opened my mouth only to have it slammed closed by Samlil's open palm. Pain exploded from my jaw and fissured around my head.

"Tsk, tsk. Even after all these years, you haven't learned the submissive role of women." His body moved to the side, and the sun blinded me. I blinked several times. Raised a hand to shield the glare.

"On your feet."

What was he going to do with me? I wanted to ask but dared not. The whole left side of my face throbbed with my pulse, a constant reminder of his lesson in submission. I covered the sting with my palm and attempted to push myself up off the ground with my other hand. My arm shook with my weight, my energy drained from my mad sprint to the illusion of safety.

A foot connected with my stomach, and I landed on my side. Curled into the fetal position. A groan escaped my mouth along with all the air in my lungs. I coughed and heaved. Silently prayed for a miracle.

"When I give a command, you obey. Now, on your feet."

Still attempting to suck air, I managed to make it to my hands and knees.

Not quick enough.

Samlil's hands were on me again, pressing against my head and fisting my hijab and large chunks of hair. He yanked, and I cried out from the shooting needles of pain. I was on my feet, head covering askew and body aching like I'd never felt before. His fingers covered my upper arm in a vice, bruising the tender flesh there. He jerked me forward. I stumbled behind.

The other man trotted up, his full beard rising and falling as his mouth opened and closed. His eyes moved from me to Samlil a few times before resting on Samlil. "What are you going to do with her?"

Samlil stopped. The gleam that twisted his features caused my blood to cool.

"I overheard her last night breaking the law. Blasphemy against Islam and proselytizing to get Muslims to convert from Islam is punishable by death." He pinched my chin and rattled my head back and forth a few times. "I am a law-abiding citizen. For the sake of Islam, she will be a warning to any who dare to even think of converting to Christianity."

My vision blurred as my pulse quickened. This was it. I was going to die. The grave would swallow me before I had a chance to tell Karim how I felt about him. How much I loved him. Before I got to tell my parents goodbye.

My chin trembled, every muscle in by body tightening in preparation. But then, just as quickly, as if a supernatural blanket of peace was draped over my shoulders, my fear drained away. My shallow breathing deepened, racing heartbeat slowed.

In the name of Christ.

"Death where is your sting, grave where is your victory." The verse from First Corinthians escaped my lips on a whisper but contained within it the power of a roaring lion.

Samlil shook me. "Shut up, whore."

Though logic said otherwise, demanded that I not do anything to anger this madman further, submit as he wished, humble myself in a slim chance he'd show mercy, I lifted my head. And looked him straight in the eye. "You may kill my body, but you can never destroy my soul. Like martyrs throughout history, my blood will be the water that nourishes the planted seeds. You may try, but you cannot stop the work of Christ." *Like Stephen, Lord, let me see heaven. Let my death be not in vain but a means for your eternal harvest.*

Samlil laughed, the sound as rancid as the garlic and onions on his breath. "When you die, Islam wins. Your voice cannot be heard from the grave."

My body hurt and naturally folded in on itself from the fatigue and pain. Inch by inch I straightened my spine and forced my shoulders back. "I serve a Father God who is the resurrection and life. All who believe in him will never die."

A vicious tug on my hair caused me to cry out, my back

and neck bending at an odd angle to try and alleviate the pain. My beautiful head covering slid down my back.

"Oh, you will die, make no mistake of that. Karim, fool that he is, is not here to save you." He bent over me until his hooked nose almost touched mine. "Not even your God could save you now."

I stumbled after him, and he pulled me by my hair to the center of Daher's village. He threw me to the ground and lifted his voice. "Brothers and sisters! Gather around and witness the fate of any who wish to turn their back on Islam."

My knees and palms stung where they'd slid into the hard-packed dirt. Small pebbles embedded themselves into my flesh. I raised my head and looked around at the crowd that had gathered in a circle around Samlil and me. Some faces familiar from our own tribe. Others I recognized from the few days we'd camped and worked among them. I could hear my heartbeat, but still it remained calm. Assurance rested in my breast, and I closed my eyes and savored the feeling.

Pain exploded in my shoulder, a hard blow knocking me back to the ground. My cheek rested against the hot surface, and I raised my eyes to the crowd again, searching out Radina. She had to know Jesus held me in his hands, cradled me like a loving mother does a newborn child. One by one my gaze landed on the spectators' faces. Some of the women turned away, horror in their eyes. Some faces hardened, obviously displeased with the display yet not willing to say anything against it. A few did little to hide the delight in their expressions.

Another blow landed on my lower back, skin tearing. Dizziness brought on by pain fogged my brain, had me reaching and groping for the stillness of calm that had surrounded me.

Lord! Like a rush, the quiet returned. As I looked back out at the crowd, my heart broke. "Lord!" My prayer was vocal this time. Like Stephen and Jesus, I would die praying for those who took my life.

The smack of wood against flesh echoed in the courtyard, but no blows hit me.

"Cease!" The command held no small amount of threat. "How dare you administer justice within my walls without my consent."

"My pardons, Daher."

With my face in the ground, I couldn't see the conversation that took place right beside me. But I could hear. Samlil no more sought forgiveness for his actions than I sought to travel the globe on a camel's back.

"What are your charges against this woman, Samlil?"

"She has sought to spread her evil poison of Christianity and Western thinking among the people. I heard her myself just yester eve."

"Are you the only witness, or are there others?"

I couldn't move even though I wanted to. My body refused to summon up the strength to even lift my head.

"I alone heard her in her mother's tent last night."

"Then it is your word against hers."

"My word as a devout Muslim and brother against this"— his spit landed in the dirt by my nose—"American? I think it enough."

"As this woman is the wife of your sheikh, it is not enough. He will judge this matter."

"But he is not here."

"Then it waits!" Anger threaded with warning in Daher's shout that shook the ground beneath me.

"As you wish." Samlil's response sounded like it had traveled past clenched teeth. "In the meantime, maybe you would like to investigate just who it was that listened to the whore's heresy. I'm sure the authorities would be interested in the outcome."

I swallowed hard, the sand in my mouth scratching my throat on the way down. Samlil had been satisfied with my demise. Now thwarted, he sought to destroy Radina, Qitarah, and Bahia as well.

The slimy, oily son of a serpent!

Fingers snapped before Daher boomed, "Radina."

In a flash, my friend was by my side, cooing and clucking over me like a mother hen.

"As leader, I will proceed with my people as I see fit."

"Of course. As long as your leadership adheres to the law, right, Daher?"

"Do not threaten me, Samlil."

"I wouldn't dream of it."

Footsteps crunched away from me, followed by those at a longer distance. Samlil had left, and the crowd dispersed.

Radina placed a hand on my shoulder. I winced.

"I'm so sorry," she apologized. "Are you okay?"

I was alive, and that was a better outcome than I'd predicted. "Help me up." I managed to raise an arm, which she hooked over her own and then lifted. Another arm wrapped around my waist from the other side. I turned and tried to smile at Qitarah, who'd joined us.

"You both are in danger because of me. I'm so sorry."

"Shh," Radina hushed. "It's not safe to talk out here. Besides, you have nothing to apologize for."

"But—"

"Not another word." With slow steps we trekked down the main street. "You'll be safe with us until your husband returns."

What would Karim do? He'd warned me against sharing my faith, had made me promise not to try and convert him. How would he react when he found out about the women's Bible study?

Samlil would not be satisfied until blood was spilled—mine, my parents'. If Karim didn't gratify Samlil's expectations and give in to his threats and demands, what measures would he take in his quest to "uphold Islam," as he called it?

A rock on one side, a hard place on the other, and there we sat wedged right in the middle. Pressed anymore, and we'd all be crushed by the pressure.

Chapter 28

KARIM

The knot under my breastbone grew in diameter with each kilometer the old Toyota trekked. Its threadbare tires bounced over the stones in the unpacked road, the lack of shocks causing me to bounce like a cork upon the waves. Jostled from without, expanding from within. Even so, I kept my focus razor sharp directly in front of me, as if my vision could tunnel across the distance and see what lay ahead of me.

What would I find? Mother had only said her dream meant Hannah was in trouble. Would I be too late? Or maybe—I held on to the thin hope—her dream was simply brought on by medication the doctor had given her and I'd drive up and everything would be as I'd left it. Hannah would greet me hardy and whole, and we'd all have a good laugh at my mad dash back based on the sleep patterns of a medicated woman.

Except that knot that warned otherwise. As well as the

pit in the bottom of my stomach that continued to open and devour that hope.

The mountain that towered over Daher's village grew in height as I sped toward it. Trees dotted the beige landscape, the buildings of the village itself coming into view. I pressed my foot against the accelerator, coaxing even more speed from the decades-old automobile. More details were added to the landscape ahead of me the closer I got, and soon I could make out people walking about their business. My foot shifted to the brake, and my momentum slowed to a halt, a brown dust billowing about and then swallowing the vehicle. I jumped out and ran past the dust cloud, gaze darting in search of Hannah, feet moving just as swiftly.

People stopped and stared, but I didn't slow enough to process their expressions. If Mother's dream was correct, I hadn't a moment to lose, or I'd lose it all. Everything—or rather, everyone—that mattered most to me.

No matter where I turned, Hannah's unique features didn't stare back at me. I longed for a glimpse of her peach complexion and sapphire-blue eyes. Like a hunter, I searched for my precious treasure, but kept coming up empty.

A woman stepped in my path, and I made to move around her, anxious not to stop. No delays.

"Excuse my forwardness," she said, her voice a whisper.

I stalled enough to glance down at her, but all I could see was the top of her head covering. If she broke social convention enough to speak to a strange man in public, maybe what she had to say was worth my attention. "Speak."

"Your wife—"

"You know where she is? Where? Is she safe?"

Her head lowered even further, and I had to strain to pick

up the words she dropped. "She is safe under the sheikh's protection and resides at his home."

Daher. Of course. I should have looked there first. The man would not allow harm to come to Hannah, not after promising to bring her into his household in my absence.

My chest deflated, the knot there unraveling. My breaths came deep for the first time in over an hour. I nearly laughed in relief—and in embarrassment. Daher would surely tease my mad dash based on the slumbering whims of my mother.

Still, I ached to hold Hannah again in my arms. She should be in the date groves doing her duty and helping in the harvest, but I couldn't muster any desire for correction. In honesty, I was pleased she was within Daher's walls. It allowed for a private greeting.

My lips spread wide in a grin.

One I couldn't wait another moment to experience.

"Your name?" I asked of the brave woman. For I did appreciate her actions and thought her brave, though others would say foolish and disrespectful.

"Qitarah."

"*Shukraan*, Qitarah."

She whispered a "you're welcome" as she continued down the dusty street with her eyes downcast. I turned and, with long strides, walked to Daher's home. Stopping in front of his wooden door, I lifted my fist and knocked.

Feet shuffled on the other side before the door swung open with a creak. Daher stood on the other side, his face pinched and eyes sunken in their sockets.

"Karim." He looked and sounded relieved to see me, his weight sagging a bit against the door. "It is good you are back, my friend." He waved a hand behind him. "Your wife is in the back room."

I didn't wait. Couldn't. Even though I knew he wasn't done speaking. But I needed to see Hannah. Touch her. I needed my treasure back with me. Where she belonged. Forever and always. So I stepped around Daher and into his house, dashed to the room at the back, and halted at the doorframe.

She faced away from me, but I knew it was her. Her height that fit every contour of my body just right, her smell—a light fragrance of jasmine—the colors of her clothing—a soft pastel blue that matched her uniqueness better than the bright red Daher's wife was known to wear.

"Wife," I said, and hoped she could hear the love in the title.

She spun, her blue eyes wide. "Karim."

The distance grew too much. I had to slay it for simply keeping us apart. One moment my shoulder rested on the doorframe, the next I wrapped Hannah in my arms and pressed her to my chest with my hands at her back. How I'd dreamed of this moment, couldn't wait to tell her how much I loved—

"Ah!"

Her cry of pain ripped through my thought with a serrated edge. I gentled my hold on her, leaned back to peer into her face. Tears coated her lashes, making them appear thick and long. "What is it? Did I hurt you?"

Of course I hurt her or she wouldn't have cried out. But how? The physical labor of harvesting the dates should not have taxed her muscles so greatly.

She looked up at me, the muscles in her face relaxing until her mouth bowed in a small smile. "I'm fine."

Her reassurances did not erase the echo of her cry. Still it ricocheted around my heart, pricking at its walls. My brows furrowed as I stared down at her.

"Please." She rested her hands on my shoulders and leaned her head against my chest. "Hold me again, but"—she paused—"be gentle."

Instead of placing my palms against her back again, I rested them on her hips. Her hands moved from my shoulders and wrapped around my waist. Pressed tighter to me. Whatever rationale I'd used to convince myself Mother's dream had been an illusion vanished.

I was too late. In some way, Hannah had been hurt, the proof in my arms. Her tears dampening the front of my cloak, her shoulders rising and falling with silent sobs.

Falak himself, the legendary powerful serpent that lived under the Realm of Fire, might as well have been slithering through my insides, igniting the flames within. Just as he sought to swallow all creation, my wrath took on the quest to devour the person responsible for whatever had happened to cause my wife this pain.

With gentle movements so as not to snag her hair, I pushed back her head covering and combed my fingers through her silky strands. My fingers grazed her hairline then followed the waterfall down her back. The shaking of her shoulders slowed, and I continued playing with her hair until they ceased all together.

I pressed my cheek against the top of her head and closed my eyes. Twice I'd failed in my vow to protect, but Allah had been gracious and saved her when I did not. For that alone I renewed my dedication to Him and would prostrate myself even more fully before Him tonight during prayers.

I kissed her crown and then stepped away, though I left my hands on her shoulders. I didn't know if she'd meet my eyes willingly or if I'd needed to tilt her chin in encouragement. I shouldn't have worried. She looked up, so much hidden beneath those blue depths that I wished I could wipe away the memories as easily as I had her tears. Her throat worked as she swallowed, and I stilled the serpent Falak inside lest she see my anger and turn away in fear.

"Let me see." My voice cracked, and I cleared my throat of emotion.

Her eyes clouded.

"When I hugged you, I caused you pain. I would see your injuries and hear an account of all that transpired when I left."

Her chin fell, as did her hands. Then her fingers began to crawl the material of her dress up her legs, exposing the round flesh of her calf, then the bend in her knees.

I took another step back, though I didn't know why. The adrenaline that had pumped into my system as I'd sped across the deserted land to get here in time returned with the rage of a monsoon, stealing my breath and heating my blood.

I tempered the thing that had killed Falak in me, and now the serpent threatened to consume me with its power. If I didn't control it, it would control me. I knew its name, familiar with it, as all men were. The thing we call desire. Though not evil, it did have a time and place to be allowed to be unleashed.

And in the midst of examining my wife's injuries was not the time, my friend's house not the place.

But control, a dear companion, sought to betray me, and I fought to keep it by my side, confused by my struggle. Hannah and I had not been married long, it was true, but we had connected our souls, and I had drunk from her well. Why did I feel like a weary traveler who had lost his way, on the brink of death if he didn't soon taste sweet water on his tongue?

Maleka and I had been married far longer, had taken every opportunity to make an heir, and never had my body or spirit longed for her or responded to her presence the way I did for Hannah.

Hannah still faced me as she slipped her clothing up over her head, and I marveled at her form, the handiwork of a creator god.

An explosion went off in my gut, desire circling and squeezing, my breaths coming in labored gasps now.

Hannah raised her eyes to meet mine. I could stand it no longer. Everything in me cried for everything in her. I ate the distance between us in a single step, cupped the back of my hand behind her head, and drew her face up the same time mine came crashing down, our lips feverishly meeting in the middle. I couldn't get enough of her, and the way she tunneled her fingers through my hair and gripped the edges said she couldn't get enough of me either.

Control sauntered out the door with a little wave and a smirk, but I didn't care. I could think of nothing but this. My love pouring out of me and into the woman.

I groaned and wrapped my arms around Hannah, lifting and planning to carry her to the bed in the corner.

Her mouth wrenched from mine the same time that her back arched. "Ah!"

Then everything that control had taken when I'd let it leave came barreling back, bringing with it self-loathing, shame, and disgrace.

I let Hannah's feet slide to the ground. She looked up at me with a wobbly smile, but I could see the grimace she tried to hide.

I tucked a strand of hair behind her ear. "I'm sorry."

"You have nothing to be sorry for."

But I did. So much. "I lost control and hurt you." Again.

"Karim."

But I couldn't listen. Didn't deserve her absolution. "Turn around. Let me see."

She stood and stared at me for a few seconds, then let out a huff of a breath and pulled her hair over her shoulder. She turned around until her back faced me.

My stomach clenched, and Falak roared to life. Dark bruises contrasted against Hannah's white skin like ink on a fresh sheet of paper. They traveled the length of her back from shoulder to hip, their ugliness a mirror of the one who'd inflicted them.

I reached out and ran the pad of a finger over one of the offenders, my touch as gentle as if handling the wings of a butterfly.

"Karim?"

"Who?" I tried to keep the anger inside, but it colored my vision red. Its bite was not for Hannah to feel. I swallowed hard and tried again to remain in control. "Who did this to you?"

"Why did you leave me here? Why didn't you take me with you?"

The rawness in her voice cut through me as if she'd unsheathed the dagger at my belt and sliced my skin.

I needed to know. The drive to obtain a name consumed me. But Hannah's emotional pain took precedence.

"I wanted to be there for you. Didn't..." Her shoulders sagged, and I thought she would stop. Would keep the rest of what she wanted to say to herself.

My mind went to the cave. Our cave. The place where we'd go to talk and make sure no secrets lay between us.

Her chin rose. "Didn't you need me there?" Strength infused her voice, stopping the quake of before. She turned and studied my face before resting her gaze in mine. "Have I disappointed you? Are you sorry you married me?"

Chapter 29

HANNAH

Why had I said it? Now that the words were out there, they couldn't be taken back. Karim would see me for the insecure little wife that I was, when I should have been exuding the strength he needed from someone by his side.

More importantly, I should have immediately told him of Samlil and his poisoning the sheep. Instead I'd derailed the conversation from a life-or-death matter to one of no consequence. All because I couldn't bear to find myself lacking when compared to others.

I stood, and Karim's hand fell from my shoulder. He'd seen the bruises, the evidence of Samlil's staff. But I hadn't died, and so far Samlil hadn't identified Radina, Bahia, and Qitarah as the other women in the tent with me that night. Hopefully, he'd never discover who'd been there.

I should've been thinking of them, not myself. The sooner Karim knew of his friend's betrayal and sabotage, the sooner he could deal with the problem. The focus would shift from the women and land directly where it belonged—on the man who'd sought to ruin them all.

I turned and pulled my clothing back over my head. Let the hem fall to the ground and skim my ankles.

Karim's eyes softened and his jaw slacked, the hardness of both dying like the embers of a fire left all night to cool. No! I needed him to feel the burn of anger. To wish to engulf and consume those who sought to harm him. If I poked and prodded, could those embers reignite back to life?

A knock on the door preceded its opening, and Daher's large frame filled the opening. "I take it you've learned all that transpired?"

Karim turned toward his friend. "We were discussing an equally important matter."

Daher's mouth thinned. "I'm afraid this cannot wait. Come. We will discuss it together." Without waiting for a response, he turned and walked to the front room, expecting us to follow.

I let out a long breath, thankful Daher had interrupted. Karim would listen with respect to the leadership and advice of one who had been sheikh to his people for more years than himself. Daher had effectively taken the reins back and steered us off the course my self-doubt had taken us and back to the road we never should have left.

A finger hooked under my chin and brought my face up. Karim's black eyes seemed fathomless as they bore into mine. "This is not over. There is much I have to say on the matter, and much you need to hear."

I tried to keep the floor of my stomach from bottoming out, but it slipped through my fingers, my heart sinking to my toes. I didn't wish to hear how much of a disappointment I'd been. How different I was from the wife he needed me to be. One befitting his position and legacy.

I followed him down a small, dark hall and into the main room, where Daher sat on a low couch with Radina. Karim lowered his tall frame to the seat barely raised above the floor, and I sat beside him.

For a second I indulged in a daydream, pictured Karim reaching over and plucking my hand from my lap and threading his tapered fingers through mine. He'd squeeze, a secret message that all would be well. One I'd foster in my heart until we were alone once more and he could verbalize his reassurances.

And his love.

"Have you seen her bruises?"

Daher's question shattered my daydream and chastised me. Again, I'd left the path of importance, if only this time in my mind.

"I have and would like an answer for it."

"I could never apologize enough and offer my own back to receive your anger. Blow for blow as I failed to keep your wife safe in your absence."

"Were you the one to strike her?"

"No, but I was too late in preventing it."

Karim cut a look in my direction before facing forward again. "As I have been, as well. You are forgiven, but I'd have the name of the man responsible and his reasons."

Daher shifted his weight on the couch, drawing even closer to Radina until their shoulders touched. "His name is easy enough to give. His reasons are not."

Karim stiffened beside me. "You do not know them?"

Daher's chin dipped. "I do."

"Then?"

The big man's chest sunk in, and he looked away.

Radina, on the other hand, squared her shoulders. "Hannah was teaching me the truth as found in both the *Taurat* and the *Injeel*."

I honed in on my peripheral vision to gauge Karim's reaction without giving myself away. How would he react to the news that I'd shared with Radina from both the Old Testament and the New?

He sat like a statue, not a muscle moving. Slowly he turned toward me, and the tender look he'd showered on me in private had been replaced with one of accusation.

"We agreed." His voice was controlled and low, his lips barely stirring, as if afraid too much movement and he'd lose the restraint he held on to with a firm grasp. "We agreed you would not strive to convert others from their beliefs."

"If your wife made such a promise, she did not break it." Radina's words brought Karim's head back around. "It was I who approached her to learn."

"And not just for herself." Daher sat up straight again. "I, too, wished to learn about Isa, and her father was not around, having left with you."

Only the tilting of his head by a fraction witnessed to any reaction by Karim. "You, Daher?"

"Yes."

He paused, and I offered a silent prayer for him. It was risky, admitting any sort of interest in Jesus and Christianity. Even if to a friend. Brothers had been known to kill brothers; fathers, sons. Blood that flowed through veins to unite families too often spilled by their own hands.

I watched Daher as courage enveloped him and steeled

his resolve. As he chose to be true to himself and the man who'd been visiting him during the night. "For almost a year now, I have been having Jesus dreams."

"They're just dreams, my friend."

"You know they are not." He settled back against the cushions on the couch. "Last year I went on Hajj." His eyes shifted to include me. "That's the pilgrimage to Mecca that all Muslims are required to take at least once in their life."

I smiled, but Karim cut in. "She has lived here since she was seven. She knows the five pillars of Islam."

Shaahada—faith. Salat—prayer. Zakat—charity. Sawm—fasting. Hajj—pilgrimage to Mecca.

"I went on Hajj thinking I would get closer to Allah through the experience." Daher continued to recount his experience. "One night in my tent, a man appeared to me out of nowhere. He wore a white robe, but it wasn't a thawb like we wear. He held up a hand in greeting and was covered in light. The light seemed to reach from Him and enter me with an unearthly warmth. I felt a peace I'd never felt before. He smiled, and I knew who stood before me even though I'd never seen Him before and He never spoke his name. It was Isa. I was filled with love as if a vessel filled to overflowing. Jesus looked at me and spoke two words before he vanished into thin air."

"What did he say?"

I tried to detect an emotion from Karim's question—curiosity, scorn, rebuke—but he might as well have asked about the weather, for all the interest he showed.

"He said, *Follow me.*" Daher tugged at his full beard. "But how does one follow if one does not know the way?" He leaned forward. "I needed someone to show me the way, my friend. I have so many question. Why did Isa appear to me? What about Him brought so much peace? How is the Bible different from the Qur'an?"

"And in your search for answers, you risked my wife's life." The accusation fell like an executioner's scimitar. He shook his head and shifted his body away from me.

I immediately felt the absence of his warmth. Like condemnation, his rejection, disapproval, hammered down upon my heart. A judge's gavel echoing my guilty sentence. But when I gathered enough courage about me to look into his face and bear the disappointment, all I saw was weariness.

I was torn. Ripped in half with ragged edges exposed.

Anyone who loves their father or mother more than me is not worthy of me. That went for husbands and wives as well. But obedience didn't mean the absence of pain, and my heart wept as I stared into Karim's face. Already he took too much upon himself, not knowing the release of giving burdens over to the Lord. As his wife, I was to be his helpmate, someone to help shoulder the load. Yet my faith had only added to the weight that threatened to crush him.

He rubbed at his temples. "Let me guess. Someone overheard you."

I stared at my hands clasped in my lap. "Yes."

His head fell back, face to the ceiling, and he whispered under his breath, "What am I going to do?"

My chin dropped to my chest, not in defeat but in prayer. Karim might not know what to do, but God did. We needed His wisdom now more than ever.

A warm palm slid behind my neck, the pad of a thumb across my cheek. "Foolish woman." A rebuke in the words, a caress in the tone. And I caught the question he didn't voice: What was he going to do *with me?*

His hand dropped away, and he stood. "I need to think. To pray." A second later the door shut with a click. The three of us sat there in silence with our thoughts, each one consumed with what was and what could be.

What *would* Karim do? Samlil was his best friend...

I shot to my feet, Radina and Daher staring at me with wide eyes. "We never told him it was Samlil who overheard. Samlil who is behind the mysterious illness in the flocks."

"Maybe you should give him some time to process the information he does know," Daher advised. "When he is ready, he will return, and then we can inform him of the rest."

Would that be the best? The inside of my cheek caught between my teeth.

There should be no secrets between us, if love is to grow.

Funny how one's mind could talk, even bringing back conversations and letting you hear them in the other person's voice. Karim's words, spoken in our cave before we were husband and wife, when we were just friends and naïve in thinking marriage vows could somehow shield us from the winds of strife set against us, came to me. They coated me with the tenderness in which they were spoken, warmed me like the sun to a delicate shoot.

But I wasn't a fragile sapling any longer. Nor was my love for Karim. It had grown roots, deep and strong, like the massive white oak tree planted in the middle of campus at the university in Tennessee. The one whose shade shielded me from the sun while I'd studied, its trunk a perfect cradle for my back. I'd literally stumbled upon it, my feet tripping over its exposed roots that spread out far and wide. Not even the strong gusts from storms threatening tornadoes could topple that stalwart tree.

Daher said Karim needed space to deal with everything. His feelings for me, the disappointment and confusion I'd brought on a part of that. If I approached him before he was ready, before he had everything under his control once more, there was a chance I could feel the lash of his unrestraint. Even so, my love for him could weather it. Could weather anything. It was stronger than my fear, and now I found an opportunity to help unburden some of his load. When he found out Samlil had been poisoning the sheep, he'd no longer have to worry about the tribe's livelihood and preserving their way of life. The threat on that front would have vanished.

I dashed across the room and opened the door.

"Hannah, you really should—"

Click. The door shut. What I really should be doing, I was. For once this day I thought of others instead of myself. The sheep and the whole tribe must be saved. Who knew how much more their small bodies could take or how long before Samlil gave them a lethal dose, blaming both me and my parents with the excuse of righteous retribution?

Which way had he gone? I looked down the road to the right, then to the left. The mountains loomed above, still kilometers away. If we'd never come here, had stayed at the encampment pitched when I'd first arrived back, I'd know exactly where to look. Caves called to my husband like the ocean calls sailors. But he'd never shown me a special place to him here, and I couldn't recall any from my childhood memories.

Lord, I could use some help here. It wouldn't be safe for me to wander around the village alone. Samlil or another with views bent to the same extreme could happen upon me. The chances I'd come away with my life a second time were slim.

I needed to use my head. My heart. Let the Holy Spirit guide me. Being in the desert, I wouldn't object to a cloud or a pillar of fire to lead me like Moses. But no supernatural phenomenon appeared.

I looked again down the long, dusty road to my right and then to my left. Felt a tug. A Scripture song my parents and I used to sing flooded me with lyrics.

I lift my eyes to the mountains—where does my help come from?

A grin stretched my mouth. "My help comes from the Lord, the Maker of heaven and earth." I'd look for Karim in the mountains.

A door opened and closed behind me, footsteps approached. "Follow the trail along the canal to the base of the mountain where the water pours out the mouth. You will find him there, if I'm not mistaken."

I looked up at Daher. "How far?"

"Too far to walk. You'll need to take a camel or horse, unless you have the keys to the Toyota?"

If only. Which left an Arabian stallion I couldn't control or the camel that had tried to kill me in the dunes. "Camel it is."

Daher whistled, and a small boy popped around from the back of the house. He received some instructions, then ran off.

"Asoud will deliver her in a moment." He hesitated. "Are

you sure about this?"

Since I'd arrived back, when had I ever been sure of anything? If I wanted to put on the mantle of Esther, that Bible story that had never been too far away from my thoughts of late, I'd quote the famous line *for such a time as this*. The phrase seemed...momentous. A culmination of events that climaxed in a great cosmic script. Brave Esther had been chosen as the new queen, and she'd saved her people. Me? Well, I was just going to find my husband to tell him something I should have told him an hour ago instead of wallowing in my personal insecurities. A small thing. Nothing grand or heroic.

I took a step back to wait under the shade of an awning, and my sandal caught on the ground, scooping up a mound of dirt between my heel and sole. It crunched when I put my weight down, and I lifted my foot and shook to displace the grains. They fell in a thin line like from an hour glass, one on top of the other. Insignificant and yet I felt a push within, an inaudible voice to look harder, to grasp a meaning, learn a lesson.

I squinted but didn't see anything different. A small pile of sand in an ocean of it. If I'd brushed it away, erased it somehow, it would make no difference. Not like if one of the large dunes just suddenly vanished. That would change the landscape forever. But what was the difference between my small mound and a towering dune? They were both made up of the same thing.

Which was I? No question, I was the few grains stuck to my heel. Those big dunes? Those were people like Moses, Elijah, and Esther. People who changed the landscape of history with their faithfulness.

I bent down and brushed my fingers across my heel to dislodge the last bit of clinging sand there only to look down and find them now on my fingers. They glistened in the sunshine, begging not to be ignored.

I squinted as I glanced up at the sky. There was an object lesson here that I feared I was missing. Looking back down, I studied my fingers and the tiny beige granules attached.

"For such a time..."

If that was a culmination, then that meant building. Moments built on each other. Decisions along the way. Small ones. Little by little.

What was a looming dune but the substance of its smallest member?

Noah choosing each day to put hammer to wood. Joshua choosing to continue the march around Jericho. Rahab choosing to lower a scarlet cord. Hammering, marching, placing a rope out a window—not difficult or momentous things. But the outcome of those small decisions gave witness to God's amazing power.

To be faithful in the big, one must be faithful with the small. Jesus had said something like that in a parable to his disciples.

One choice at a time. Moment by moment. The surrender of will. It was the only way God could use any of us.

Use me, Lord.

Maybe one day the grains of sand that made up my decisions for God would amass and make an impact that would change the landscape of time forever. Even if only in those that I loved.

Chapter 30

KARIM

The water flowed through the canal, its trickling sounds magnified by the dome of the cave like I'd remembered. The temperature dropped the farther inside I trekked, and the reprieve of the heat cooled the sweat on my skin.

Caution had my feet slowing, then stopping altogether. I had no light source, and if I went any farther, I'd be swallowed in total darkness. A part of me played with the idea of throwing off the cloak of responsibility and plunging deeper into the cave. I felt wild, and the risk appealed. If I closed my ears to the voice of reason, the excitement of toying with danger almost wrestled the anger within.

I turned my back to the darkness and faced the light shining into the mouth of the cave. I'd come seeking to silence the anger long enough to hear out wisdom, but the path behind me wasn't the way.

If only the peace I usually found in caves would wash over me the way the water ran over the rock dug and carved out centuries ago. Instead a dam had built, and I was dry and parched for the quietness of spirit.

I should have stayed. Should have faced Hannah, Daher, and Hannah's accuser. But with each revelation it had felt as if a physical blow to my body. When I realized my grasp on control was slipping, I'd left to regroup. But now, alone, I still seemed to be faced off against three opponents, each one vying for my attention, for a piece of my flesh. Three against one, I fought a losing battle.

Hannah had endangered herself to share her faith. A sucker punch to the ribs right above my heart. In truth, I'd only made her promise not to try and convert me, but how could she put herself in danger when I'd done all I could to protect her?

Daher interested in converting from Islam to Christianity? Left hook to the jaw that caused me to stumble backward. A blow I'd never seen coming. How could this faithful mentor turn his back on all he held true?

My failure yet again to keep Hannah from harm threatened to knock me out cold. If anything, this opponent attacked the most viciously.

Bruised in spirit, I lifted my head, no closer in knowing what to do, how to win this fight.

"Karim. I saw you enter, my friend. Where are you?"

A silhouette outlined the center of the mouth of the cave while Samlil's words bounced off its walls. Weary, I walked forward. No use pretending I wasn't there if he'd already seen me. Besides, maybe I needed a friend by my side. One who could add a perspective I hadn't considered before. Heaven knew I wasn't getting anywhere on my own.

I let the light touch my feet but kept the rest of my body

within the shadows of the cave. My soul needed respite more than my body, but I'd take what I could get. Already heat built from the friction inside me. Add the temperature of full sun exposure, and I'd burn like paper to a match.

"How is your mother?" Samlil asked, his brows lowered in concern.

"Better. She and Ethan should be returning to us shortly."

"Good. That's good. I was happy to learn that you had returned. Much happened in your absence." Samlil looked at me with a steady regard, and unease crept into my stomach. The feeling had tiptoed across my skin, making the hairs on my arms rise, pushing out the report I'd known with him all my life. The feeling had come slowly, gradually, over the last several months, but I'd been loath to face it and confront the reason. Still was. Samlil had done nothing that I'd seen to cause this hesitation in his presence. But unlike a dog's ease to shake off water from his furry coat, this feeling clung to me, refusing to be shaken.

What was Samlil looking for in my expression? Maybe he wished to fill me in on the events if I was still in the dark. "I am aware."

"Are you?" His voice rose, though he tried to hide it. A little cautious. A little excited.

Alertness prickled my skin, but I cast my voice in a tone of no consequence. "Tell me, do you know who left those marks on my wife?"

"You do not know?"

A gleam entered his eye for a moment but then was gone. Had I imagined it?

"I do not."

Samlil leaned against the cave's wall in a languid manner. He lifted his hand and inspected his fingertips. An air of superiority hovered around him. He knew. He knew, and he reveled in the knowledge like a pig wallowing in the mud.

Though they twitched, I refused to allow my fingers to curl into themselves. To reveal that anything about my friend's behavior set me on edge.

"Tell me, do you know why your wife was beaten?"

I had to swallow down the anger. Keep Falak, that consuming serpent of the underworld, inside. "I do."

He let his hand drop. "And?"

"She is my wife."

Nostrils flared, and Samlil pushed off the wall. "You will choose that...that..."

"Careful how you speak of my wife, Samlil."

His face reddened as his lips compressed. "You will choose her over Allah?"

He held my gaze, challenging. That was not the choice in front of me. Prayers to Allah that was not the choice. But my conviction wavered, and doubt caused me to look away.

Samlil took a step toward me. "You know what the Qur'an requires of you."

My head snapped up. "I know what you believe the Qur'an requires of me. I am beginning to think we do not interpret the honored book the same way, my friend."

His body seized, then relaxed. He lifted his hands palm out, as if approaching a skittish stallion. "You love her. I understand." His voice was placating. "You do not want to live without her. Then be as our father Abraham and take another woman. One you can make sons and heirs with. One that will prove to Allah and our tribe your faithfulness to him. Maybe then he will lift his hand of judgement from our necks and allow our flocks to flourish once more."

A shuffle sounded from outside the cave, rocks falling and rolling down the mountainside. A camel brayed, then feet thudded to the ground.

"Don't listen to him, Karim." Hannah's covered head popped into view around the mouth of the cave. She looked first at Samlil, then to me. Her shattered expression revealed the answer to the unasked question that had formed the moment she'd revealed her presence. She'd heard. How much, I wasn't sure. If all, wouldn't she rejoice over the knowledge that I loved her? Or would that declaration not be believed from another's lips? Or perhaps overshadowed by the fact Samlil wished I would set her aside, diminish her title as wife, and take another.

That would never happen.

An evil twinkle blinked on Samlil's face. A star quickly burning, then snuffed out in the night sky.

But the sky didn't stay in darkness forever. It was chased by the vibrant rays of the morning sun casting light into every shadow. Understanding dawned in my consciousness, and a sickening twist squeezed my gut as I peered at the one who'd been my best friend. The one who'd simultaneously lifted a staff and dagger in hand, landing blows on Hannah's back while jabbing a blade into my own.

His body swayed toward her, and my twisted gut tightened more. Twice I'd failed to protect Hannah. That would not be the case a third time.

I sharpened my gaze on her face, communicating my love with my eyes while I let my tongue lash like a whip. "Why did you come, wife?" I only prayed she'd listen with her heart and not her ears.

Samlil stilled, his lips tilting in a delighted grin.

Hannah faltered, her expression drowning in pain. She licked her lips, cut a glance to Samlil before raising her chin and looking back at me. "You left before you heard all you needed to."

"I heard enough. Wait for me at Daher's." *Please, Hannah. Turn around and get out of here.*

"Karim—"

"Obey me at once." My command echoed in the cavern, each time coming back to me with a slap. Hannah flinched, her eyes widening as if feeling the sting. But she didn't move. Didn't turn. Didn't mount her camel. Didn't leave.

"Know your place, woman." Samlil sneered.

If possible, Hannah's chin lifted even higher. "I do." Her face turned until her gaze rested in mine. "It is with my husband."

I looked at her and knew. The way I'd always known with her no matter the circumstances or situation. A silent connection that pulled us together, speaking though no words were spoken. We were adrift in our own private current, one that drove us toward each other and washed us away.

I'm not leaving, her look said. *No matter what you say or how loud you bellow, I'm staying wherever you are.*

The skin around her eyes softened as her scowl receded. She'd seen what I'd tried to hide. That I didn't truly want her anywhere but by my side.

She turned back to Samlil, and the chords around my heart stretched toward breaking. Too soon she'd severed our connection, never seeing my silent direction to slip behind me. She was out in the open, exposed. A single leap away from being held in Samlil's clutches.

"Did you tell Karim about the sheep?" Her question reeked of accusation.

I inched toward her, half wanting Samlil's attention to remain on her so I could get closer and half wanting to draw him toward me and forget her entirely. I could care less about the sheep. Not when compared to Hannah's life.

"Did you tell him how you've been poisoning them all along?"

Samlil's arm thrust forward to his belt, and the sound of metal siding against leather filled my ears. I jumped, pulled my dagger from its sheath, and drove it upward horizontally to block his downward blow. Metal clashed, and my arm vibrated from the strike. With a shove, I drove his dagger from mine, pushed him from me.

He circled, and I pivoted to keep him in front of me, Hannah behind. I would be an impenetrable wall between the two. One that would protect my wife at any cost. And yet as part of me shored up my strength, pumped adrenaline through flexed muscles, another part bled out from the mortal wound of betrayal. "You, Samlil?"

His lips curled even more. Any feelings of love or friendship, whether genuine or faked, fell to the ground at his sandaled feet.

"Why?" The most anguished word of any language tore from my lungs.

"Though you were fool enough not to see what was right under your nose, do not lower your intelligence further in my eyes. You know the answer to your question."

I did, and my heart broke for it. Gone was my childhood

friend. A man bent on fighting a jihad now stood before me. The sun glinted off his steel blade, and I had no problem imagining a more powerful weapon in his hand. He'd taken his first steps as a wayward warrior through a more passive route, hoping to undermine and sabotage. A battle plan comprised from the mind more than muscle.

His fingers around the gold hilt of his dagger squeezed, and the weapon rotated. A whetted appetite toward violence could never be quenched. His eyes blazed. Falak was inside him as well, but Samlil had no control. The monster had consumed and now possessed.

He looked at me in a cold, hard stare. "For our friendship, I will spare you. But if you do not step aside, I will be forced to end your life along with hers."

"No one will be dying this day, Samlil."

"That is where you are wrong." His jaw dropped. A mighty war cry charged from his mouth as he rushed toward me, his blade aimed at my belly.

I shifted my weight and leaned back. Gripped his wrist as the dagger sliced through the material of my thawb at my hip and spun him around. I tried to twist his arm up and back, but he pulled free of my grasp. He didn't wait a second before attacking again. Short jabs this time. Their mark to pierce my vital organs and spill the life flow from my body. *Clang.* My blade met Samlil's upward thrust with a downward arc. *Clang.* Again.

I kept my breathing even, my attention focused. "I don't want to hurt you."

Sweat beaded on Samlil's brow. "Yet another area in which we differ." He sliced his blade at my face. I deflected, our wrists slamming into one another. He sliced again, and I jumped back. If I didn't disarm him, and soon, one of his attacks would eventually hit their mark.

When the hand with the dagger slowed to his side, I lunged for his wrist. Samlil crouched and jerked his hand back, but my reach was farther than his, and I was able to wrap my fingers around the lower portion of his arm. Using all my strength, I pulled his hand toward the outside of my hip, bringing his body closer to mine. His musky scent, a mixture of adrenaline and fear, filled my nostrils. I wanted nothing more than to push him away, but distance from an enemy wasn't always the wisest course.

He struggled in my hold, and my arms quivered with the exertion of keeping him pinned to my side. I squeezed my grip as tightly as I could. If I could press tight enough, his fingers would loosen around the dagger hilt and it would drop to the ground.

Hannah's shouts penetrated my hearing as if from a long distance, but I closed my ear to them. Any waver of focus and I could lose more than this fight.

Samlil wrapped his other arm around my neck and shoved my head down at the same time as he brought up a knee. Pain exploded from my nose, lights danced in my vision, and my hold broke. I stumbled backward as a metallic liquid washed down the back of my throat. Blood dropped over the curve of my top lip. I shook my head to try and regain the sharpness of my sight, the dark and bright spots fading in time to see the sharp edge of Samlil's blade whooshing down on me. I brought my arm up, the skin on my forearm slicing open from his attack. I sucked in a breath through my teeth. Took another step back.

Samlil came at me again, this time the back of his fist

swiping and colliding with mine. My hand opened, and my dagger skittered to the floor with a clang. He kicked it across the cave, an evil grin twisting his mouth.

"I should have done this a long time ago, found a way to cleanse our people of the immoral corruption the Americans brought to our family." The dagger rose. "You should have found a way, Karim. But you didn't. Instead you lay with the enemy. Now your immortal judgement will be the same as theirs. Goodbye, my friend."

His free hand cupped the back of my neck, and with quick foresight I saw the scene play out. In another second, his blade would plunge into my stomach.

Chapter 31

HANNAH

I wasn't sure what happened first, my scream or the thrust of the knife. My ears rang with the sound of my cries and the pumping of my heart. I stared, eyes wide though tears still coursed down my cheeks. Two bodies lay in a heap atop each other, a crescent of light outlining the destruction, the handle of a knife sticking from the back of the top person.

"Karim!" I rushed forward. Had to know. Was he still alive? Did Samlil's dagger protrude from my husband's body like the one along the betrayer's spine?

Who had thrown the knife? Where had it come from? At the moment, I didn't care. Even if the angel with the flaming sword who'd caused Balaam's donkey to stop along the road had materialized to release the fatal blow, I didn't care. None of it mattered. Not when I didn't know if Karim lived.

I fell to the ground beside the two men, got the heels of my palms under Samlil's shoulder, and pushed with all my might. But my strength was no match for Samlil's dead weight. His shoulder lifted a little, but the men still lay chest to chest.

"Dear God, please don't let him be dead." How could I get Samlil's body off Karim? If I grabbed his heels and pulled to slide him off, would that cause more damage if Karim was hurt?

A shadow fell over us, and I looked up. A tall man with a full beard and a red-and-white checked keffiyeh towered above. He looked familiar. Yes I'd seen him before with the flocks.

"Please." I begged, my voice cracking. "Please help me."

Without a word, he straddled the bodies and bent at the knees, his elbows hooking under the hollow pits of Samlil's arms. The man lifted and pulled Samlil off of Karim.

Against the stark whiteness of his thawb, the pool of red widened at Karim's side. The weave of fabric soaked in the crimson liquid took on a vibrancy that reached into my lungs and snatched the breath from my body. I reached forward and plunged my fingers through the slice in the fabric, pulling my hands apart, a satisfying rip sounding in the hollow space. I pulled again, widening the tear enough to see my husband's side from the bottom of his ribs to the top of his *sarwal* that rested at his hips. A cut about six inches long traveled from the curve of his rib to the bend of his waist. Blood oozed out in a continuous flow, and I winced. If only Dad were here.

But he wasn't. I was. With a prayer, I closed my eyes and covered the wound with my hands, applying pressure to help stem the blood flow.

A groan pressed through Karim's compacted lips, and his body shifted under my hands.

Praise God! He's alive!

My hands lifted as they started their glorious journey to his face. His beautiful, wonderful face.

But Karim's mouth twisted, and his head listed to the side, causing my hands to still, hovering above his chest. I wanted to thread my fingers through his closely trimmed beard. Shower his lips with a thousand kisses. Whisper to him how much I loved him and how thankful I was he was still alive.

I cut a glance back to his side. Blood spurted out like an underground spring emerging from the ground. If I didn't stop the flow, he'd lose too much. I leaned down and gave him a quick peck on the cheek, then replaced one of my hands over the wound. The long lengths of material from his thawb would serve as a bandage, his legs still covered modestly by his *sarwal* underneath.

A knife entered my peripheral vision, and I sucked in a breath, my pulse kicking me in the chest. My eyes flew upward and landed on the shepherd.

"If it is okay?" he asked as he pointed to my unconscious husband.

I nodded and shifted to the side. "*Shukraan.*"

He knelt beside me and sliced through Karim's clothing faster than I could have done. Long strips of material were handed to me, and then he helped lift Karim so I could wind the bandages around his middle. Under his back, over his belly, again and again.

Karim shifted again with a groan, and his eyes fluttered open. Ever dark, they seemed midnight with the dilation of his pupils. He blinked to focus and lifted his head off the hard ground, turning his face toward me. The painful twist of his mouth slackened as he took me in. "My treasure," he breathed.

"You're going to be okay." My voice caught, and I wiped at an errant tear that escaped. Truth be told, I wasn't sure. Doctor's daughter though I be, I didn't know all that much about anatomy. Samlil could have nicked an artery or something. There was a lot of blood. But I had to believe that he'd be okay, and even more importantly, Karim had to believe it.

Karim nodded, then let his head fall back to the ground. He looked up, noticed the other man for the first time.

"Mahabat."

"It's good to see I wasn't too late. For you or the sheep."

My chin jerked in his direction. "You knew about the sheep?"

Mahabat ignored me. Didn't even look in my direction. "Samlil had an accomplice." He spoke to Karim alone. "I've taken care of him as well."

Karim tried to sit up, but I pushed his shoulder back to the ground.

His eyes flicked to me in that unreadable way of his. If he were upset with me that I cared more for his health than for him showing strength at this time, then so be it. I wasn't going to let him bleed out simply because he didn't want to appear weak to another man.

Karim's hand lifted. "The same way you took care of Samlil?"

Mahabat bent over Samlil's still form and pulled his long knife from the dead man's back. The nine-inch blade gleamed red. I turned my face away.

"They try to kill my sheep, I kill them." Mahabat

shrugged like it was a small matter to take another man's life. Two men's lives.

Karim licked his lips, the only sign of his struggle. But I knew. Felt the queasiness in my own stomach that churned in his own. That struggle of gratefulness for saving Karim's life and grief over the loss that had been both necessary and unnecessary.

I squeezed Karim's bicep and looked up at Mahabat again. The man sheathed his long knife, then looked out of the mouth of the cave. Whether he wished to ignore me or not, he no longer had a choice.

"We need to get Karim back to the village."

I felt Karim's bicep harden under my touch, knew he thought to sit up, even walk out on his own strength. I put my weight into my hands to hold him down and continued to talk to the shepherd. "He needs to stay as still as possible so the bleeding doesn't start up again."

Not even a look in my direction, but Mahabat stepped up above Karim's head, bent, and hooked his elbows under Karim's shoulders just as he'd done with Samlil.

"Careful!"

Mahabat's brows dipped at my outburst, and a second later Karim was on his feet. Mahabat moved to Karim's side.

Karim's face thundered a mixture of pain, indignation, and warning. I stepped up and lifted his arm, draped it over my neck. Though it would be better if Mahabat could carry Karim, I wasn't sure if the sheikh's pride could bear that burden, or the shepherd Karim's weight.

Mahabat mimicked my position on Karim's other side, and the three of us shuffled into the full light, pausing at the rim of the cave's mouth.

The camel stood where I'd left her, my husband's truck a few yards below that. If we could get him to the Toyota, we could lay him in the bed. Not the most comfortable, but our best option. But first we had to traverse the path made up of rounded rock and ledges.

Karim paled, the muscles in his arms and back tightening with each jolted step we took. When we made it to level ground, I unhooked his arm from my neck and rushed forward to lower the tailgate of the truck. If only we had some pillows or something to cushion the ride.

Mahabat helped Karim into the back, then took off his outer cloak, which he handed to me without a word. I wasn't sure how many times I'd thanked the man today, but I did so again, balling up the cloak and then lifting Karim's head to place it under.

I jumped down from the back of the truck and opened the driver's-side door. I paused and turned, my palm still on the handle. "The camel?"

The shepherd waved me away, and I took that to mean he'd take care of her. I hopped into the truck and started the ignition, then headed down the mountain as slowly as I could so as not to jar Karim too much.

I reached my hand back behind my head to the window there and slid it open.

"You're going to be okay." I shouted so he could hear.

The truck hit a small hole in the ground and bounced. Karim groaned behind me.

"Sing to me. Help me keep my mind off—" It sounded like he sucked in air between clenched teeth. "Keep my mind off the pain."

I blinked hard and swallowed. A song? Then it came to

me. The lyrics to "Without You" by King and Country. The one Luke Smallbone wrote and sang with his wife when he nearly died.

My voice started wobbly and cracked on the chorus, but I kept singing. Put my heart into the words. I didn't want to live without Karim either.

Finally, we pulled up to the outskirts of town, where a crowd had formed in a circle. As I approached, the people turned, and my heart skipped a beat at the sight of the two in the middle. My dad and Karim's mom.

Thank you, Jesus.

Dad lifted up the lengths of his thawb from around his ankles and sprinted toward where I'd let the Toyota roll to a stop. His hand batted away the dust as he opened my door.

"In the back. Quick!" I dashed to the truck bed and lowered the tailgate.

Dad used the side of the truck to vault himself into the back, and he crouched beside his new patient.

My mother-in-law stepped up to my side. Covered my blood-stained hand with her own. The warmth there tore my gaze away from my husband's anguished expression and the prodding fingers of my father. I looked down at her, surprised to see a small smile grace her lips, when I'd expected her face to mirror mine. One filled with worry.

She patted my hand, then squeezed my fingers. "He made it in time. I am glad."

Wha—

Karim groaned, and my head jerked back in his direction. Any questions about his mother's statement were erased from my mind. Dad curved his arm around Karim's back and helped him sit up.

"The wound needs to be cleaned and will require some stitches, but I don't think any major damage was done."

I looked to my husband and prayed that was true. His physical body would heal, but the wound had plunged deeper than the eye could see. Only one Physician could heal those types of injuries, but He didn't take on unwilling patients.

"I'll take care of it." My father's voice filtered through the walls, though his volume wasn't pitched loud. Whether they wished me to hear their conversation or not, I would be privy, though I wasn't purposefully eavesdropping.

I stared down at my husband's restful face. Dad had given him some medicine for the pain before administering the stitches, and Karim had fallen into an exhausted sleep. I'd refused to leave even at my father's insistence that I needed rest as well. Nothing could give me as much peace right now than to watch the rise and fall of this man's chest, hear the beat of his heart under my ear when I laid my head against his ribs, felt his skin beneath my fingertips as I traced the grooves responsibility had dug into his forehead.

"Even after all that man did to you and your family. After all he tried to do. You would still do this?" Daher said from the other room.

Karim's head covering had been taken off, his dark strands a mass of soft curls on top his head. I moved my fingers up an inch from his forehead and ran them along his hairline, down his beard along his jaw. My stomach constricted as I studied his face. In rest, I could see a bit more of the boy I'd grown up with, his muscles relaxed as they were in his youthful, carefree days.

"I would. Isa asked God to forgive those who were crucifying him, and He is my example. How could I do any less?"

My dad paused, and I wondered if he had made some sort of gesture with his hands.

"I know your customs regarding death. Let me do this. Let me bring his body back so his wife can bathe him, shroud him, and we can bury him in the required time frame."

Daher's sigh was audible even through the wall. "I do not understand this grace and forgiveness you speak of, but go. Do this, if you must." Footsteps sounded. "But, Ethan, when you return, perhaps you can tell me more about Isa and why you think your prophet is truer than Muhammad?"

"Not a prophet, my brother. God's son."

A door clicked shut as my lips curved. Daher would have much to think about with that one.

My smile dropped as my fingers continued their journey over Karim's still, full lips. Would he ever ask such questions? Be interested in knowing Jesus? Or would his mouth remain as it was now, a reflection of his closed heart?

Closed to me as well? Before he'd left to take his mother to the hospital, I wouldn't have thought so. If anything, I'd have said our feelings toward each other had shifted, as he'd assured me they would. I knew mine had. Without a doubt, I loved this man. Not as a friend loved a friend, but as a wife loved her husband. Wholly and completely.

But would it be enough?

Every logical question I'd posed to myself before our marriage about being unequally yoked with an unbeliever came back to me. We were two completely different people raised to view the world through two completely different lenses. I felt the knit of my heart with his, the fabric of our lives woven together on a weaver's loom. Would that cord be strong enough, or would we eventually be ripped apart as easily as Samlil's dagger had torn through Karim's clothing?

My inadequacies cramped my gut, and I doubled over. I loved him, but I feared it wouldn't be enough. Could never measure up to what he needed. Compared, I'd fall short.

My gaze traveled from his face down his motionless body. His hand curled at his side, and I picked it up and cradled it in my own, slowly stroking my thumb across his palm. So strong. With that hand he'd saved me. Had fought but had also been willing to give his life for mine.

I bent my head and pressed a kiss to the center of his palm. Would it one day be full as he held our child? Or by then would he realize the error in his decision to make me his wife? Would he take Samlil's suggestion to marry another and have children with her instead? A woman who shared his beliefs and knew his ways, not as an adoptee but one born with the culture flowing through her veins?

A sigh compressed my chest as I closed my eyes.

"My wife measures me, studies me in silence as she paints my face like an artist, and when she makes a sound, it is weighted with despair." Karim's eyes opened and pinned mine. His lip twitched, then fell back flat. "My pride is pierced that your breath does not leave you on the wings of a dreamful lightness. Is my face not so comely as to make you swoon?"

I blinked slowly, then shoved his shoulder. "You tease."

One side of his mouth tilted, but I wouldn't call it a smile. Too much sadness hinted in the curve. "I saw my own serious expression reflected in your eyes. It fits me, but not you, my *kanz*. Something had to be done, even my poor attempt at a joke, since I'd never have that shadow eclipse your brightness." He gently held my chin between his thumb and forefinger. "Now, tell me what troubles you, wife."

How could I? If our happiness were but a dream of reality, one to be shattered when he realized his mistake when he'd asked me to marry him, then I'd not be the one to rip out my heart and make shards of a joy that had an expiration date. I needed to bask in it now so I could feel the glow of my memory when that was all I had to keep me warm. When the cold facts of our differences become too strong to ignore.

"You have that look about you. The same one you had when last we were in this room."

With my chin in his grasp, I couldn't turn my face away. Could only avert my eyes. Hope whatever wreckage his words caused in my heart, that I'd be strong enough to pick up the pieces. No woman was worth the trouble I'd caused. Not in any culture.

"Whatever voice is speaking to you now in your mind, turn it off. Heed my words alone."

He waited, and my chin lifted, then dipped. "Who are you, Hannah Pratt, now Hannah Al-Amir?"

A nervous laugh tickled the back of my throat as my eyes lifted to meet his. He dropped his hold on my chin, and my shoulders sagged a bit with relief. I still had time. Unless I was seriously mistaken, his speech would not be the one I'd feared. "What are you talking about? You've known me since I was seven. You know who I am."

"Who are you?" he asked again without inflection. As if he thought I didn't know the answer.

"I'm me." Simple.

"Yes, but who are you?"

I squirmed a bit, not knowing what his point would be. "Why don't you tell me who you think I am?"

"Very well." He dug his elbow into the mattress and grimaced as he shifted his weight so that he was sitting up against the pillows piled behind him. "You say I have known you since you were seven. Practically all your life. Do you think I know you well?"

My cheeks heated at how well he did know me. More intimately than anyone else ever could or would. "Yes."

"And you will believe me when I tell you who you are?"

I hesitated a moment but then nodded.

"You are more than you think. Better than you believe."

"I don't—"

He pressed a finger to my lips. "Heed me. Who created you?"

"God."

"Yes, Allah, in his image. Who created the mountains, the oceans?"

"God."

"And which, in comparison, do you believe is better? Which do you believe God loves more?"

My mouth opened, but no sound came out. How did he know? How could he possible know my inner struggles?

"As you said, I *do* know you. You may be from the left and I from the right, but ever since the first day I laid eyes on you, I felt a new world existed in the middle. A reality all our own. Differences faded, and all that was left was the sameness between us. Your spirit and mine communicating in a language all their own."

"But..."

"Hannah, my love, my treasure." He cupped the side of my face. "The mountain's height does not belittle the ocean, and the ocean's depth does not tear down the mountain. They are both Allah's creation, made for their own perfect work and reason."

As I was God's creation.

Though I knew my worth, that Jesus died on the cross for my sins, something Karim had not yet accepted, it was he God used to remind me of this undeniable truth—I was His workmanship, and when I belittled myself or compared myself to others, it was His creation I deemed not worthy.

God, forgive me.

"It pleases me to know that you now see what I see." Karim smiled. "There is one more thing you must hear from my lips."

Something else?

He sat up straight, his face as serious as I'd ever seen it as his gaze bore into mine. "We married as friends, but you have become so much more to me. More than a confidant, more than a lover. You have become my whole life." He took my hands in his, the back of mine resting on his palms. "My heart is yours, my *kanz*. I place it in your hands with all my love." He curled my fingers into my palms as if closing them over an object. He lowered his mouth to my ear. "I love you," he said in accented English.

There were many ways to say love in Arabic, and as I turned my head and my lips to his cheek, I was filled with each one. *Shawq.* Wild affection. *Shaghaf.* Passion. *Hanaan, sabaaba, gharaam.* Tenderness, longing, desire.

Framing his face with my hands, the stubble of his beard

sending delicious prickles along my palms, I looked him in the eye. "*Ana behibak.*" I love you. My eyes drifted closed as I pulled his head down, anticipation swirling in my center for his kiss.

My first language would always be English and his Arabic, but our hearts spoke to each other in a language all their own. One where our love would never be lost in translation.

Chapter 32

HANNAH

I should be elated. Overjoyed. Completely giddy. And I was. Mostly. If not for the stone that sank in the middle of my stomach. Everything was returning to normal. To the way things were supposed to be. The sheep were gaining their strength. I liked to watch them from the hill prancing about and kicking up their heels. They were gaining weight, and their coats were returning to the healthy sheen they'd had before.

Once word had spread that Samlil had been responsible for all the troubles among the flock, the demonstrations and threats against my family stopped. No more whispered words that Allah was punishing them for harboring us all these years. If anything, the people seemed more gracious to me and my parents, offering smiles of welcome and returning to the hospitality they were known for.

At Daher's insistence, we'd stayed camped outside his village for longer than Karim had planned. But after everything the sheikh had done for us, my husband was more than willing to concede to his request of sojourn. It benefited us as well, Karim and me. Our lives as a married couple had been rushed, with barely days before the wedding, then a crazy trek across a desert wasteland, separation due to sickness, and then the escalation of Samlil's attack. We spent our days getting reacquainted after the six-year absence from each other, as well as settling into our new roles as husband and wife. I still struggled with finding fault in myself and turning off the internal voice that whispered my failures and others' successes, but I was working on it. Karim helped, as he loved to remind me who I was—God's creation and the woman he loved.

But in all that brightness, a small shadow still marred the landscape. Karim refused to listen to any talk of Jesus. My father and Daher met often, as did Radina, Qitarah, and I. Karim never forbade the gatherings, but neither would he reside anywhere within earshot.

So I prayed. I'd promised even before we'd married that I wouldn't convert him, but I never agreed not to pray for him. The Holy Spirit would have to do the work I could not.

The reeds rustled against each other as a bird soared down, his wings flapping at the last minute to slow his descent. He glided over the smooth surface of the oasis lake.

Karim had his caves, but I had my oasis. Here I came when my heart was full. Of joy, of sorrow, of worry. Here I petitioned the Lord.

Father God, hear my prayer. Reveal yourself to my husband...

Karim

My forearm and fingers tingled, the weight of Hannah's head on my bicep. She'd fallen asleep curled into my side, my upper arm for a pillow. Her golden hair fanned out over my shoulder and chest, her face relaxed and peaceful. I wouldn't risk waking her to ease my limb's discomfort. Wouldn't trade this closeness. Not for the return of blood flow to my fingertips.

I closed my eyes. Night had fallen hours ago, and my body needed rest. Even though the clan's future seemed more secure than it had in a long time, the flocks thrived and the Pratts' safety was no longer threatened, the weight that had hung on my shoulders like an oxen's yoke hadn't lifted. I still felt burdened beyond what I was capable of carrying.

Daher's face, so filled with joy and free of care, filtered through my mind. Under the cloak of darkness, not even a crescent moon to illuminate the night's sky, Ethan had dipped my friend under the water the oasis provided. Baptism, he'd called it.

I hadn't wanted to be there. Didn't want to witness the fall of a powerful leader, the heresy of a friend closer than a brother, the beginning of the end to a man who chose to break Sharia law. But though I hardened my heart, I couldn't turn away from his request, and so I stood beside the reeds, arms crossed and teeth clenched lest I say something that would wound those I loved. He'd gone under, the man I knew, the water running over his head doing some sort of magic in his soul. He'd come up changed. Visibly. So much so that it shook me at my foundation. A radiant glow shown from his face as if the water had slicked the cares right off his back. He'd locked eyes on me and smiled brightly, nodded as if answering a question I'd never posed. One formed against my will at my center.

He'd exited the small body of water, clapped a firm grip around my forearm, and then left without a word.

My eyes grew heavy, my mind thickening around all the questions that had swirled there the last twenty-four hours, and I drifted off to sleep.

A blinding light pierced my eyes from behind closed lids. I blinked against the brightness, holding up my free hand to shield my sight against white blazing brilliance. I glanced down, but Hannah lay undisturbed. Could she not see the room illuminated as if the sun itself had decided to cast its orbit within our dwelling? I slid my arm from under her head, flexed my fingers, and looked up. The brightness hadn't dimmed, but no longer did I squint from it. My hand lowered, and a man stood in the center of the room, the light emanating from his person.

My heart kicked against its internal cage, knowing without a doubt that I wouldn't survive this encounter with the divine.

The man lifted his palm toward me. "Fear not."

His voice had the power to command my emotions as every ounce of terror leached from my body, replaced by a flow of peace that originated from the man before me, every cell of my body soaking it in.

Isa, whom my wife called Jesus. I didn't know how, but I knew that fact more than I ever knew anything in my whole life.

"Karim Al-Amir, follow Me."

Author's Note

While this story is purely fiction, a lot of truth and research went into it. The 10/40 window, the geographical region between ten and forty degrees north latitude, is a major space of land where those unreached by the Gospel reside. Many of these people have never even heard of the name Jesus before. There are missionaries working in countries in this area where Christianity and evangelism are illegal. They do so through friendship and working to meet the physical needs of the people. I'd highly encourage you to support these missionaries through prayer. If you'd like to learn more about these missionaries and ways you can help, check out http://afmonline.org/missionaries/.

I learned a lot about the Muslim faith while researching this story. Two books that helped me understand some of the trials and exciting things happening among believers and nonbelievers alike are *Killing Christians: Living the Faith Where It's Not Safe to Believe* and *Dreams and Visions: Is God Awakening the Muslim World?* Both written by Tom Doyle. Another great resource I found were these Bible studies written specifically for sharing your faith with Muslims. They have subjects ranging from Jesus in the Qur'an to showing how the Bible is true. If you're interested in learning more, check out http://leavesoflifeministry.com/.

Lastly, I just want to say that I understand this story may have been difficult to read for some of you. With the political climate in which we live, I recognize the sensitivity of the subject. But remember, "God has not given us a spirit of fear, but of power and of love and of a sound mind" (2 Timothy

1:7). Love has the power to cast out all fear. So let that love grow. Cultivate it until it takes up residence in your heart and is felt by all around you. We are all brothers and sisters, created by a powerful God and ransomed by a loving Savior. "Love one another, as I have loved you" (John 13:34).

Thank You Readers!

I sincerely hope you enjoyed this story. I'd be forever grateful if you'd leave a review on Amazon and/or Goodreads—just a sentence or two. http://amzn.to/2iTVV3j You can find me on Facebook at www.facebook.com/sarahmonzonwrites . I'd love to hear from you!

Free Novella!

Sign up to my newsletter at http://www.sarahmonzonwrites.com/subscribe.html to receive a free Christmas novella!

Twelve days. That's all Lucy Nel has left before her foster daughter, Abby, goes back to live with her biological mother. Twelve days to make this the best, most memorable Christmas of Abby's young life. Lucy plans to provide a snowman for each day—no easy feat with Florida's unseasonable temperatures. When an attractive new coworker nursing a wounded heart offers to help Lucy, she reluctantly accepts his generosity, determined not to let his friendship sway her from giving Abby her undivided affection.

Can twelve days of snowmen turn into a lifetime of love?

Made in the USA
Middletown, DE
11 November 2018